The Organisation

A
Fairy
Tale

TREVOR CROFT

The Organisation

First published in Great Britain as a softback original in 2019

Typeset in Dante MT Std

Editing, design, typesetting and publishing by UK Book Publishing
www.ukbookpublishing.com

ISBN: 978-1-913179-22-9

Illustrations by *Brian*

For *Jan* and *Steve*

About the author

After taking a Honours degree in physics in the 1960s from the University of Hull, followed by a Masters degree in laser physics from the University of Essex, Trevor Croft spent his working life teaching physics and mathematics in colleges of further education. He is now retired and has been for over a decade.

Contents

Chapter One

Yes, the realm of fairy-tales does have a history. This is the story of one of its kingdoms, Areho. Its capital city, Arcue, had a variety of buildings of varying size and purpose, all with the usual features to be found in the world of make-believe. Prominent at Arcue's heart stood the royal palace with its lofty towers, open balconies, ornate gardens and gilded gates. Nearby there were a magnificent cathedral, an assortment of splendid mansions and an imposing castle where the king and his councillors met, all overlooking an open space where people from far and near wanting to buy and sell goods regularly met. One of the mansions was particularly sturdy, built to be both a home in times of peace and a fortress in times of conflict. It belonged to Harry Indolder, a shrewd, nonchalant, well-built man in his early forties who was very fond of the comforts of home.

Arcue Cathedral, overlooking the market place.

1

Our story begins one day a long, long time ago, long before portable telephones with catchy jingles had been invented. When carts pulled by donkeys rolled along on solid wooden wheels. Harry, as usual, was at home in a large upstairs room sitting in his favourite chair by the fire in the company of his two friends, Eric Schemowt and Frank Telslow. Outside the sun was shining brightly and it was fine and warm, but Harry liked to have his fire lit, he liked to watch its flickering flames. Eric, a younger man, handsome, fair and with a slight hint of determination in his eyes, was quietly sitting opposite, and Frank, looking out from an open window, was watching people below busily buying and selling goods in the market place. Frank was roughly the same age and build as Eric, but usually not so carefully groomed. He had a keen enough intellect, but was not quite as perceptive as his two companions.

Frank was watching people busily buying and selling goods in the market place.

The afternoon drifted along lazily.

'The market has a lot more stalls than it had only a few years ago. It seems a lot bigger,' Frank idly remarked.

'It is bigger,' Harry replied. 'There's a lot more stuff to be sold. It's because of all the fine summers we've been having. The crops have been good and the chickens and pigs have all grown fatter.'

'And there's not been any serious wars for quite a while – that has helped,' added Eric.

Frank continued watching the people below busily going about their business. After a while he commented, 'There seems to be a lot of money changing hands. I can see lots of gold coins glistening in the sunlight. Some of the traders have sold out already and are going home with very full pouches.'

'Yes, and some might end up not having such a good day,' Harry responded. 'Recently some traders have been robbed of their takings after a day at the market. Some returned home with very nasty injuries and no money.'

'You'd think they'd take more care of their money.'

Traders were robbed, and their donkey frightened away, after a day at the market.

'Yes, but what could they do? Some have to pass by the forest on their way home to farms and villages.'

Frank and Harry continued exchanging comments about the market, the traders and the robbers who lurked in the forest, but Eric didn't add anything more to the conversation. He was thinking. Later, at home in bed, he was still thinking. Nancy, one of his kitchen maids, snuggled up to him, trying to arouse his interest, but Eric, quite uncharacteristically, had no enthusiasm for what she had in mind. When she was unable to gain the attention she desired, Nancy turned her back to him and sulked before going to sleep. Eric continued thinking. He stayed awake for most of the night. The following day, back in Harry's place, he told Frank and Harry of a plan he thought they would find interesting. He started by asking Harry, 'How's the old dungeon down in your basement?'

'It's fine I guess, probably a bit dirty and damp,' Harry answered. 'I've not been down there for quite a while. Why do you ask?'

'Let's go down and have a look and I'll tell you,' Eric responded.

'Alright, if that's what you want.'

They looked around the dungeon, knocking cobwebs away and trying to avoid standing in the worst of the grunge scattered about the floor.

Down in the dungeon they looked around knocking cobwebs away and trying to avoid standing in the worst of the grunge scattered about the floor. After a while that seemed far too long to the others, Eric said, 'You know, this place could be converted into a very fine strong-room.'

'What for?' Harry asked.

'Yesterday you were talking about market traders who were robbed of their takings, do you remember?'

'Yes,' the other two responded.

'Well I've been thinking. For a modest fee, we could offer to store their gold safely in a secure strong-room; this dungeon.'

Harry thought about it for a while. 'There are quite a few market traders. It would only be worthwhile if a good number of them wanted to use the service. And gold coins all look the same, how would we keep track of whose gold we were storing?'

'I've thought of that,' Eric responded. 'We'd give them written acknowledgment of having received their gold - receipts, or vouchers, or whatever you want to call them - showing how much they'd deposited with us.'

'And do you think they'd trust us?'

'A lot of market traders have known us for a long time. Of course they'd trust us. They'd know we wouldn't be able to run off with their gold. We'd give them vouchers with elaborate hard-to-copy printed patterns, each bearing our signatures and a promise that it could be exchanged for their gold at any time.'

'There's a lot more people in the city besides market traders who might want us to store their gold,' Frank added to the conversation.

Eric looked directly at Harry. 'What do you think?'

Harry thought for a while, and then said, 'Why not? Let's give it a try.'

Frank nodded his approval. Feeling pleased and excited by their agreement the three shook hands before hugging together and heartily patting each other's shoulders.

When they had discussed and decided what needed to be done, Harry called for his carpenter and other minions. He gave instructions for the dungeon to be cleaned, plastered, painted and provided with sturdy shelves, and for an imposing wooden door, with robust hinges and heavy-duty locks, to be fitted to its entrance in addition to the existing iron bars. The dungeon had originally been built to keep people in; the modifications were designed to keep people out. As the dungeon was being converted, new ideas occurred to Eric and Harry, ideas Frank keenly supported. To create a welcoming reception area for clients, the entrance hall of Harry's mansion was to be reassuringly decorated and provided with a long, sturdy table to act as a counter, and, for the benefit of any clients wanting to view the security arrangements, the stairway from it down to the basement was to be suitably spruced up and furnished. Also, a printing press able to churn out eye-catching vouchers was to be obtained, and a suitable room prepared for its accommodation.

When the printing press had been installed and they had become familiar with its operation, they set about designing vouchers. Conveniently sized pieces of paper bearing the promise that they could be exchanged for stored gold at any time were planned, each with ornate patterns surrounding spaces into which their three signatures and the amount of gold being stored could be entered. After printing a few sample vouchers and being satisfied they were just as they wanted, they found another job for their printing machine. It was set-up to print flyers inviting market traders, and any others who might be interested, to come and learn about their gold storage service and to inspect the security arrangements. Also, large attention-catching posters to be shown outside Harry's mansion and at other suitable places around the city were printed. When all the refurbishment and decoration works had been completed and a good stock of vouchers had been printed, the three entrepreneurs were ready for business. On a day chosen because there would be few other attractions to distract potential clients, the posters were pasted, the flyers were distributed and a large placard saying 'Open for Business' was placed outside Harry's mansion above the large double doors to the entrance hall. Eric, Harry and Frank anxiously waited to see the results.

Until people started to walk in, Frank felt a little uneasy waiting at the reception counter. He'd prepared a short friendly speech intended for potential clients, rehearsed it to himself several times and was uncertain of how it would be received, but when people started to walk up to the counter he was able to relax, abandon his speech, answer their questions and make them feel welcome, before passing them on to Harry to be shown the basement and strong-room. At first he was able to deal with inquirers in this way before others arrived, but after a while the volume of visitors started to build up. They strolled around the reception area, curiously looking at pictures and notices, waiting to be dealt with. When their numbers had swollen, they started to bunch together in groups, noisily discussing what was being offered. The hum of their conversations started to dominate the lobby and Eric, who'd been observing, weighing up the prospective clientele and watching out for any hitches, realized they were becoming impatient. He tapped loudly on the counter and in a commanding voice said, 'Welcome everybody. We're very pleased to see that so many of you are interested in our new, secure gold storage facility. I'll briefly describe how the service is designed to operate and explain why we think it is needed. Then, when you have all had an opportunity to inspect our security arrangements, refreshments will be provided in the room to your left where we will be pleased to answer any questions you may have.'

After Eric had described the vouchers, shown examples and explained how they were to be used, he went on to tell the gathering, which had become quiet and attentive, how in recent years he and his colleagues had observed the growth of trade in the city and the parallel increase in the occurrence of violent robberies. When he felt he had suitably convinced them of the need for a secure gold storage service, and how they would be unwise to risk not using it, he asked them to go downstairs to where they would be able to meet Harry and inspect the strong-room. When the inquirers were making their way to the basement area, once again noisily chatting, he told Frank to tell Harry's domestic staff to quickly arrange suitable refreshments and seating in the room he'd told the budding customers to return to, and then return to the reception counter to greet any late-comers. Frank went looking for domestic staff, and Eric went to the improvised refreshment room to supervise its hasty preparation before returning to the reception lobby to address another batch of inquirers that had started to assemble soon after the first had gone down to the basement.

The three were kept busy well into the evening, with several sizeable gatherings of inquirers being addressed in the lobby, conducted to the basement, shown the strong-room and invited to ask questions in the refreshment room. The level of interest shown in their scheme exceeded their most optimistic expectations, and when the last of the visitors had left they were able to lock the large double doors to Harry's lobby knowing they were in business. They felt exhausted, surprised and delighted. When they collected together all the pieces of paper on which they'd noted appointments arranged with potential customers they knew they would need to be better organized before the next day of business. They would need an appointments book, an interview room and a few suitable trusted employees, selected from each of their household staff, to welcome new inquirers, answer their questions and make appointments for any wanting to deposit gold. In the following days, gold stored in the strong-room, and money taken from customers as fees, steadily increased. Eric, Harry and Frank were very pleased. They thought storing other people's gold was the best scheme they'd ever devised. Eric considered reminding the others that it was he who had concocted the idea but decided against it.

Several months later their business was functioning smoothly and profitably. Trusted employees, promoted from domestic responsibilities, carried out routine tasks - welcoming inquirers, arranging appointments, printing blank vouchers and generally ensuring the venture was operating as intended - but whenever deposits or withdrawals were made, Eric, Frank and Harry always took charge of handling the gold. They signed and issued vouchers, or accepted and destroyed them, and counted the *arets* (as the lowest valued gold coins were known). Frank particularly enjoyed taking new deposits down to the strong-room; he liked to see and touch all the glistening gold. Few customers ever wanted to fully redeem their vouchers, and Eric and Harry knew if business continued as it had been then either the strong-room would have to be extended or an additional one would have to be built. They also mulled over the possibility of trusted employees managing the responsibility of handling gold and issuing or redeeming vouchers, but decided to leave such an important change until later; for the time being, although it was tedious, they would continue counting gold coins and signing and issuing, or redeeming, the corresponding vouchers. The money they took as fees adequately compensated for the tedium.

Down in the strong room, Frank liked to handle all the glistening gold coins.

A few years later, however, the question of employees issuing or redeeming vouchers, and counting gold coins, needed to be addressed. News of the business and its popularity had spread throughout the kingdom, and people far from the capital were asking for similar gold storage services to be made available locally. The three knew that if they didn't provide the facilities called for, others would copy their ideas and set-up their own businesses. There would be competition. To forestall this possibility, they needed to open branches without too much delay. This, however, presented a few difficulties. If they were not going to manage local offices, an option allowing only one or two branches, then trusted employees who could manage the responsibility of issuing and redeeming vouchers and counting gold would be needed, employees who would need to be highly dependable and totally trustworthy. After discussing the situation, they decided to hand over such responsibilities to the most reliable and trusted of their staff, to see if any problems arose, before opening branches elsewhere. Before doing so they identified two things that needed to be addressed. Firstly, staff with such responsibilities would need to be well-paid to ensure loyalty and reduce the temptation of dishonesty. This was not a problem. The business was very profitable. The second was the question of signing vouchers. To deal with this they engaged the services of a skilled engraver. He made copies of their signatures to produce plates, adorned with highly intricate patterns, with which new vouchers that didn't need to be signed could be printed. The required signatures would be printed. All that would then need to be entered on each voucher would be the value of the gold being deposited. Also, with just a few modifications to the printing machine, each new voucher was to have an exclusive serial number. When issuing vouchers appropriate members of staff would then be required to enter serial numbers, dates and the amounts of gold being deposited into a ledger. A similar ledger would be used for redemptions. When these matters had been attended to, responsibility for dealing with vouchers and gold was handed over to selected members of staff. Soon it was clear that the business was operating smoothly and efficiently without the three having to do anything more than stroll about occasionally, asking staff members if everything was alright. They were then able to turn their attention to the question of opening branches. Harry had trusted friends in most major cities, who in turn had friends in other cities and large towns. He would be able to quickly learn if there were any rumours of copy-cat businesses being planned. Upon such information, if any came, the three planned to decide where to open their first branch office.

However, before any need to hurriedly open branches arose, a disturbing problem became apparent. Fewer large new deposits were being made. Since this reduced the business's profitability it was a matter of grave concern. The need to extend the strong-room, or build another one, had not occurred. Placing a sturdy table in the strong-room, to supplement the shelving, had been sufficient while the amount of deposited gold was steadily increasing, but as space on the table was being filled the number of people wanting to make large new deposits started to decrease. Eventually, such depositors declined to a trickle. Eric in particular had been aware of the impending problem for some time. He was aware that there was a limited amount of gold in the kingdom and occasionally wondered if it might be important, if it could be the reason for fewer large deposits. Also, from the earliest days of the business he had noticed that depositors often came wanting to withdraw a portion of their gold, leaving the remainder on deposit. When this first occurred the three considered redeeming the customer's voucher in full and then asking him to make a fresh deposit with whatever portion of his gold he wanted to remain in the strong-room. This would have involved issuing a fresh voucher and charging an additional fee. Aware that the success of their business depended largely on maintaining good relations with customers, they decided against it. Instead, they simply wrote the amount of gold withdrawn, and the amount remaining, on the back of the customer's existing voucher, along with the date and their three signatures. No fee was charged for this. At the time the business was still very profitable, but later, when it became clear that very few large new deposits were being made, the wisdom of dealing with partial withdrawals in this way seemed far less clear. Many vouchers, after several such withdrawals and endorsements, came to have values of just a few arets. Also, for some time, depositors had been bringing quite small amounts of gold to be securely stored, in some cases just two or three arets. Since fees were a percentage of the value of the gold being deposited, this did little to stem the business's flagging profitability.

One afternoon Eric and Harry were upstairs, relaxing in the sitting room. They were talking about the business's difficulties, about its long-term prospects, when Frank burst into the room. 'Guess what?' he asked. 'I've just been browsing around the market and could see people buying things with our vouchers. Sometimes market traders gave vouchers as change. Would you believe it? People are using our vouchers as money.'

Eric looked up with interest and asked, 'Are you sure?'

'Yes I'm sure, I asked quite a few people about it, and they all said the same; vouchers are being used as money.'

'Did you find out anything more?' asked Harry.

'Well yes, I asked how long it had been going on. I was told it had been going on for quite a while. For large purchases at first, but as vouchers of lower value became common they started being used for buying less expensive things. People said it was a lot easier to carry pieces of paper around than bags of heavy gold coins. I was told it started soon after people found that anyone could redeem vouchers. Also, I found out that some people have started to call Harry's house *the bank*, and vouchers *banknotes*. Don't ask me why, no one seemed to know. No one could tell me why the word *bank* was used or where it came from. Some suggested it was from an old word for a long table, like the one we use as a counter.'

When Eric heard that vouchers were being used as money the reason fewer large new deposits were being made became a little clearer to him. Traders were being paid for their goods or services in vouchers, or banknotes, not gold coins. They no longer needed to deposit large, heavy pouches of gold after a day at the market. Eric thought about it for the rest of the day and for most of the night. Nancy, by then his personal secretary, had another night of sulking before going to sleep. The following day, when all three were in Harry's sitting room, Eric said, 'I've been thinking. If people want to buy and sell things using our vouchers then we should do all we can to make it easier for them. If they want to use vouchers, or banknotes, as money, they should be encouraged.'

Frank thought about it. He was a little perplexed. He asked, 'But if they use banknotes as money instead of gold coins won't that mean they'd no longer need our services?'

'That's a good question, Frank,' Eric responded. 'It would, but they're already bringing fewer new deposits to us, and I can only see it getting worse. As I see it, most of the wealthy people in and around the city have already deposited with us all the gold they don't need immediately, gold they regard as savings, gold they want protected from thieves, and are using vouchers, or banknotes, for day-to-day spending. New deposits are already down to a trickle, and soon they are likely to dry-up altogether. What we need to do is to offer new services, profitable services, services that will bring life back to our business.'

Frank and Harry glanced at each other with puzzled expressions and Harry asked, 'What do you have in mind?'

'First of all, I suggest we design and print new vouchers - sorry, banknotes; if that's what people like to call them, then that's what we should get used to calling them. The new banknotes will be very similar to the old vouchers, with our signatures and the promise that they can be redeemed in gold on demand at any time, but they will not have a space for writing in the value of gold being deposited. Instead they will have the value of the gold for which they could be redeemed already printed. We can have one aret, five aret, ten aret, twenty aret, fifty aret and even half aret banknotes. With such notes we'll be able to provide for any amount of gold customers want to deposit. If necessary, we can print hundred aret banknotes, or ones of even higher values. We can print the different banknotes in different colours and with different patterns. Also, to make it clear that banknotes can be redeemed by anyone we can address the redemption promise *to the bearer.*'

Harry was interested. 'But how will this help us?' he asked. 'I can't see how it will stop the decline of our gold storage scheme. How will it bring extra gold to our strong-room and extra fees to our coffers?'

'Perhaps it won't bring very much extra gold to our business, if any at all, but what it will do is prepare the public for an even better scheme. Once we start to issue the new vouchers - sorry, banknotes - they'll go into circulation in the market place and more people will start using them. Paper money won't attract thieves' attention as much as swollen pouches of gold coins and will be a lot easier to carry around. People will get used to the new banknotes. There'll still be plenty of old vouchers in circulation, but I suspect that when people see the convenience of the new paper money they'll come to hand in their vouchers wanting to exchange them for banknotes.'

'But how will that help?' asked Harry. 'Do you think we'll be able to charge fees for such exchanges?'

'No, we don't want to do that; we don't want to discourage people from exchanging their vouchers. We want banknotes to become popular. We want everyone to start using them.'

'You think that when people get used to paper money they'll want to deposit more gold with us - they'll realize how convenient banknotes are and won't want to continue using gold coins - is that what you have in mind?'

'Well, as paper money becomes widespread, there might be a helpful boost to our gold deposits, and associated fees, but that's not going to make us fabulously rich. I've a far better scheme for doing that.'

'So what's this new idea you keep mentioning?'

'We know that from the start very few people wanted to fully redeem their vouchers. Traders and others with expenses to pay to people who would only accept gold occasionally made withdrawals, but there was always plenty of gold left in the strong-room. I think that as banknotes become generally used and accepted people will rarely, if ever, want to exchange them for gold coins. They'll get used to banknotes. They'll start to think of them as proper money.'

'Go on, we're listening.'

'Well, once banknotes become commonplace we'll be able to take advantage of the situation.'

'How?'

'We'll be able to print some extra banknotes and use them ourselves.'

Harry paused. Eric's suggestion was surprising and he needed to think. Frank, however, who'd been quietly listening, was more puzzled than anything else. 'You mean we'd make some banknotes for ourselves without putting any gold in the strong room?'

'Yes, that's exactly what I mean.'

'But if we spent them it would mean there'd be more banknotes in circulation than gold coins in the strong-room.'

'Yes, it would; but would it matter?'

'Well I'm not sure. It would mean we were creating money out of pieces of paper. We'd be printing money. I don't know why, but it seems a bit creepy. How could we just create money like that? It doesn't seem possible.'

Eric could see Frank was struggling. He answered, 'People are gullible and like to conform, and as long as others are doing the same they'll use banknotes for buying and selling things without worrying about what money is or where it comes from. They won't think about it. They'll accept whatever form of money is in general use, be it metal coins or paper banknotes, unaware of how it gets its value. It's not at all likely, but if any oddballs do bother to think about it, and one or two start to worry, there'll always be enough gold in the strong-room to redeem their banknotes and put their minds at rest. They'll never know if there are a few more banknotes in circulation than gold coins in our strong room.'

Frank inhaled deeply, trying to absorb and digest Eric's words, but Harry, who'd been listening carefully, looked at Eric and said, 'You crafty scoundrel, you've surpassed yourself this time. Creating money out of pieces of paper, what a scam! I think we'll do well with this one.'

'Yes, but we'll have to be very careful. No one must ever suspect that there's not enough gold in the strong-room to redeem all the banknotes in circulation. If such a suspicion was to spread it's likely that people in droves would come clamouring at our doors wanting to redeem their paper money. We'd have to lock the doors and try to bluff, or run out of gold and risk being lynched. So we'll have to be very careful and very secretive.'

Frank and Harry nodded in agreement and Harry asked, 'What do you suggest? How will we use this money?'

'I think we should aim to have a branch in every city and large town. If everyone in the kingdom was using our banknotes, it would make things difficult for would-be competitors wanting to copy our business. Harry, have you heard anything from your friends; any gossip of possible rivals?'

'No, I've not heard anything recently. I was told people living far from Arcue were fascinated when they first heard about gold being stored safely in our strong-room, but it seems they soon lost interest. I've not heard anything more, and if any rumours of potential rivals had cropped up I'm sure I'd have got to know about them.'

'In that case, I think we should first concentrate on getting the new banknotes into circulation here in Arcue. In addition to tendering banknotes to people making new deposits, I suggest we distribute flyers to inform customers that we were responding to the increasing number of people using vouchers as money by introducing new banknotes. The flyers will describe the new notes, persuasively emphasize their convenience and include an invitation to call at reception to exchange old vouchers for new banknotes of equal value, highlighting that this will be done entirely free of charge.'

Harry thought for a moment. 'But what about the banknotes we're going to print for ourselves? What are we going to do with them?'

'Initially, when our staff asks to be paid in banknotes, as I think they will when many people are happily using them in everyday transactions, we can start printing extra ones to pay their wages. I don't think any of them will suspect anything, I don't see any reason why they would, but if one does, I think he'll be smart enough to keep quiet about it – he'll not want to lose his well-paid job, and, if everyone in the city was happily using banknotes, he'll not want to risk being ridiculed by making claims he'd have no way of substantiating. Then, if all goes well, we can start printing extra notes for our own use.'

'So banknotes become commonplace in Arcue; then what?'

'Then we'll spread our business throughout the kingdom. We'll open branches in every city and large town in the country. To obtain and furnish the necessary premises we'll either cautiously print the money required, or, if in some places banknotes are still not fully acceptable, we'll borrow gold from our strong-room. Either way, no one will know or worry about it. They'll go on thinking enough gold was stored safely in our vaults to back all the banknotes in circulation. They'll have no reason for thinking otherwise.'

'But when everyone in the kingdom with gold they want kept away from the risk of theft has it all safely stored in our strong-rooms won't our revenues dry-up? Wouldn't we then run into the same problems we found here in Arcue?'

'Yes, we probably will, but when we have branches in every town and city, and our banknotes are accepted throughout the kingdom, we can progress to the best scheme of all.'

'And what will that be?' Harry asked.

'Lending money and charging interest. We'll print extra banknotes and let people borrow them, even ones with no gold in our vaults, and until they'd re-paid their loans the borrowers will have to go on making regular interest payments.'

Frank, who'd been listening carefully, trying to grasp all that had been said, felt uncertain and uneasy. 'But we'd be charging interest on loans of money created out of pieces of paper; we'd be lending claims to other people's gold. How could we do that? How could we get away with it?'

'By not telling people about it,' Eric replied. 'We'll only run into difficulties if everyone came at the same time wanting to exchange their banknotes for gold. Trust me, Frank; they're not going to do that. They'll only flock to our doors wanting gold if they found out that there wasn't enough gold in our vaults for them all to exchange their banknotes, and since we'll be the only ones who'll know about it, they'll never find out about it.'

Although he was still a little uncertain, Frank replied, 'Yes, I can see that. I can see that we'll need to be very secretive.'

'That's right, Frank; very, very secretive!'

'Let's do it,' Harry added. 'I can't see any way it could go wrong.'

So, the three went ahead with their scheme. It turned out exactly as Eric had envisioned. They opened branches throughout the kingdom, banknotes became commonplace and they printed more and more of them so they could make more and more interest-bearing loans. It was the best scheme ever invented. They became very rich. And because they were very rich people thought they must be very clever; and because they promised to exchange banknotes for gold at any time people also thought they must be very honourable and trustworthy; and because people thought they were honourable, trustworthy and very clever, they accepted their banknotes as proper money without ever thinking very much about what money was or where it came from.

Chapter Two

Soon after the money lending scheme had become operational, Harry's sitting room started to show signs of increasing affluence. His favourite chair remained, but recently acquired thick rugs scattered around the floor, elaborately painted ornaments, intricate woven tapestries and expensive paintings hanging on the walls gave him an added sense of well-being. They made him feel snug and secure. Surrounded by such opulence, Eric and Harry often sat leisurely chatting as the headquarters of their business empire quietly hummed below.

Eric and Harry often sat leisurely chatting as the headquarters of their business empire quietly hummed below.

One afternoon they were sitting by the fire discussing Eric's forthcoming marriage. Nancy, his long-term house-maid, aide, companion and lover, had managed to become pregnant, and the thought that he might soon have a son or daughter made Eric feel good. However, the impending marriage and birth brought home the certainty of death and the question of who would then inherit the business. Harry's wife had died two years before the start of the gold storage scheme, and when the business started to flourish the prospect of a second marriage, and children to pass his share of the partnership on to, increasingly occupied his thoughts. Eric's and Nancy's matrimonial plans brought such concerns into sharp focus. As he sat casually discussing it, his friend pointed out that he was attractive, very wealthy and still had many years of active life to look forward to, and would therefore have little difficulty in finding a young woman who would brighten up his life and give birth to children who would grow up to be his heirs. Harry, feeling a little uncomfortable, said he would think about it. The two then turned their attention to Frank and his enduring, but slightly erratic, affiliation with a woman called Fiona. They decide to encourage the relationship and steer the two to marriage and the production of offspring.

The conversation then wandered into the question of how, when events made it necessary, the business was to be handed over to their successors. They decided, provided Frank agreed, that the business was to go equally to however many heirs they had with the intelligence, skills and strength of mind to manage it diligently. The possibility of one, two or all of them having daughters led them to conclude that equal shares of the business should be allocated, irrespective of gender, according to ability, aptitude and determination to run it successfully. They also decided, if destiny decreed that there were to be numerous heirs with a wide range of abilities, possible disputes over where the dividing line would be drawn between those with the necessary skills, and those without, would have to be settled when they arose, with the understanding that, provided circumstances allowed, they, Frank included, would have the final say. This led to the possible problem of disagreeing wives. This, they decided, would also have to be settled if and when it arose.

Their rambling conversation drifted easily into discussing the possible advantages and disadvantages of splitting the business into separate organisations when it was time to hand it over to their chosen heirs. Operating divisions of the business as seemingly disconnected firms, with differing trade-names, they thought, would alleviate possible leadership disputes amongst inheritors, and would lead the public into believing it had a choice. It would create an illusion of competition. They were coming to the view that splitting the business in this way would be the best option, when Frank walked in. He was clearly excited.

'Guess what?' he asked theatrically. 'There's going to be a war.'

'You what?' asked Harry in disbelief.

'There's going to be a war. Everyone's talking about it.'

'Why, what's happened?'

'I don't know the full story, people are confused and uncertain, but it seems the King's upset because King Arnold of Isconsia has laid claims on the Duchy of Arvin.'

Harry and Eric looked at each other with uneasy expressions. They knew there'd been rumours of friction with Isconsia, a neighbouring kingdom to the north of Areho, but they'd never thought it would come to war. Addressing Harry, Eric said, 'I think you'd better get round to the palace to see what this is all about.'

'Yes, I think you're right. I'll send someone over to find out if and when the King can see me. I'm well in with him at the moment so I don't think there'll be any problems.'

Don't bother with all that bowing stuff, take a seat and tell me how you've been.

The following day, in the King's parlour, the head butler announced, 'Mr Harold Indolder, your majesty.'

'Come on in, Harry,' the King responded. 'Don't bother with all that bowing stuff, take a seat and tell me how you've been.'

Harry chose a seat facing the King and replied, 'I'm fine, your majesty, how are things with you?'

'Arr, things haven't been too good recently, but I'm very pleased and impressed by the success of your money lending scheme. It seems to have livened up my kingdom considerably. The markets are all busy, and blacksmiths, carpenters and the like all seem to be fully occupied. I think your business has had a lot to do with it.'

'Thank you, your majesty. That's very kind of you. But I'm sorry to hear things are not too good with you. Is it anything to do with rumours I've been hearing about you having a bit of bother with Isconsia?'

'A bit of bother! A bit of bother! It's a lot more than that. That swine King Arnold is trying to take the Duchy of Arvin from me.'

'How has that come about, your majesty?'

'Don't keep on saying *your majesty*. I keep on hearing it all day, every day. It gets on my nerves. I get sick of hearing it.'

'I'm sorry. I didn't mean to upset you.'

'I know, Harry. I know. I'm sorry too. It's just that damnable Arnold, he gets me really rattled.'

'So what's it all about? How come he's trying to take Arvin from you?'

'It's a bit of a long story. You know that Duke Forbim of Arvin married Arnold's daughter, Emma?'

'Yes.'

'Well, when Forbim died Emma took control of the Duchy and somehow Arnold got it into his head that this gave him the right to claim it as part of his kingdom. At first he sent a handful of knights, supposedly to ensure Emma's safety, but now he's sent more men to Arvin. They're going around telling people Arvin is now part of Isconsia and Arnold is their king. Well, he's not going to get away with it. I sent a message to him saying that if he didn't get his men out of Arvin by the end of the month a state of war would exist between Isconsia and Areho.'

'Has he taken his men out?'

'No, he has not.'

'So what's going to happen? Has there been any fighting?'

'Nothing's happened yet, but it's going to. I've sent writs to all my barons telling them to prepare for war.'

'Do you think they'll all support you?'

'They'd damned well better. I'll have any that refuse tortured and executed for treason.'

'I was just thinking about your father. I remember being told as a child that when he wanted to go to war with Otel, the hostility withered away before he could get the fighting underway because so many barons quibbled and dallied.'

'Well that's not going to happen again.'

'I know it's not, but even so, it's going to take some time for them all to get their forces organised and assembled. That'll give Arnold time to flood Arvin with seasoned troops. It'll then be much more difficult to drive him out.'

'Well that can't be helped.'

'I think it can. If you had the money you'll need for the war available without delay you'd be able to get the barons mobilized much more quickly. You'd be one step ahead of Arnold, and you'd be able to drive him out much more easily. All you have to do is ask. I'll then make sure you have that money before the day is out. And if you needed more, there'd be more. You won't have to worry about running out of money.'

'Yes, but that would mean taking out one of your loans; a very big one. How will I ever be able to pay it back, let alone pay the interest?'

'That's easy. You're the King. You'd have every right to tax your people so you could pay it back.'

'Yes, I could do that, couldn't I?'

'Of course you could. Just tell the people that they had to pay income tax. Tell them it was their patriotic duty to help you to pay off the national debt.'

'Income tax, I like the sound of that.'

'Well just say the word and the money will be delivered to you before the day is out. You'll be able to drive Arnold and his bully boys out of Arvin before he'd had time to think about it.'

'Yes, you're right. Let's do it. I'll show him he can't insult Areho and get away with it. Get the money to me and I'll see to it that you're re-paid in full, with interest.'

So, without knowing it had been created out of nothing more than pieces of paper, King Walter II borrowed the money he needed for the war. Arnold's forces were easily driven out of Arvin, or captured and held as hostages. To secure the release of his favourite knights, all of noble birth, Arnold not only had to pay a hefty ransom, in gold, he also had to kneel in Arvin's cathedral and, under oath, solemnly relinquish all claims on the Duchy. King Walter was very pleased. Harry, Frank and Eric were also very pleased. Previously, all the loans they'd made had been to people who needed relatively small amounts. They'd made loans to replace worn out carts or dead donkeys, for marriages, funerals and other family occasions, and for many other events requiring modest amounts of money; amounts ordinary people, nevertheless, would not usually have readily available. The war loan to the King was in a different league. It far exceeded any loans they'd made before. It was so profitable that Harry persuaded the King to borrow more.

Just as Harry said it would, the loan enabled the war with Isconsia to be won quickly and easily. Accordingly, the costs had been much lower than the royal accountants had predicted, and King Walter suggested re-paying the unused part of the loan back to the bank. To this, Harry responded, 'Don't do that, your majesty. People are jubilant and patriotic after your glorious victory. They think you handled the war brilliantly. They're filled up with nationalistic fervour and they don't mind the income tax. They'd be proud and happy if you borrowed a little more to bolster the kingdom's defences. They won't mind if the national debt was increased just a little so you could have a standing army. With a professional army, commanded by expert generals instead of dithering, argumentative barons, you'd be able to have soldiers permanently ready to defend your borders. Potential enemies would then think twice before invading your lands, and when they weren't fighting or training you could have some of the soldiers march up and down in nice bright uniforms outside your palace.'

King Walter liked the idea of smartly dressed soldiers marching up and down outside his palace.

King Walter liked the idea of smartly dressed soldiers marching up and down outside his palace. It would, he thought, make him feel like a proper king. He agreed to Harry's suggestion and borrowed more money. No one was bothered very much by income tax and the national debt. People were triumphal in the wake of the war and happy that the kingdom was prosperous. There was plenty of food and fuel for sale in the markets, and there was plenty of money in circulation with which they could be bought, much of it a consequence of the war and defence loans. Moreover, King Walter, by depositing the gold he'd received from King Arnold and taking out banknotes, had indulged in a bit of personal spending. In addition to buying magnificent horses to restock his stables, he had his palace splendidly refurbished throughout. He had every room redecorated and adorned with thick rugs, painted ornaments, expensive paintings and fancy tapestries. All-in-all it meant that Harry's, Frank's and Eric's business was doing really well. In the wake of the war its profits soared, but at night, as Nancy slept peacefully beside him, Eric's thoughts were sometimes a little uneasy.

After the money lending scheme had been running for a while, Frank had noticed that the prices of goods being sold in the market had started to rise. The increase was trivial, barely noticeable, but Frank, always eager to pass on information, told Harry and Eric about it. They considered it unimportant, a symptom of a briskly operating market place, and thought little more of it. But when the war was over and things had settled down, the prices of goods started to rise a little more noticeably. It was this, along with recollections of Frank's earlier observation that sometimes occupied Eric's thoughts at night. He wondered what, if any, was the connection between the price rises and the activities of the bank.

One night, just as he was drifting off to sleep, a vague answer started to form in his mind. In the morning it gradually became much clearer. The total amount of money spent buying things in the market had to be directly related to the total amount in circulation. The bank, by creating extra money and letting people borrow it, had increased the total amount in circulation. Prices had increased accordingly. Suddenly the answer to his question was obvious. The bank, by creating extra currency, was causing the value of money to fall. When this had become clear in his slowly awakening mind, Eric sat up in bed abruptly. His sudden movement awakened Nancy.

'What's wrong?' she asked.

'It's nothing, my love, just an unpleasant dream. You go back to sleep, it's still very early.'

But Eric didn't think it was nothing. He could see that if people started to become aware that banknotes were losing their value - that they no longer bought the same goods as they did earlier - they would probably want to redeem them. They would want their gold back. But there wouldn't be enough to redeem all the banknotes the bank had printed. The money it had so easily created would just as easily turn into worthless pieces of paper. The kingdom would be plunged into chaos. There'd be violent riots, and the people's anger would be focused on the bank and its owners.

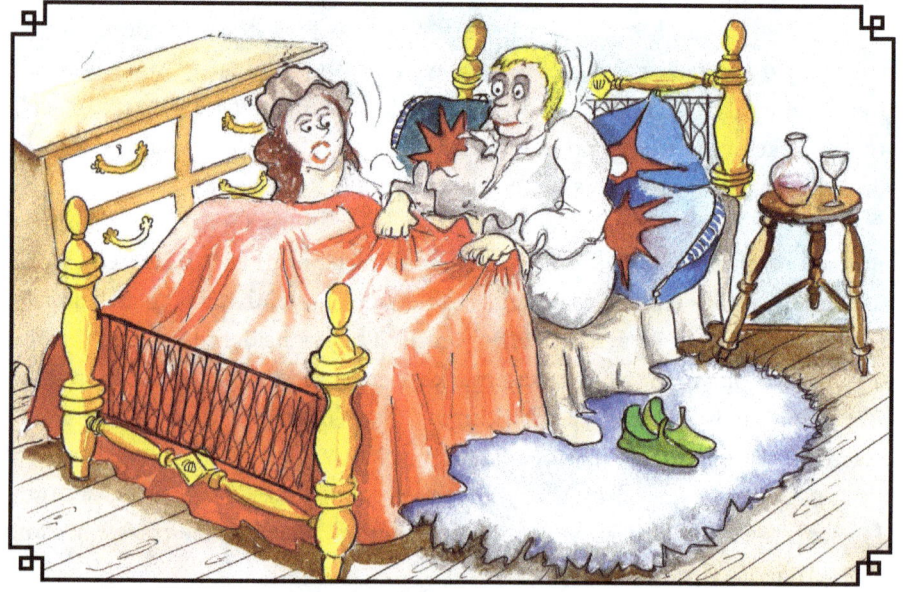

Eric's sudden movement awakened Nancy.

Later, when all three were in Harry's sitting room, Eric informed his friends of his nocturnal musing. He told them the value of money was decreasing as a result of them printing extra banknotes. They were putting extra currency into circulation. It was the reason prices were increasing. He went on to explain why he feared it could easily give rise to serious difficulties for the bank. Harry listened carefully. He easily understood Eric's reasoning and made the comment, 'Although I can't recall its name, I vaguely remember being told of a kingdom where a very rich seam of gold was found in one of its mines. It quickly gave rise to widespread price increases. If my memory serves me correctly, the phenomenon was called inflation.'

'Yes, that's the same sort of thing. That's what I'm talking about. The extra gold would have gone into circulation as extra money, and this would have caused the price increases.'

But Frank was unsure. His friends' conversation made him feel a little excluded. He asked, 'Why do prices have to increase if there's an increase in the amount of money? Why can't people just enjoy the extra money without having to pay more for the things they want?'

'Look at it this way,' Eric answered. 'If there was a fixed amount of goods for sale in the market and every item showed the price its owner thought it could be sold for, then all of a sudden all the money in people's possession magically doubled, what do you think would happen?'

'People would buy the things they wanted and have plenty of money left over.'

'How do you think the sellers would have decided on the prices they'd offered to sell their goods for?'

'I suppose they'd have based them on what they thought people would be able and willing to pay.'

'I think you're right, but they'd have done this before the amount of money suddenly doubled. Do you think they'd have set the same prices if they'd known the amount of money people had to spend was about to suddenly double?'

'No, they'd have set their prices higher. Oh, I think I see what you mean. If there was plenty of spending money in people's pockets, other people with things to sell would be able to sell at higher prices.'

'That's right. If there was an increase in the amount of money and the number of things for sale was fixed, then prices would increase. Now, just as a check, let's imagine the amount of goods for sale was fixed and all of a sudden half the money in circulation suddenly disappeared. What do you think would happen then?'

'Well, if there was less money available, people with things to sell would have to lower their prices.'

'There you are then. I think you've got it.'

'So, if the amount of money in circulation doubled, would that mean prices would also have to double?'

'Well, the extra money might persuade people to spend more liberally, and others might be encouraged to offer more things for sale, but, yes, if these didn't happen and nothing else changed, then prices would double if the amount of circulating money doubled.'

'And increasing prices would be a threat to our bank?'

'Yes, that's right. If people started to see that banknotes were losing their value they'd probably want to exchange them for gold, and you know what that would mean.'

Eric continued explaining his thoughts to Frank. He went on to say that because rising prices would put them in great danger they would have to stop lending. They would have to stop putting extra banknotes into circulation. But Harry, who'd been listening and thinking, said, 'It doesn't have to be that way.'

'What do you mean?' asked Eric.

'You said prices would increase if the amount of money increased and there was no change in the things offered for sale in the market.'

'Yes.'

'Well what do you think would happen if the amount of money increased and the number of things for sale also increased?'

'If they both increased by the same proportion then prices would remain unchanged.'

'There you are then. There's your answer. Prices won't change and we won't have to stop lending if there's an increase in the number of things for sale.'

'Yes, but how are we going to arrange that? We can't just wave a magic wand and conjure up more goods for the kingdom's markets.'

'Well I don't think we'll need to do that. I remember talking some time back to a man called Albert who sometimes does a few jobs for me. He makes wheels for carts and wagons and he told me about a suggestion someone had put to him about making strong, light-weight wheels. The proposed wheels were to have stout wide hubs able to turn on sections of steel rod called axles, outer rims made up of shaped wooden sections each connected to the hubs by radial rods called spokes, all held together by steel rings that are placed around the rims after being heated in a fire. The steel rings shrink as they cool, so holding all the parts of the wheels firmly together.'

'Go on, we're listening.'

'Well, Albert told me he was very interested and had a go at making a few. He liked them. They were tough, sturdy and much lighter than solid wheels, but making one took him more than a week, even after practice. Such strong, light wheels, he thought, if he'd been able to make them more quickly, would easily become very popular. But as it was, he'd have to ask too much for them, he'd never be able to sell enough to make it worthwhile.'

'So what are you getting at? What's your point?' Eric asked.

'I told Albert about someone's ideas I'd had described to me a short while earlier. They were about dividing manufacturing into a series of steps so that making things could be undertaken more resourcefully. By having each step performed by a person skilled in a particular task, it was argued, making things could be achieved much more quickly and efficiently. Albert responded by saying it was alright for armchair theorists to dream up such ideas but they never consider the difficulties of putting them into practice. How, he asked, could he get enough people, each making the same part of a wheel over and over again, into his small workshop? And how would he be able to pay them? Would they be willing and able to wait until sufficient wheels had been sold before they were paid? Of course not, I said. But that was before we'd started the money lending scheme. When you said increasing prices would put us in great danger if we continued creating money and there was no change in the quantity of goods offered for sale, my talk with Albert came back to me. It occurred to me that we wouldn't have to stop printing money if, by lending, we helped to increase the quantity of goods for sale.'

Albert was in the business of making wheels.

'You mean we could offer to lend money to Albert so he could set up a bigger wheel-making workshop?'

'Yes, that's what I was thinking. I'm sure Albert will be interested if I suggest it. He's not as young as he used to be so I think he'll welcome the idea of employing other people to make wheels while he oversees the process. But I wasn't just thinking about Albert and wheels, I was thinking about manufacturing in general, about increasing the number and variety of goods for sale in the markets. If we made loans available to people who wanted to open workshops and employ people to make things for sale, and if the money they got by selling the things was greater than the money, and interest, they needed to pay back to us, they'd have some money left over for themselves. They'd make a profit, and so would we.'

Even after a few trials, it took Albert more than a week to make one spoked wheel.

Frank commented, 'And if they could go on making profits they could open more workshops and become richer.'

Eric added, 'Harry, I think you've got something. We certainly can't go on creating money without causing inflation unless there's a lot more things for people to spend it on, so lending money to people who want to open workshops is an excellent idea.'

Harry replied, 'I'll see what Albert has to say. If he takes a loan and is able to make a profit selling spoked wheels we can then see about lending to other people with industrial ambitions.'

Albert borrowed, bought a bigger workshop, employed a blacksmith and a team of carpenters, and, after his staff had become familiar with their respective tasks and working together, was soon able to produce nine or ten wheels a day. Spoked wheels quickly became very popular. They were sturdy, durable and much lighter than ones made of solid wooden boards. Customers frequently asked for spoked wheels to be fitted to their carts and wagons. In response, Albert took on an additional employee, a wheel fitter, to provide the service requested. Wheel sales and fitting soon provided sufficient income for Albert to pay his staff's wages, service his debt, pay his income tax and comfortably provide for his personal needs. After a while he was ready to employ another person, someone to replace him in the manufacturing process, so allowing him to spend more time overseeing his business and planning its future. More and more he toyed with the idea of building coaches. He sometimes dreamed of a business empire centred on the manufacture of luxurious carriages. He imagined them being pulled by teams of thoroughbred horses, transporting finely dressed people to important places and being carried along on elegant, steel-rimmed, spoked wheels.

After becoming familiar with their respective tasks and working together,
Albert's staff was able to produce nine or ten wheels a day.

The bankers observed Albert's progress with interest. His success encouraged them to proceed with their plans to promote borrowing as a means to increase the production of saleable goods. They were particularly encouraged when they realized that by taking interest payments from Albert they were, in effect, taking a share of the wealth created by the people who worked in his workshop. As a scam, it was almost as good as creating money out of pieces of paper. However, when they considered their plans carefully, they could see that lending money to people who wanted to build and operate workshops was not as straightforward as creating money. Eric alerted the others to this when he said, 'If borrowers were not able to sell all, or most, of the things they made in their workshops, they might not be able to re-pay the money, including interest, they owed to us.'

*Albert dreamed of making luxurious carriages with elegant spoked wheels,
and of them being pulled by teams of thoroughbred horses transporting,
finely dressed people to important places.*

Harry responded, 'Yes, I see that. Large sums will be needed to set-up and operate workshops, so we don't want to lend to people who might get into such difficulties. We'll have to be very careful about who we lend money to.'

'People who are already very rich won't be a problem,' Eric replied. 'If they want to set-up manufacturing workshops with employed workers, but don't have the necessary cash readily available, we can let them borrow whatever they need. If they get into difficulties they'll be able to sell some of their assets. It's people who are not so wealthy that we'll need to be careful with.'

'You're right,' answered Harry. 'We'll have to tell them we're only willing to let them borrow part of the money they require, and that they'll have to provide the rest from their savings, or from someone else's.'

Eric added, 'And we'll only lend if the project they have in mind seems likely to succeed. They'll have to convince us that the business they planned was feasible and likely to be profitable.'

The others agreed and Frank added, 'We could also require them to pay higher interest rates.'

'That's a good idea,' Eric replied. 'The extra interest will offset the additional risk we'd be taking in agreeing to their loans.'

So the bankers agreed that very rich people who wanted to operate large industrial concerns would, within reason, be able to borrow whatever they asked for; less rich people who wanted to operate smaller manufacturing workshops would be able to borrow smaller amounts, at higher interest rates, provided they were able to provide a proportion of the money they needed and their proposals were viable; and poor people would not be eligible to borrow anything at all, not even very small amounts. Having so agreed, they turned their attention to a matter they knew would need to be addressed before they embarked on their industrialisation programme. It was an issue requiring the King's collaboration.

A few days later, in the royal palace's main parlour, the King and Harry exchanged polite pleasantries. A relaxed, friendly conversation followed. Before broaching the request he'd come to ask for, Harry prepared the King by first saying how good the soldiers parading outside the palace looked in their smart uniforms. This pleased the King. By following Harry's advice things had gone well for him. The success and glory of an easily won war, his splendidly refurbished palace, his standing army and impressive royal guards and the high regard his people had for him - people who were enjoying unparalleled prosperity - he attributed to Harry and his friends at the bank. He expressed his gratitude to Harry for helping to make his good fortune possible, mentioning each beneficial achievement in turn. In response Harry thanked the King for his kind words. He then asked, 'How's the income tax scheme going?'

'Oh, it's just fine,' the King replied. 'In fact it's bringing in more than I need. My accountants always err on the safe side when making estimates, so you've no need to worry about your re-payments.'

'I wasn't worried about that, your majesty. I was just wondering if you'd like to borrow a little more. People seem very relaxed about the national debt and paying income tax. They think you spend their money very wisely. I think they'd be very pleased if you spent a little more on something they could see and appreciate. How about the sea-front and jetty? The sea-walls are getting old and dangerous; they're long overdue for renewal. Just think how the fishermen in the harbour would feel if you announced that the quayside was to be rebuilt and extra landing stages were to be added. I think they'd love you for it. And since you already have a surplus tax income, you won't need to increase the tax rate until next year.'

'That's a brilliant suggestion. A renewed harbour front! Yes, I like the idea. I'll see to it'

'And if you agree to my next suggestion,' Harry continued, 'it's probable that you won't need to increase the tax rate in the foreseeable future, your tax income will increase automatically as economic activity in your kingdom increases.'

'What is it, Harry? What do you want me to agree to?'

'I want you to introduce a law allowing the bank to take property from people who are not willing or able, to repay borrowed money.'

'That seems fair and reasonable.'

'Yes, I think so too. Without the protection of such a law, the bank will not be able to carry on lending as it has been. Commerce will no longer remain prosperous and buoyant. I can't see your kingdom continuing to flourish unless there's a law designed to protect the bank from bad debts. And it will be a just law, your majesty, for the value of property seized will be no more than the amount, including interest, owed.'

'Yes, that does seem just and fair. I'll see to it that a new law is introduced as soon as possible.'

'Thank you, your majesty.'

'I thought I told you to stop saying *your majesty*. Never mind, let's move on to less serious matters. What's this I hear about your friend Eric planning to marry his housekeeper, Nancy?'

'They're both looking forward to it. All the details are more or less arranged, and on the big day they're planning to have a lavish celebration at Eric's place. They'd both be deeply honoured if you were to attend.'

'Oh, that would never do. It wouldn't be fitting. But thank them all the same. What about Frank, what's he getting up to? Has he got a lady friend?'

'He has, a young woman called Fiona. They're both excited about Eric and Nancy, and I think they'll be announcing their own engagement very soon.'

'Give them my best wishes. What about you? It's quite a while since your wife died. Don't you think it's time to be thinking of marrying again?'

'I'm getting a bit too old for that.'

'Nonsense! Nonsense! You're still a young man, and you've got a lot to offer.' The king paused, and then said, 'Come along with me, I've something to show you.'

In front of the King and Harry was a painting of a striking woman
still blessed with the beauty of her younger years.

The King walked to a far corner of the room, and Harry followed. In front of them, mounted on the wall, was a painting of a striking woman still blessed with the beauty of her younger years.

'Do you know who that is?' the King asked.

'No, but whoever it is, she's very attractive.'

'Yes, she is. She's Emma, the Duchess of Arvin.'

'I've wondered what happened to her. Is she still in Arvin?

'She is. I'm not too sure if she played any part in her father's plot to seize the Duchy, so I've not yet decided what to do with her, whether to send her back to Isconsia, or allow her to remain in Arvin. In the meantime, I've ordered that she is to remain confined to her palace.'

Harry paused. When they first looked at the picture he wondered why the King had taken him to see it, but he had his suspicions. They became firmer when the King agreed that she was very attractive. He thought it was time to ask, 'Why are you showing me this picture?'

'I just thought you might like to see what the Duchess looked like. After all you did help me to drive her contemptible father out of my kingdom.'

'Come on, there's more to it than that. Were you thinking I might be interested in her?'

'Well, it might have crossed my mind.'

'But she's a royal princess. She's out of my league.'

'Nonsense, you're far richer than any of my noble barons.'

Harry wondered what to say. He managed, 'But…'

'Never mind your 'buts', Harry. I'll be having her sent to Arcue soon, so would you like to meet her while she's here?'

'But I'm not a baron or earl, or anything like that, I'm an ordinary person.'

'Don't worry about that. If you want a noble title I'll give you one. I'm the King, remember.'

'But that's not the point. If I was to marry someone, it would have to be because I really liked her, not because of a duchy or a title. I couldn't do it. It wouldn't feel right.'

'How do you know that? And who said anything about marriage? All I'm suggesting is that you might like to meet the woman. In spite of her depraved father, I understand she's very agreeable. And from what Duke Forbim told me, she's - well, err, how shall I put it? She's very well accomplished in bedroom talents. Somehow I think you and Emma will get on very well together.'

'But what if she was to tell me she'd supported her father in trying to annex Arvin?'

'Don't worry about that. If I found she'd been involved I'd probably send her back to Isconsia, but if you took a fancy to her it wouldn't matter. After all, the war's over and nothing's better for sealing the peace than a good old fashioned love story.'

'I don't know what to say. You're asking me to take up with a woman I've never met. I like to think I'm patriotic, but you're asking for something I wasn't expecting. I feel as if my loyalty is being questioned.'

'Good God, man, I'm not asking you to marry the woman, I'm asking if you'd like to meet her. Look, call round while she's staying here in the palace and, if it seems right, ask if she'd like to accompany you at Eric's wedding. How's that? You could do that, couldn't you?'

'Yes, I suppose I could. Alright, I'll come to see her, and, if she agrees, I'll take her to Eric's wedding.'

'Well then, that's settled. Now, is there anything else you want me to deal with?'

When it was finished, the King proudly inspected the new harbour.

'Yes, there is one more little thing I'd like you to do. Banking, as I'm sure you appreciate, is a complicated business. It took years to gain the skills and experience needed to run the bank. Yet I hear rumours that people with no idea of what's involved are thinking of trying to copy our methods. They,

I'm told, are considering opening banks in competition to ours. Please don't misunderstand me, we've nothing against competition, it would help to keep us from becoming complacent, but, as I'm sure you'll agree, banks need to be run by people who know what they're doing. Think of the harm inexperienced amateurs could do to commerce and trade if they tried to open banks. They could easily upset the delicate balance of your kingdom's financial system.'

'So what is it you want me to do?'

'I want you to issue a decree making it illegal to open a bank without a licence. To obtain a licence, a would-be banker would need to show he was sufficiently competent to handle the complicated business of finance.'

'And who would decide if someone applying for a licence was sufficiently competent?'

'We could do that.'

'That seems fair enough to me. I'll get my lawyers to draft the necessary papers and I'll issue the decree as soon as possible.'

'Thank you, your majesty.'

'Stop saying your majesty.'

When it was time to leave, Harry thanked the King for the laws he'd promised to introduce. Both thought their conversation had been very fruitful. Harry was pleased with what he'd accomplished. As he walked away, he was also profoundly thoughtful of the prospects of meeting Princess Emma, The Duchess of Arvin.

Chapter Three

As expected and intended, people who were able to satisfy the bank's lending criteria, regardless of the lawful risks to their property, started borrowing in order to expand their trades. It started slowly at first. Aware of the success of Albert's spoked wheel venture, a few craftsmen followed his lead and borrowed. They were able to enlarge and develop their workshops profitably, and this inspired others to extend and upgrade theirs. The industrialisation programme then unfolded more rapidly than the bankers had anticipated. Soon, in a time that was very short when compared with how long people had lived in the realms of make-believe, new or upgraded workshops, many using division-of-labour methods, started to appear in most parts of Areho. Everyday articles, including pots, pans, clothing, tools, shoes, candles, crockery and many others, became plentiful. Moreover, the growth of manufacturing encouraged creativity and invention, and many previously unseen products, including luxurious carriages carried on elegant, steel-rimmed, spoked wheels became familiar in Arcue. For the bankers, the expansion exceeded their most optimistic expectations. As they thought it would, it enabled them to continue lending paper money without causing undesirable price rises. Money introduced into circulation increased in step with increases in the quantity of saleable goods, so ensuring stable prices. But the bankers did not anticipate the rapidity with which the growth of industrialisation would occur. The success of the first wave of artisans to reap the benefits of borrowing inspired a larger second wave, and this in turn inspired an even larger third wave, and so on, giving rise to a rapid growth of manufacturing, and since borrowing grew in step, the bankers' profits increased in the same way. They became extremely wealthy. Many years later, after studying historical records of the industrial growth, intellectuals described it as a revolution.

Amid the excitement and commotion of the early stages of their industrialisation scheme, the bankers became married men. Eric married Nancy, Frank married Fiona and Harry, after a little hesitation, married Princess Emma. Powerful feelings of love, fulfilment and ambition that normally accompany marriages stirred in all six; as usual in the three women, but strongly infused by recurring thoughts of raising and instructing heirs in the three men. The bankers were not disappointed. In the course of their respective marriages, Nancy gave birth to two sons and a daughter, Fiona to two sons and two daughters and Emma to one son and one daughter. With one exception - Harry and Emma's son James - the children showed keen interests in their parents' business. James spent much of his early years at his mother's Duchy, and there, in the company of the estate's managers, gardeners and gamekeepers, he quickly developed interests in agriculture, forests, mountains and open country. Unlike his sister, Miranda, he disliked the city and showed no interest in the bank, preferring instead hunting, riding and fishing. His rustic inclinations were reinforced by his tutors who, with the best of intentions, tailored his instruction to his personal preferences. The other children grew up in Arcue, and there, in addition to gaining broad general educations, were prepared by their parents for careers in banking. However, until they showed signs of being curious and were thought to be sufficiently mature to appreciate the need for complete confidentiality, they were not told the secret of where money came from.

Harry and Emma's wedding.

The creation of money out of pieces of paper, the mainstay of the banking system, was necessarily kept from the general public, principally by encouraging the widespread belief that banking was a highly complex activity understood only by gentlemen of great intelligence, experience and integrity. When considering how this essential deception could be maintained when it was time to pass their business on to their successors, the bankers initially gave little thought to the extremely high probability that their heirs would, in the fullness of maturity, form intimate relationships with members of the opposite sex. But when the children approached puberty it became an issue of considerable concern. Would heirs be able to keep the bank's secrets from their spouses? Could they be trusted to keep secrets from their intimate partners, or to choose ones who could be trusted with them? Possible answers didn't inspire the bankers with confidence. Nancy and Fiona never inquired too deeply into their husbands' business affairs, happy with the wealth they provided and the freedom this gave to pursue their own interests. Only Emma, able to sense that something was being kept from her, repeatedly questioned Harry until he had fully satisfied her curiosity. She was sufficiently wise and self-interested to understand the need for strict confidentiality. Nancy and Fiona, without showing Emma's inquisitiveness, intuitively understood this need. None of this lessened the bankers' concerns for the security of the bank's secrets when in the hands of their successors. They disregarded their own experiences. However, before the bankers had given much thought as to how they might forestall problems that would arise if their heirs intended to marry untrustworthy partners, their fears were resolved effortlessly, agreeably and unexpectedly.

The bankers' sons and daughters enjoyed themselves as playful children normally do. With the exception of James, they shared the same tutors and interests and they happily played together. They were content with their friendships and tended to have little interaction with other children in the city. Unsurprisingly, as they grew into adolescents each developed a keen closeness with one friend in particular. They became four loving couples. Nancy's first son, Alan, fell in love with Fiona's second daughter, Pauline; Fiona's first son, William, fell in love with Nancy's daughter, Caroline; Nancy's second son, Tom, fell in love with Fiona's first daughter, Margaret; and Emma's daughter, Miranda, fell in love with Fiona's second son, George. When the appropriate time came, the young couples married. As well as pleasing their parents in the usual way, the marriages dispelled their fathers' and Emma's fears of their heirs falling in love with unsuitable spouses.

As the years passed by, financed by loans, many new workshops appeared, many making innovative products. The bank flourished. Harry, Eric and Frank, happy that their business could be passed on to capable successors, decided it was time to consider retirement. Nancy, Fiona and Emma concurred, so, in accord with earlier agreements, it was decided that the bank was to be split into parts. Ostensibly independent and roughly equal in terms of trading volumes, four new banking businesses with different trading names were formed, each with branches throughout the kingdom. When all the necessary arrangements had been made, the new businesses were handed over to the bankers' heirs. Alan and Pauline took control of Schemowt's Bank, William and Caroline took Telslow's Bank, Tom and Margaret took Indolder's Bank and the fourth bank, headquartered in Harry's city mansion, was entrusted to George and Miranda. Their bank, in view of it holding the palace's account and Miranda's mother's regal background, was, with the King's approval, called The Royal Bank of Areho. The King also approved of James' entitlement, after being given possession of his mother's Duchy, to be known as the Duke of Arvin. Harry, Eric, Frank, their wives and their progeny were all pleased with the new arrangements. The original bankers retired to relax and enjoy all the comforts great wealth was able to provide, but they still took a keen interest in their successors' banking activities and were always available if advice was asked for.

James became the Duke of Arvin.

The four new banking corporations easily slotted into the role their parent organisation had previously monopolised: lending to households and industry. Also, the King, encouraged by his old friend Harry, continued borrowing in order to develop his kingdom and bolster his popularity, dividing his requirements equally between the four new banks. Tax revenues, which, as predicted, increased in line with economic growth, enabled him to re-pay his debts, with interest, without income tax rates needing to be increased. So, the new bankers found they had little to do but administer divisions of a fully functional and carefully planned enterprise. In practice, management of each bank was handled mainly by one of its two owners. Alan directed Schemowt's Bank, William handled Telslow's Bank, Tom managed Indolder's Bank and Miranda took charge of The Royal Bank of Areho. Pauline, Caroline, Margaret and George were happy to take passive roles, but still had keen interests in the world of banking.

In addition to the need for strict secrecy, they had all been frequently told by their parents that competition would be wasteful and lead to ruin while cooperation would ensure prosperity. This advice was totally unnecessary. All eight banking heirs retained the close friendships they'd enjoyed from childhood, there was more than sufficient business for them to share and they intuitively understood the need for cooperation without being told. They met frequently, to discuss banking issues and to socialise generally, but after a while it was realised that this risked violating confidentiality. It was not the secret of where money came from that was at risk, it was the public's belief that the four new banks operated independently and competitively, an illusion the banks were keen to encourage. Banknotes issued before the four banks were formed remained in use for a while, and the public seemed unconcerned when new ones bearing the names of the new banks entered into circulation along with them. The mingling of different sets of banknotes didn't cause the public to think the four banks were not operating independently. People looked at the new notes, made comments about their designs, but thought little more about them. Banknotes were money, that was all that mattered. Nevertheless, the new bankers agreed that they should be seen together in public as little as possible. They continued meeting unobtrusively in one or other of the various palatial country mansions their three sets of parents had retired to, but they knew that before too long they would have make more satisfactory arrangements. They would have to consider how they could continue meeting to discuss their common interests without arousing suspicion. The issue, however, was not pressing and was not seriously examined until several factors brought it into focus. One factor was the increasing number of very rich borrowers.

Previously, apart from ones taken out by the King, loans had been arranged predominantly with people who were involved in the business of making and selling things. Typically, they borrowed moderate sums in order to expand and develop their existing workshops, and then worked along with paid craftsmen to produce plentiful supplies of traditional and newly devised goods. Other than consuming the merchandise so produced, very rich people - the aristocracy - had not been involved. However, the proliferation of manufacturing workshops created a large and growing demand for the basic materials of which things were made. Steel, timber, coal, leather, textiles and many other essential resources became needed in quantities requiring previously unseen levels of industrialisation. A few very rich individuals, recognising the need for such facilities, and being able to provide the collateral needed for very large loans, borrowed in order to set them up. Their ventures were observably successful, and other would-be business magnates with wealthy backgrounds quickly followed. Very large industrial organisations producing large quantities of essential basic materials soon started to appear throughout the kingdom. The bankers quickly found that dealing with very rich individuals was not as straightforward as arranging, or refusing, loans for small workshop owners. Usually, no more than brief interviews and property surveys conducted by branch employees were required to ascertain if ventures proposed by applicants for modest amounts were likely to succeed, but requests by candidates for much larger loans needed to be examined in far greater detail. Their business proposals and prospects had to be carefully studied, their credentials and collaterals had to be scrutinized and, if loans were approved, detailed contracts had to be agreed and drafted. Technical matters were handled at bank headquarters by employed experts, but with very wealthy individuals the bankers usually preferred to discuss contractual details cordially, in relaxed, informal settings. One such conversation, in combination with other factors, in due course led to fundamental changes in industry and banking in Areho.

Baron Ranty, wanting to take advantage of his extensive forests and the vigorous river running through his huge estate, approached Telslow's Bank seeking a substantial loan so he could have a dam and water-powered saw-mill built in a secluded part of the river's valley. He wanted to start a timber business. To discuss the proposal, William Telslow, the Bank's chairman, dined with the

Baron in one of the capital's exclusive restaurants. Having agreed terms, the two chatted as they enjoyed the chef's special delicacies and the kingdom's finest wines. As the evening passed William became acutely aware that as soon as possible he would need to tell his fellow bankers of his conversation with Ranty. Helped by the food, the wine and the atmosphere, the conversation became increasingly relaxed and the Baron started inquiring about the bank, its business, its organisation and its profitability. His questions became increasingly searching and William's answers became increasingly cautious. Guarded responses and avoidance of giving direct replies revealed William's discomfort, and Ranty's incisive mind and wide experiences made him a skilful judge of people. He decided it was a good time to take the conversation to a new level. He looked at William directly and said, 'I think I know what your game is.'

Baron Ranty had ideas of a water-powered saw-mill.

'What do you mean?' William spluttered.

'I know that you and the other bankers have printed far more money than you could ever redeem in gold, as promised on your banknotes.'

'How could you think such a thing?'

'It's not too difficult. I've long been aware that there's a lot more money in circulation now than there was not so many years ago and, after thinking about it I took the trouble of making informed estimates of the total amount of gold and the total amount of paper money in the Kingdom. There was a wide gap between my two evaluations.'

'How could you make such assessments?'

'Don't be concerned, they were much more than educated guesses. I've lived and done business in Areho for many years and I know what I'm talking about.'

'But how could you be sure they were accurate?'

'Relax. Don't worry. Your secret is safe with me.'

William was feeling very uneasy in the restaurant.

William was feeling very uneasy. He asked, 'Why do you say that?'

'That's simple,' the Baron replied. 'It wouldn't be in my interests to reveal it. You and the others are clearly doing very well out of your audacious scheme, but so is the country, and so am I, and I hope to do even better in the years ahead. If it became widely known that the promises on your banknotes are worthless you'd be in trouble, serious trouble, but so would the country as a whole. After the masses had finished venting their fury on you and your fellow bankers, probably with very unsavoury consequences, they'd find the prosperous economy they'd learned to enjoy and take for granted crumbling rapidly into chaos. Without a plentiful supply of trusted money, workshops and factories would cease production, busy markets would disappear and, in all probability, desperate bandits would take violent control of formerly peaceful communities. None of this would be of any benefit to me; on the contrary, I would find it extremely unsatisfactory. I'd, for example, no longer be able to enjoy dining in fine restaurants such as the one we are now sitting in. I'd no longer be able to travel safely to the capital, to stay in its splendid hotels and to visit the charming theatres and opera houses that are now springing up in the better-off parts of the city. I'd no longer be able to appreciate all the remarkable improvements the King's development plans are producing throughout the kingdom. And I'd have to abandon my plans for building my saw mill, and my future ambitions of developing the artificial lake its dam will create into a lucrative boating and fishing tourist attraction. So, you see, I'm going to keep very quiet about the things I've been able to figure-out about your banking business. As I said, your secret is safe. Moreover, I must thank you for substantiating my analysis. Although I was confident in the accuracy of my estimates and the correctness of my reasoning, until I was able to observe your reactions this evening I couldn't be fully certain of my conclusions, the ramifications were too great, they were overwhelming. I could hardly believe my own deductions. You've put an end to any lingering doubts I had about the powers of my own reasoning.'

'I don't know what to say to that.'

'There's no need to say anything. Your predecessors' clever scheme has transformed the country. You've clearly done well out of it, but so has the kingdom as a whole, and for that they have my fullest respect.'

The two continued discussing banking issues in particular and national, industrial and political matters in general well into the evening. William became reassured that Baron Ranty was a man he could trust and respect; nevertheless, the following morning he took urgent steps to arrange a clandestine meeting with the other bankers. They all agreed to meet the following day at Harry Indolder's country mansion.

Designed with regal splendour by Emma's personal architects, Harry and Emma's purpose-built country mansion was situated beside a wide lake that stretched far to the south. With its magnificent gardens and miles and miles of dense forest and gently sloping hills beyond, it allowed the two to enjoy retirement in considerable comfort. Its seclusion made it also an ideal location for the bankers' meeting. When they had settled in the main hall and servants had been dismissed and told not to disturb the conference, William summarized his tête-à-tête with Baron Ranty. His words gave rise to a general hum of uneasy conversation until Harry brought the meeting to order. In a loud and clear voice, he said, 'Let's approach the situation calmly and rationally. We need to talk one at a time.'

The meeting became hushed for a while until Eric looked at William and asked, 'Are you absolutely sure this Ranty has no intention of revealing our secrets?'

'Oh yes,' William replied. 'He made that very clear. As I said, he fully understands how his own interests and well-being depend on the continued operation of our banks. I think we can trust him.'

Harry and Emma's purpose-built country mansion was situated beside a wide lake.

'I'm sure you're right,' Eric replied. 'But it opens up the question of how many others might have come to the same conclusions as his.'

'I was thinking the same thing,' Harry added. 'If Ranty was able to see-through our scheme then others may well have been able to do the same, and some may not have decided as he did, that self-interest stipulates secrecy. I think it's something we'll need to look into without too much delay.'

'I agree,' Eric responded. He then looked again at William and asked, 'Ranty claimed to have a good grasp of all aspects of business in Areho?'

'Yes, he said he knew enough to be able to see that there was far more paper money than we would be able to back with gold, but he refused to explain how. I got the impression that he was able to make his claims from having done business with very many big-shots over the years. I think all these barons and earls and the like all stick together and make deals with each other.'

'Be careful what you say, young man,' Emma responded playfully.

'Did he say anything about discussing money and gold with others?' Eric asked.

'No,' William answered, 'he never mentioned other people.'

William told the other bankers about his meeting with Baron Ranty.

Eric then looked at Harry and asked, 'Harry, you've lots of well-placed friends in Areho, have you heard any rumours from any of them, any chitchat that might suggest others may have been thinking along the same lines as Ranty?'

'No, I'd have told you if I had. I'll ask a few discreet questions. There are one or two people I think would know if there are any such ideas being aired, and I'll pop round to have bit of a chat with the King. I'll get him talking about the state of the nation's economy, casually asking for his opinion about the mood in the country to see if he has anything interesting to say. I know toadies approach him whenever they can, bringing any gossip they think might ingratiate themselves with him, but I don't expect I'll find out anything worth knowing. What I was thinking is that we should be having a bit of a chinwag with Ranty himself; asking, for example, if he'd figured-out our scheme alone, or if he'd discussed it with others. I suggest we have a friendly word or two with him, to find out how we and he stand.'

Harry's suggestion won unanimous approval. It was decided that a cordial letter was to be sent to Ranty and his wife inviting them to be, at their own convenience, guests at Harry and Emma's mansion. The delights of the country palace and its magnificent surroundings were outlined in the message, and the invitees were assured of a very warm welcome. It was hoped that during the visit Harry and Ranty would find opportunities to discuss matters of common interest. Other than everyone giving serious thought as to how the new situation might be handled, it was decided that nothing more was to be done until after Harry's anticipated meeting with Ranty.

When Ranty received Harry and Emma's invitation he instantly realized its purpose. He and his wife, Juliet, responded keenly and, after making appropriate arrangements, arrived to stay for a while as welcome guests. Each of the two couples quickly found their new acquaintances to be very agreeable, with Ranty and Harry in particular gaining good understandings of each other's points of view. They discussed at great lengths all the issues William and Ranty had broached during their conversation in the restaurant, and went on to explore how their mutual interests might best be served in the years to come. Emma would have liked to have been involved in the talks, but she was at ease courteously entertaining Juliet knowing Harry would be more than capable of conferring with Ranty appropriately. When all issues of mutual concern had been fully examined, and it was time for the visitors to leave, warm assurances were given that the meeting had been very enjoyable and fruitful, and that newly formed friendships were to be sustained and nurtured.

As planned, soon after Ranty and Juliet had left, the banking families made arrangements to meet. A different location, Eric's country mansion, with its loyal and discreet staff, was chosen in order to reduce the possibility of arousing unhelpful suspicions. After telling everyone that his talks with Ranty had been very interesting and helpful, Harry followed by saying, 'He told me he'd figured-out our modus-operandi alone and had not discussed it with anyone else, but he also said he thought it likely that anyone with enough curiosity and sufficient powers of observation and deduction would be able to do the same, and, for all the reasons he made clear to William, it was as much in his interests as ours to determine if there are any such persons. The ease with which he'd been able to undertake his investigation into our affairs, he said, had brought home to him the very real dangers that threatened his security and prosperity. Like William, I felt I could trust him. We agreed to cooperate in trying to find out if there are any dangers to our common interests from people inclined to asking too many questions, and, if there are any such risks, how they might be reduced or eliminated. After a lengthy discussion we decided that one approach to the problem would be to establish a clandestine club, or association, or whatever it might be called, into which persons showing signs of ominous curiosity might be invited. We talked about how such persons might be recognized without arousing their suspicions. We surmised that in relaxed informal settings, by means of casual friendly conversations that didn't reveal their inquisitive purpose, it should not be too difficult to identify intelligent individuals with undue levels of unwanted curiosity.'

Alan, feeling a little confused, asked, 'You mean the club will be where such exploratory conversations will be held?'

'No, no,' Harry answered. 'That's not what I meant. The club we had in mind will be one into which suitable individuals will be invited after the informal, easy-going chitchats; after it had been established that they had dangerous suspicions about the trustworthiness of our banknotes. We'll want to know if they could be trusted, if they realized their welfare, and the kingdom's prosperity in general, would be threatened if their doubts became widespread. We'll look for such individuals in the numerous societies and guilds that already exist, in business associations, local interest organizations, trade circles, friendship fellowships, that sort of thing. Ranty told me he felt confident he would be able to inconspicuously identify anyone whose thoughts were following the same lines as his. He said he expected them to have an inner urge to seek signs of confirmation of their suspicions, as he had, and he thought this could be uncovered bit-by-bit, without recourse to leading questions, by means of casual, friendly conversations. We intend to try the tactic initially on several individuals we know, including one or two known to both of us. Ranty and I thought it was worthwhile casually asking what they thought about the obvious changes in commerce and industry that have occurred in their lifetimes, and discreetly encouraging them to talk about it if they seemed in any way astonished, uneasy, curious, or in any other way that suggested they'd given it more that passing thoughts. We decided to start circulating in their favourite haunts. If they, or any others we might encounter, show any signs of having questions about the credibility of our banknotes, we'll endeavour to gain their confidence and, if they show themselves to be fully suitable, we'll cautiously ask, "If there was to be an exclusive, secretive meeting of individuals who think as you do would you be interested in being involved?" If enough show a positive response we'll then be able to think further about forming some sort of club.'

Tom interrupted and asked, 'What about the possibility of smart-alecks who figure-out our business practice but don't think they should keep it secret?'

'We considered that and thought that anyone smart enough to fathom out our system would also be intelligent enough to see that it was in his or her interests to keep quiet about it. If the increasing prosperity our banking scheme has brought to the kingdom aroused their curiosity, and I can think of nothing else that could possibly do this, they are not likely to want to ruin it all by revealing their suspicions publicly.'

'Yes, I can see that,' Tom responded. 'But there still might be a few cranks who think people should know about their ideas. Perhaps they might have eccentric notions of the public having an entitlement to be told, or maybe they might simply want to be famous.'

'If we come across any such individuals we'll simply have to gently persuade them that they are wrong, that they had not fully considered the likely consequences of revealing their mistaken ideas and that they would not become famed celebrities but would, instead, become notorious heralds of chaos and rebellion.'

'What if gentle persuasion is unable to change their minds?' George inquired.

'Then, I guess, not so gentle methods will be needed,' Eric responded.

Eric's comment aroused another buzz of edgy conversations causing Harry to again bring the meeting to order. After firmly tapping a glass on the table before him, he addressed his friends and relatives saying, 'I think we're getting way ahead of ourselves. As far as we know only one person has been able to figure out our methods, and he seems to be fully committed to keeping it secret, so it's a bit premature to start thinking about what we'll do if we think someone might be planning to spread unhelpful rumours. So, before we go any further, let's first see if anything interesting comes to light after Ranty and I have sounded out the individuals and places we have in mind. We'll perhaps then have a better picture of the problem we face, if indeed there is one. As soon as I have anything interesting to tell you I'll call another meeting. Now, is there any other business?'

Eric went out and about visiting popular taverns.

Those eager to express their thoughts took Harry's question to signify that the meeting was over and again the room became filled with the hum of lively conversations. Eric, who did have something more to say, sensibly allowed the chattering to go on for a while before standing up to show he was waiting for everybody's attention. When the room was quiet, looking particularly at the new generation of bankers, he said, 'While Harry and Emma were entertaining Ranty and Juliet, I did a little bit of discreet investigation myself.

Without being recognized, in simple clothing, I simply went out and about visiting popular taverns, inconspicuously talking with anyone willing to chat. It soon became clear that a lot of ordinary people hoard banknotes. They put away any they don't need right away with the intention of using them later, perhaps after a sizeable amount had accrued. Some don't have a particular expensive purchase in mind but simply like the feeling of security they gain from having a sizeable store of readily available cash. It made me think back to the time when Harry, Frank and I started the gold storage scheme that gave birth to the banking scheme we all now enjoy. We recognized then that there was a need for a place where people could safely store gold. I think you should consider offering the same sort of facility for banknotes. Tell people that they can safely deposit their money with you, away from the danger of theft, and that you'll keep records of how much money they'd deposited. Make it clear that they'll be provided with copies of their accounts and will be able to withdraw all, or some, of their money at any time.'

'And charge a fee, just like you did when you first started storing people's gold?' Tom asked.

'No, no, you don't want to do that. In fact, I think you should offer to pay interest to customers with special accounts, ones from which they agree not to withdraw money until after a specified time had passed. You can call them savings accounts, and the others, instant-access accounts.'

'Pay interest?' William asked. 'Why should we do that?'

'First let me say that the interest I'm suggesting will be at much lower rates than the ones you charge on loans. Secondly, I think by encouraging savers to have bank accounts that pay interest you'll gain far more than you lose. Let me explain why. I know people bring banknotes to you when they make regular payments on their loans; nevertheless I bet that more often than not you don't have enough notes readily available when customers take out new loans. You then have to print new ones. Am I right?'

Several voices replied, 'Yes, that's right.'

'Well, I think if savers bring their banknotes to your cash desks for safe keeping, you'll be short of them far less frequently. As you know, printing banknotes is not cost-free, so I think you'll find by encouraging people to have savings accounts you'll save more by not having to print so many new banknotes than you'll lose by paying a little interest. Banknotes not actively in circulation should be in your vaults, not under savers' mattresses. However, I think by encouraging people to open accounts, both instant-access and savings, there's another, even greater, benefit to be gained. You've come here today because you are concerned about the possibility of it becoming widely known that you don't have enough gold in your vaults to redeem all the banknotes in circulation. If Ranty was easily able to figure out why there's so much money kicking about, then it's more than likely that others with sufficient curiosity and intelligence will soon do the same, if they've not already done so. After they'd noticed that there's far more money in circulation now than there was not so long ago they're going to ask, where has it all come from? The answer they're going to come up with is *the banks*. Then they're going to ask, where did the banks get all the money from? At this stage of their pondering, if they're smart enough, they'll come up with the same answer as Ranty. But if they know that lots of people keep money in bank accounts they'll be far more inclined to think you are able to issue loans because of the savers' money you keep in your vaults. They'll probably think you make profits because of the difference in the rates of interest you pay savers and charge borrowers. Most will then ponder no further. Few are likely to think you simply print banknotes that are not backed by sufficient gold. It's possible that Ranty wouldn't have thought as he did if he'd known that you had lots of banknotes in your vaults, banknotes deposited there by customers with bank accounts. I don't think he'd have realized, as he did, that you simply create new money out of pieces of paper. So, for the two good reasons I've given, I think you should encourage customers to have bank accounts.'

Eric's suggestion was accepted by everyone at the meeting as an excellent idea. It would restrain people from asking too many questions about where money came from. It was decided that it was to be tried initially by Miranda's bank, The Royal Bank of Areho. Then, after any unseen difficulties had been ironed out, it was to be put into operation by the other banks. Miranda's evaluation of the trial was to be reported at the next full meeting, planned to be after Harry and Ranty had completed their inquiries and were ready to give their report. Having made such resolutions, their anxieties largely toned down, the bankers were able to put aside their formal business personas and relax. They retired to the music room; summoned musicians ordered for the occasion and instructed the servants to bring refreshments.

The third full meeting of all the bankers called in the wake of Ranty's conversation with William was held in Frank's splendid country mansion. It equalled the magnificence of Harry's and Eric's rural retreats, and its seclusion and well trained loyal staff made it equally suited to hosting clandestine conferences. Harry opened the meeting by saying, 'As we planned, Ranty and I mingled in exclusive gathering places casually chatting with any perceptive individuals we happened to come across. In doing so we encountered many interesting characters. We didn't meet anyone willing to open up as Ranty did, saying they knew that banks must be printing un-secured banknotes, but we did come across quite a few inquisitive individuals who wondered widely about the kingdom's recently attained prosperity. Not only were they curious about how it had come about, one way or another, and with a range of unease, many seemed concerned about its permanence. Will it last? Will it go on increasing? How should I plan for the future? Could it all decline as easily as it developed? What should I do if it all ends? These and many similar questions arose as we nonchalantly chatted with well-heeled individuals whose newly gained wealth was a consequence of the country's increasing prosperity. It's unclear if any of them had figured out the secret of paper money, for if they had the concerns they expressed suggested that they would know, as Ranty does, that it wouldn't be prudent to talk about it.'

Harry paused to take a sip of water and to see if anybody wanted to comment. No one did, so he continued, 'When we took stock of our findings we decided to put aside our original plans and instead think about forming some sort of association for the people I've just described, for individuals who are interested in the kingdom's economic welfare and its future prospects. We'll promote it mainly as a social circle in which they'll be able to mingle with people who think as they do, expand their networks of business contacts, develop their wider interests and support the economic system from which they all benefit. In addition to this rather formal aspect, we'll suggest a more relaxed side to the club, one in which they'll be able to unwind and enjoy social fellowship.'

Harry waited a while, allowing his audience, many clearly eager to express their views, to consider the issues he'd presented. When the meeting seemed ready to hear more, he cleared his throat loudly to gain attention and continued, aiming his words directly at the new generation of bankers. 'As you know, until you found love and marriage as you did, we, your parents, were concerned that you might find unsuitable partners. We were concerned that you might find loving relationships with individuals with whom our business secrets could not be safely entrusted. When it became clear that you intended to marry as you did, keeping the bank's secrets within our three families, we were very pleased and relieved, but we also realized that exceptional circumstances had made it possible. In recent years you've made us grandparents, and we all are extremely proud of our lovely grandchildren, but as they grow up we'll all have to face renewed anxieties about the possibility of one or more of them finding love with unsuitable partners. It would be far too optimistic to hope they will pair up within our families, within our banking community, as you did. It would be too much of a coincidence for it to happen again. And if by some stroke of good fortune the difficulty was surmounted, there would still be the problem of keeping our banking secrets secure when in the hands of subsequent generations. It would be too much to hope that knowledge of where money comes from could be contained within banking families indefinitely.'

Harry's words surprised his audience, particularly the women. They were expecting to hear of plans to form some sort of business club, not about their children's future prospects. A hum of whispering could be heard, and Harry allowed it to subside before continuing. 'I talked with Ranty at length about the issue, and he had many interesting things to say. Basically, in so many words, he talked about how the privileged elite, over very many centuries, has created a system by which individuals from non-aristocratic families, with very few exceptions, are excluded from their social circles. Although it's something we are all vaguely aware of, it's something we wouldn't normally express in such explicit terms. Ranty described it in its basic essentials in order to make the point that we, and other individuals from non-aristocratic backgrounds who have recently amassed considerable wealth, need to learn from the habits of the nobility. Getting directly to the issue we are now concerned with, in order to ensure that their sons and daughters meet and marry suitable partners the aristocracy arrange numerous grand social occasions, particularly magnificent formal balls. Some are held at regular intervals, others are occasional, but they are always splendid and exclusive. Displays of wealth and other enjoyments are associated with such events, but they are principally held to facilitate marriages, for marriages bond noble families together so constructing an interconnected, inter-generational network of privileged, powerful and influential families, the backbone of the ruling elite. This, then, provides a model, a template, for the association we require. I said earlier that we need to build up a social group, a club, or whatever it might be called, in which individuals with concerns about the welfare of the economic system will be able to mingle with people who have similar apprehensions. After several lengthy discussions with Ranty it became clear that, modelled on the methods of the nobility, the basic organisation we need is one with the principal purpose of facilitating suitable marriages. Hopefully such an association will be fully established before your children - our grandchildren - have grown up.'

Again, murmurs of surprise spread softly around the room. Anxious to get on with his announcements, rather than allowing the murmuring to take its course, in a loud clear voice Harry asked, 'Are there any questions anyone would like to ask?'

Alan responded, 'I can see the advantages of making arrangements for our children to meet suitable partners when they are older, and the benefits of thereby nurturing strong inter-family bonds, but isn't the association you are proposing widely different from the one originally intended? What about finding out if other people have figured out where all the extra money came from?'

'I was just about to come to that,' Harry replied. 'As well as providing a means by which your children, and their children, and subsequent generations of our families, will be able to meet and marry suitable partners, the network of bonded families so formed will comprise perceptive, inquisitive and self-interested persons, for only such individuals will be invited to the social gatherings we have in mind. The principal invitation criterion will be an interest and concern for the well-being of the economic system by which they have prospered. Once established, we expect anyone within the group with an unhelpful interest in banking and the nation's currency will be easily identified. If thought to be trustworthy they'll be invited to join an elite section of the club and urged to keep its existence confidential.'

William asked, 'An elite group? What will it do?'

'It'll do several things. From time to time the group will meet covertly to exchange ideas and discuss matters of common interest, and they'll socialize generally within the larger group, nonchalantly injecting helpful views and identifying individuals either suitable for inclusion in the elite group or in need of being gently guided away from any unhelpful notions they may hold. By *helpful views* I mean ideas generally supportive of the economic system, particularly ones that takes the focus off banking. An example of this is the idea that money is created by industrial activity. This misleading notion, we think, can be made popularly believed by frequent portrayal of profitable economic activity as *making money*. Wealth in the form of goods and services is produced by industrial and commercial activity, and the distinction between money and wealth is not generally examined, so the false, but useful, impression that money is created by industrial activity should not be too difficult to propagate. I'll have a little more to say about this later. First let me say that the distinguished, astute individuals we hope will come to our social gatherings, in addition to providing a fellowship group able to facilitate suitable marriages, will also, we hope, be a source from which ideas and opinions we would like to be popular will permeate down to the general public, in much the same way in which ideas and opinions cultivated by the clandestine elite section will, hopefully, percolate down to the rest of the group.'

William interrupted to ask, 'You hope to create a comradeship of wealthy businessmen modelled on the ways of the nobility. How do you think the aristocracy will respond?'

'An excellent question,' Harry replied. 'Ranty and I talked about it. I asked him about the idea of inviting members of the aristocracy to the social programmes we envisioned. He suggested invitations to nobles should only be to ones, like himself, who have branched out into innovative business ventures. Traditional, unenterprising ones, whose income is derived exclusively from their ownership of land, tend to be scornful of new ventures and the resulting new breed of prosperous businessmen and women, especially non-aristocratic ones, whose wealth exceeds their own. So they would either not be interested or would wish to be disrespectful or disruptive. Accordingly, we agreed invitations should only be to successful, sophisticated entrepreneurs, either aristocratic or not, with a positive interest in the new, bank-loan facilitated, economic system. We then talked about how the club might evolve. We thought it possible, even likely, that it will grow to become a tightly bonded, inter-related network of very wealthy families, a rival to the traditional, un-enterprising nobility. It will, we hope, become an association from which a new ruling class will emerge.'

'Will it have a name?' Margaret asked.

'No. I'll keep calling it a club or association amongst ourselves for the time being, for convenience, but we thought it best if we don't give it a formal name. It will be something we won't want the general public to know about, and a name will not only signify that it exists but also imply that it was planned. Accordingly, we won't give it a name or publicise its meetings.'

William interrupted to say, 'You said you'll call it a club or association when talking about it amongst ourselves, but I think we should agree on a name we'll all stick to. I suggest we call it The Organisation.'

Harry responded, 'Yes, I agree, we'll need a name we can all use internally, and, unless anyone has a better suggestion, we'll call it The Organisation. Is everyone happy with that?'

No one answered, so Harry went on to say, 'Good, we'll call it The Organisation amongst ourselves, but so far as outsiders are concerned it will not exist. However, some people will, no doubt, become aware of the meetings and will, as they have done for the nobility, conjure up a variety of names for the events and the individuals who attend. So inevitably our private club, although nameless and clandestine about its internal activities, will not be able to remain unnoticed. The elite group, however, we intend to be very secretive so that even the rest of The Organisation will be unaware of its existence. Also, without the elite group being aware of it, a small section of the most dependable, imaginative and intelligent individuals of it will be selected. They will be required to swear to maintain the strictest of secrecy.'

'What will they do?' Caroline asked.

'Initially they'll examine the idea of establishing educational centres at which, with seemingly benign intentions, the workings of the economic system can be studied and promoted. As you know, every large city of the kingdom has a university principally devoted to training clergy. Religion provides beliefs that give coherence and purpose to the masses. In support of the aristocracy, it gives an explanation and justification for the nation's social structure and power and wealth distribution. We plan, under the cloak of benevolence, to provide funds and expertise to universities so they can open new departments; departments devoted to such topics as industrial production, engineering, materials and the economic system. The special, clandestine, selected group of intellectuals will watch over, influence and guide the new departments, particularly the last one mentioned. Hopefully, this will lead to the creation of a body of believable knowledge about the workings of the economic system. The need for this became clear as we mingled and chatted in exclusive gathering places and heard so many questions and concerns about the nation's new prosperity. Ranty suggested that this body of knowledge could be called *economics*. Seemingly emerging from the wisdom of universities, it will supplement religion's account of the meaning and structure of society. Moreover, it will endeavour to explain economic activity with little or no reference to banks. It will seek to sideline their role to that of supplying money when it's needed so the economy can function efficiently. Moreover, in addition to our endowments to universities, we thought about the possibility of founding a number of scholarly institutions, with seemingly benign purposes, in which intellectuals we approve of will be able to study and guide the country's affairs. They will make recommendations to the King and his advisors.'

Harry paused while his audience collected and exchanged its thoughts. When he considered it appropriate he continued. 'What I've told you is a summary of recent conversations I've had with Ranty. The overall intention of our plans is, without being seen, to shape and influence the opinions and beliefs held at every level of society. The learned institutions will seek to ensure their graduates clandestinely gravitate to all positions of power and influence in society. Also, using suitably scholastic terminology, they will churn out clichés subtly advantageous to the image of big businesses, including the dictum that profitable businesses *make money*. Their aphorisms will support the belief that the economic system is the best of all possible economic systems. People in general, unaware that their ideas of politics, economics, wisdom and righteousness have been subtly moulded by covert influences, will remain confident that their understanding of the world and its ways is the product of their own objective judgements. They will be blissfully ignorant of their ignorance.'

Harry halted briefly before carrying on. 'Our ambitions are momentous and only time will tell if they can be realized. Ranty is going to make a start by inviting a carefully selected number of successful businessmen and their spouses, some aristocratic, some not, to a grand dinner at his castle. Speeches will be made suggesting the many ways in which the people assembled, and other entrepreneurs who may be interested, will be able to benefit by banding together and meeting from time to time to discuss matters of common interest. Hopefully, further similar meetings will be planned and held, including purely social get-togethers to which sons and daughters of marriageable ages will be invited. Although we'll receive full reports of what happens, no one here will be invited to these early meetings. The Organisation's connection to banking must remain obscured. One or two of us will be able to unobtrusively attend when the belief is firmly established that The Organisation is nothing more than an association of successful businessmen. In the meantime I want you to think about the ideas I've told you about and see if you can come up with any useful suggestions. That's all I have to say at the moment but I understand Miranda has some interesting news for you.'

Miranda stood up to address the meeting. She started by saying, 'The introduction of customers' accounts at the Royal Bank has been totally successful. Soon after promoting the idea, we quickly found that many people were eager to have their money stored safely in our vault, as Eric suggested they would. Most wanted to be able to withdraw cash whenever they wished, and were happy to deposit their money with us once it was made clear that there was no charge for the service. Initially, fewer were attracted to savings accounts, but an annual interest rate of three percent, we found, was sufficient to make their numbers grow. As predicted, our vault became filled with sufficient banknotes to meet the needs of all the loans we agreed to, but we very quickly found we didn't need them. We told anyone asking for a loan that they first needed to open an account, then, when their loan had been agreed, we simply credited their account with the amount requested. It was incredible; we were able to create money out of nothing at all, without any need for banknotes. We simply wrote down the amount borrowed in the customer's account, and then started to charge interest, at much more than three percent, on money created out of nothing more than a few strokes of a pen.'

Before cheques were introduced, some customers withdrew large amounts in cash.

'That's amazing,' Tom exclaimed. 'Creating money out of little more than fresh air. It's got to be the best scam ever invented. It's a pity we didn't think of it earlier.'

'Thank you, Tom,' Miranda responded. 'But there's more,' she continued. 'After some customers had withdrawn large amounts in cash we noticed something interesting. A few days later the same amount, or very nearly the same, was deposited by a different person. After observing this a few times it became clear what was happening. The first customer, in some sort of transaction, had transferred the cash to the other person, who had then brought it back to our bank and deposited it into his or her account. After thinking about it - that money had been withdrawn from one person's account, handed to another person, and then deposited in the other person's account - a simple way of making this easier and safer for customers, and very convenient for us, came to mind. Each customer opening an instant-access account was provided with a supply of official, personal Royal Bank notes they could use whenever they wanted to pay a sizable sum to another person. On one of the notes they simply needed to write, in blank spaces provided, the amount they wanted to pay and the name of the person who was to receive it, along with the date and their signature. The note was then handed to the other person who simply then had to take it to our bank where the amount specified was deducted from the payer's account and credited to the payee's. In addition to lessening the need to print extra banknotes, our tellers were saved the trouble of twice counting large numbers of banknotes and our customers from having to carry large wads of money to and from our bank. It was very simple. We called the notes cheques. Of course, the system only worked when both persons had a bank account with us. But if you adopt the system I think we'll all benefit. I suggest you introduce the use of cheques as you start opening bank accounts, making it clear to customers that the person receiving the cheque will be able pay it into any of our four banks. There should be no difficulties in doing this. If, at the end of a suitable time period, the total value of all the cheques from one bank paid into a different one is more, or less, than the total value of the cheques from the different bank that had been paid into the other one, amending the situation will be a simple matter. It will only require a cheque for the difference being sent from one bank to the other.'

Following Harry's example, Miranda paused to allow her audience to absorb the information she'd given. When she felt the time was right, she continued. 'In addition to the advantage Eric suggested, that the existence of bank accounts will reduce the number of people inclined to asking too many questions about where money comes from, you'll quickly find, as we did, that customers with accounts occasionally withdraw small amounts for day-to-day spending and use cheques when they want to buy costly things, making things much easier for your tellers and banknote printers. You'll be able to create money by simply writing down the amounts required as loans in borrowers' accounts. It's as simple as creating money out of fresh air. Soon we'll all be able to look forward to a time, in the not too distant future, when nearly all the money there is will exist as numbers written down in ledgers. We'll still need to keep a stock of banknotes for people who want to withdraw cash for day-to-day spending, and gold coins for the occasional oddball who might demand them according to our redemption promises, but they will only be a small fraction of the money in existence. Money, in the main, will be created by our banks out of nothing more than a few pen-strokes and exist only as numbers in ledgers. That's about all I have to say right now, except I hope you'll find opening bank accounts, using cheques and creating pen-stroke money to be as easy as we did at the Royal. I look forward to learning how you get on.'

Using cheques made large transactions easy.

The meeting continued in a more relaxed but excited manner as many questions and answers were exchanged, but one question was withheld by William until he found himself alone with Miranda. Walking together after the meeting to their awaiting carriages, William asked, 'I couldn't help thinking when your father was saying how the nobility had it arranged so that persons who were not aristocrats were excluded from their social circles, how it was that your father became a close friend of the King and he married your mother, a royal princess? I'd not thought about it until Harry made those comments about the nobility.'

'Well,' answered Miranda, 'my father and mother got together with the King's approval. He, of course, had the authority to override any aristocratic customs, and he, no doubt, had his reasons for bringing the two together, but why my father and the King are close friends is something I can't answer. I've asked about it many times, but all my father would say was that their friendship goes back a long way. He was always kindly and tactfully evasive whenever I asked him to go into details, so I'm afraid I can't answer your question.'

William politely exchanged parting comments with Miranda and walked on to his carriage. As he and Caroline journeyed home, he mulled over Miranda's remarks along with all the other things he'd heard that day.

Ranty's castle.

Chapter four

Plans for forming an association of wealthy businessmen unfolded essentially as intended. Following Ranty's grand formal dinner, with its consciousness raising speakers, close friends of Ranty organised similar meetings at their own country mansions. Soon the numbers attending such gatherings increased to such an extent that it became impracticable to accommodate them all at the same place. As a result, regions of the kingdom developed their own sections, with meetings in the splendid homes of local magnates, but the unity of the association was maintained by means of occasional gatherings of selected senior members, usually held in the exclusive conference amenities of grand hotels. To avoid unwanted levels of public interest no hotel was used more than once. This need for secrecy, although largely unspoken, was generally understood. It arose mainly from subtle suggestions stealthily imparted to members by the elite group and from the means by which members were selected.

Members belonged also to one or more of the many established social groups - business circles, local interest forums, golf clubs, committees of commerce, etcetera - for potential new members were looked for within such associations. To be admitted to such associations it was usual for prospective members to be recommended for admission by at least two existing members. The Organisation, known jocularly by insiders as *Ranty's Gang*, adopted the same policy, with the added requirement that only senior members could make such recommendations. Once so admitted, recruits were regarded as initiates, and only after two years as such were they regarded as full members. Before they could be regarded as seniors, a further period, usually around five years, had to elapse in which they needed to show total commitment to the values of The Organisation, of which confidentiality was paramount. Senior members, in addition to being entitled to recommend new recruits, were eligible for selection to attend the occasional national gatherings. Moreover, only seniors were covertly considered for admittance to the secretive elite group. With this basic structure The Organisation grew and, although nameless and unpublicised, became an association to which up and coming, but not yet admitted, business magnates aspired. They were vaguely aware that very wealthy moguls met occasionally in secret in remote, up-market hotels, but were unaware of the kind of activities the tycoons undertook behind closed doors. A few astute individuals of the general public were similarly aware of the existence of a secretive association of extremely wealthy big-wigs, but could only speculate as to what its purpose might be. As intended, bankers did not go to any of The Organisation's meetings until it had been well established as a business association and they were able to attend inconspicuously. They did, of course, attend meetings of the secret elite section, where they were able to observe the effectiveness of, and help to infuse, the furtive propaganda formulated by the highly-secretive band of specially selected intellectuals.

Grand balls were held occasionally.

Fulfilling the matrimonial-agency role of The Organisation required very little effort. In its early years a few grand balls were held, but it was soon found that they were unnecessary; although they were held occasionally for the enjoyment and solidarity they produced. The intended purpose of ensuring that unsuitable marriages did not occur was mainly achieved in the same way confidentiality was secured. Inconspicuous suggestions surreptitiously infused into the membership's consciousness made it generally understood that marriage with outsiders was unacceptable. Other parts of the bankers' and Ranty's plans developed equally well. Ostensibly benevolent generous donations to new university departments and scholarly foundations produced the effects intended. Along with the ideas, opinions and clichés clandestinely supplied to the public's awareness, they helped to fashion a generally accepted favourable view of the world of industry and commerce. It blended seamlessly with the established beliefs that gave the nation a sense of purpose and unity. Unaware that attitudes and opinions had been intentionally implanted into its consciousness, the public gained a deeper feeling of belonging to a rational and coherent world. The economic system, they were frequently told, was the best of all possible economic systems.

So conditioned, people had fewer reasons for asking questions about the nation's increasing wealth; the required answers were readily available, they had seeped gently and inconspicuously into the collective consciousness. Ordinary members of The Organisation particularly appreciated their new-found awareness of industrial and commercial righteousness, for, as intended, it helped placate the widespread fears many had held, that their newborn prosperity might evaporate as easily as it emerged, that they couldn't look to the future with confidence, that the emergent economic system might be unstable or transient. They were as unaware as the general public that clandestine influences had helped to shape their ideas and beliefs, for the elite group's confidentiality was rigorously maintained. Equally, the elite group was unaware of the existence of the highly-secretive Special Intellectual Group, The Organisation's inner circle from which many of their most cherished beliefs originated. In this way, with very few teething difficulties, The Organisation fulfilled its planners' goal of blending reassuring ideas about the new-found wealth with traditional stories about the kingdom's glorious and heroic past, so heightening the nation's mood of confidence and unison. And no one suspected that the country's upbeat disposition was being clandestinely orchestrated by a cabal of bankers and their friend Baron Ranty.

With the banking system's effortless ability to create money by means of pen strokes, and the public's outlook suitably fashioned, Areho's commercial and industrial capabilities grew relentlessly. The passage of several centuries brought many changes. The Organisation matured. The frivolous moniker *Ranty's Gang,* coined by Ranty's friends, was long forgotten, and the days when Harry Indolder was able to approach and influence the old king, Walter II, was long gone, but the covert, nameless Organisation he and Baron Ranty had helped to create lived on. Its matrimonial code, as anticipated, resulted in the formation of a network of interrelated powerful families, an interconnected combination of entrepreneurial aristocrats and business moguls. The formal structure by which new members were recruited withered away. People were born belonging to The Organisation, and suitable individuals, having been steeped from birth in its beliefs and attitudes, were admitted to its various inner circles by invitation. Once so established, in addition to shaping popular opinions and averting inappropriate marriages, The Organisation was able to inconspicuously guide and ease the passage of carefully selected and suitably coached intellectuals to positions of power and influence. In this way it held a powerful sway on King Walter's descendants and the policies of their governments. Effectively, Areho's Organisation, its all-powerful industrial-financial network, became the country's unseen government. It secretly governed governments, and one of the issues it was particularly concerned with was foreign policy.

No one suspected that the country's upbeat disposition was being clandestinely orchestrated by a highly-secretive Special Intellectual Group.

As it developed and grew, The Organisation used its manufacturing, financial and propaganda muscles to influence neighbouring countries with the principal aim of ensuring that none of them could become rivals. To achieve this, it primarily used an argument designed to convince them that their economic interests would be best served by concentrating on the products they were good at producing. It was a subtle and persuasive line of reasoning developed and promoted by one of the scholarly institutions. Accordingly, if a country was good at producing wine, for example, it should focus on doing that, and not divert some of its capabilities to producing something another country was able to produce more efficiently. The argument went on to say, for instance, that if one of the other countries was able to efficiently produce corn, but was not good at producing wine, the economic wellbeing of the wine producing country and the corn producing country, assuming both required wine and corn, would be best served by trade. Neither would be diverting part of their productive resources from something they were good at to something they were not good at, but, so the argument went, the mutual benefit would only be realized if the trade was unrestricted. It had to be *free trade*; trade that was free from government involvement, free from regulations and restrictions such as tariffs and quotas. It was a powerful and persuasive argument, and, of course, it served Areho's interests by dissuading neighbouring countries from developing manufacturing industries. It ensured the unhindered export of industrial goods Areho produced in abundance and the unrestricted import of goods it wanted but was not particularly good at producing, such as wine, certain exotic foods and essential raw materials. Any country that disregarded the argument and attempted to develop its own industrial capabilities was swiftly dealt with. In the name of *free trade*, goods manufactured in Areho were offered for sale in the offending country at the basic cost of production, or less, making the development of foreign competition impracticable.

The Organisation was able to inconspicuously guide and ease the passage of carefully selected intellectuals to positions of power and influence.

Other aspects of the shadow government's foreign policy concerned monetary and military affairs. Using its agents' powers of persuasion, The Organisation induced neighbouring countries to borrow. Bank branches were opened in capital cities and loans were provided mainly for the development of infrastructure such as roads and canals. Providing interest-earning loans so a country could develop its transport systems and thereby better serve Areho's free trade policies was a brilliant scheme, and funding the construction of canals was its most profitable sector. Miles and miles had been constructed in Areho soon after its development of large scale industries. They became crucial to the country's economic growth. Soon after, exporting its skills and experience in the construction of inland waterways to indebted countries substantially added to the great benefits canals had brought to the kingdom. Areho's secret government found international banking to be very lucrative. In addition to gaining considerable interest payments, by improving cross-border transportation it expedited the import of commodities Areho required and the export of manufactured goods it produced copiously.

Miles and miles of canals had been constructed in Areho soon after its development of large scale industries.

Foreign trade and banking involved issues arising from the monies used in different countries. Each country, like Areho, based the value of its unit of currency on a fixed amount of precious metal, usually gold but sometimes silver. Countries using paper banknotes usually promised bearers of their notes redemption in precious metal on demand. With such a system, by means of economic forces acting on international currency markets, exchange rates could be established which ensured equitable balances of trade between nations. While such a situation held, trade was seen to be fair and each country's stock of gold or silver remained unchanged. But some countries quickly found they could gain advantages by altering the amount of precious metal used to fix the values of their currencies. By changing the international value of its money in this way, a country could make its goods cheaper to foreign buyers and foreign goods more expensive to buy, and, since excess foreign currency could be redeemed in precious metal, by way of such trade it could increase its stock of gold or silver. But gains achieved in this way were short-lived, for other countries quickly responded by similarly devaluing their currencies.

Countries tried to increase their stocks of gold by way of foreign trade.

None of this rivalry of currencies suited Areho's bankers and their industrial friends, and they used the powers they held over other countries to bring it to an end. They knew indebted countries would need to gain foreign currency to service their debts by way of trade or by further borrowing, or by some combination of the two. Also, countries free from debt but unable to develop industries because of The Organisation's dumping policies needed to trade with Areho if they wanted manufactured goods. The Organisation, therefore, was able to dictate terms of trade to the countries it dealt with, and it wanted the game of currencies ended. Countries were diplomatically informed that if they wanted to continue doing business with Areho they had to agree to permanently fix the amounts of precious metal used to determine the values of their currencies. Devaluations were prohibited. Also, since the relative values of gold and silver could change, countries using silver to determine their currency's value were obliged to change to gold. So it was that The Organisation, by virtue of its financial, intellectual and industrial muscle, gained access to a huge market in which it could do business, free from government restrictions and fluctuating exchange rates. It became the unseen economic overlord of not only Areho but also the countries it conducted business with.

Areho's ability to organize its armed forces, and produce powerful weapons abundantly, far outstripped any of its neighbours.

Since the time when King Walter II was persuaded to set up a standing army, Areho's military power had grown in step with its financial and industrial capabilities. Its ability to organise its armed forces efficiently, and to produce powerful weapons profusely, far outstripped any of its neighbours. It had no need to use this military strength to gain its neighbours' economic compliance – its implied threat of sanctions was sufficient – but it did use it to control their foreign policies. Aware of the tendency of significant neighbours to seek to take territory from adjacent countries by means of warfare, and the danger that one of them could become a powerful rival by such means, The Organisation adopted a policy of supporting any country threatened by aggression from a more powerful neighbour. Discreet military advice and loan-funded supplies of arms were usually sufficient, although tougher methods were available if necessary. Such measures ensured peace amongst the countries Areho did business with and averted the possibility of one of them becoming a powerful rival.

New university departments and scholarly foundations were established by means of seemingly benevolent donations.

So it came to pass that Areho became a rapacious superpower willing and able to impose its will on its neighbours and, if necessary, use its unrivalled military power to achieve its goals. Simultaneously, it was able to convince its people of the righteousness of its policies by reference to a variety of economic and moral doctrines concocted by its universities and academic institutions. But all was not well with members of The Organisation. Many years earlier, shortly after the bankers had started their industrialisation programme, people employed in newly enlarged workshops worked in harmony with their bosses. They worked together, were paid a fair share of the profits and felt a sense of pride and satisfaction in the goods they produced. But this changed as the years went by.

Huge factories employing hundreds of people appeared.

Huge factories employing hundreds or thousands of people appeared, and their workers didn't find the satisfaction their predecessors had enjoyed in small workshops. Their work was usually tedious and repetitive, and, being minor players in vast undertakings, they rarely found any interest in the goods they helped to produce. They worked only for money, and many were aware that their wages amounted to a small fraction of the income their work provided for their employers. Some said they could secure a fairer share of the profits they helped to produce by banding together and standing up to their employers, and a number of these had the personalities and communicative skills to effectively articulate their arguments to large numbers of workers.

The Organisation was aware of this threat to its interests and occasionally took measures to get rid of effective activists. The lure of money and the pressure of unrelenting propaganda were usually sufficient to persuade troublesome crusaders to call a halt to their industrial campaigns, but more persuasive methods were available if necessary. So the threat of disruptive workers didn't disturb The Organisation unduly. It had more pressing issues to contend with: the growing problem of businesses being unable to find sufficient buyers for the goods they were able to produce in abundance. The difficulty had been looming for quite a while and various methods had been used to try to ease the problem. The bankers had given birth to a system of money creation and industrial production, and, after it had been functioning for a while, they found they had control of the system as a whole because they had control of the supply of money. They could easily speed the system up, or slow it down, as they pleased. Lowering interest rates, and being more relaxed about who they were willing to lend money to, increased the rate at which new money was created. This caused the system to speed up. Increasing interest rates, and being more restrictive about who they were willing to lend money to, reduced the rate at which new money was created. This caused the system to slow down. Once they knew they had control of the economic system in this way the bankers no longer feared inflation. Prices increased when they caused the money supply to increase faster than factories were able to sell the things they made. When they knew and understood this, they knew they could make use of inflation.

Work in factories was usually hard and unpleasant.

Knowing that consumers would buy things more readily if prices always seemed to increase, the bankers created new money at a rate designed to cause prices to increase. They did this in a way that was very advantageous to themselves and their wealthy friends. Prices were caused to increase slowly, bit by bit, so as to stimulate buying without alarming people into thinking money was losing its value too rapidly. And it was not only consumers that responded to inflation in this way. Kings were persuaded - by advisors recommended by The Organisation - that they needed to borrow to pay for projects that would improve the kingdom, for if they were to delay, the costs of the improvements would increase. So every year, supposedly in the interests of the people and the welfare of the kingdom, extra roads, canals, embankments, sewers, water supply systems and other things advantageous to commerce, known collectively as public works, were built. Companies owned by members of The Organisation, as recommended to each king, were awarded the building contracts, so the bankers gained lots of extra interest and their friends gained lots of extra profits. The improvements were paid for by the crown with borrowed money, and repayments to the banks, with interest, were paid by the people by way of increased taxes; and since kings were taking out new loans faster than old ones were being repaid, with interest, the national debt went on steadily increasing. Nevertheless, the rapidly expanding newspaper industry, much of which was controlled by members of The Organisation, enthusiastically praised kings and their governments for improving the kingdom.

The public works programme increased the supply of new money to the economic system, helping to generate inflation at the rate required by The Organisation. In addition to motivating people to spend their money without too much delay, so sustaining consumer demand, inflation sustained demand for money. If money lost its value, more and more of it was needed so people could keep on buying things; and for there to be more of it, people had to keep on borrowing. This method of increasing the need for extra money was similar in many ways to another method The Organisation had devised for sustaining consumer demand: producing manufactured things that went wrong. After a while badly-made things needed to be replaced. The benefit of this more than offset the erosion of the value of debt associated with moderate inflation. The infrastructure improvements, therefore, were paid for in two ways: by people having to pay increased rates of income tax, and by the value of their money being steadily decreased. Inflation, accordingly, was equivalent to an extra form of taxation. But people didn't think of it in that way. They thought moderate inflation was normal, something that occurred quite naturally.

Work was usually tedious and repetitive, and workers rarely found any interest in the stuff they helped to produce.

Steady low inflation encouraged buying, but it did not do it sufficiently to enable factory owners to produce and sell goods as fast as they wanted to. Even with steadily increasing prices people stopped buying things when they had bought enough of them. Along with steadily increasing prices and incessant advertising, products with in-built latent faults helped to sustain buying, but it was still not enough to keep the economic system growing as The Organisation knew it needed to. Growth meant the overall level of debt was increasing, and with it the bankers' wealth and power, but astute members of The Organisation knew there was an even more compelling reason for wanting the system to go on growing. Growth was a fundamental requirement of the economic system. Without sufficient growth there would be many difficulties. If new money was not being created at a rate greater than the interest rate charged on loans, many factory owners who had borrowed heavily would become unable to service their debts. They would be unable to sell enough things because sufficient new money would not be available in the system. The economic system would cease to function effectively. It would fail and decline. There was, therefore, a minimum rate of growth below which many businesses would not be profitable and banks would not be able to continue creating money at an ever increasing rate. Growth of the system at, or above, this rate was needed, and persuasive advertising, moderate inflation and making things that went wrong and could not be easily repaired was not sufficient to ensure it. Extra consumers were needed. The ever increasing birth rate, itself a function of the expanding economic system, helped, but it was not sufficient to ensure the necessary growth.

Companies owned by members of The Organisation, as recommended
to each king, were awarded building contracts.

We pick up our story at a time when the issue of faltering growth was particularly critical. During The Organisation's annual gatherings members gorged themselves with food and drink while listening to speeches, and after each day's formal programme they customarily retired to large sitting rooms where they could continue drinking, smoke big cigars and engage in serious conversations. They usually talked about many things, about persons of interest, about all that had happened and all that might happen. We find them on this occasion discussing the lack of sufficient growth. They were all selected, seasoned members of The Organisation, and they fully understood the economic system they were deeply involved with, and totally committed to, needed to grow. It couldn't survive otherwise. So the dilemma of insufficient customers was critical. One of the industrialists, Charlie Bliggs, told the group of friends he was sitting with, 'The situation's serious. All the kingdoms we trade with are oversupplied with our goods. We've tried everything we can think of to increase sales, but to no avail. I know it's the same with almost everyone here today. So, unless we can come up with some new ploy to boost trade, I will have to dismiss workers and reduce production. I think you are all facing the same predicament.'

Insurance schemes were not always reliable.

There was a general muttering of dispirited agreement. Colin Floggit responded by telling the group about faraway lands he'd heard about where many interesting things were bought and sold. He said, 'I was recently talking to a sailor, a ship's captain, after he'd returned from a long voyage of exploration and adventure. He and his crew had sailed far from our usual trade routes and found, on the other side of the Mighty Ocean, lands they didn't know existed. People there, he told me, were friendly and very keen to learn all they could about Areho and its neighbouring kingdoms. They were prosperous and industrious and their markets were full of buyers and sellers of a wide variety of interesting goods. It occurred to me that we won't need to reduce production if we can sell our excess goods to them. I know they are a very long way away, but we have many fine ships and experienced sailors. I think we should send ships there filled with a variety of Areho's manufactured products and set up a trade deal. What do you think?'

Sailors told about faraway lands where many interesting things were bought and sold.

Everyone in the group agreed the suggestion was good and should be put to the full gathering. The following day, when heard by everyone at the meeting, it was accepted enthusiastically. It was decided that a flotilla of trading ships, filled with a wide selection of Areho's finest manufactured goods, was to be sent across the Mighty Ocean to the people of the far distant lands. There was widespread excitement and it was generally agreed that the proposal was the high-spot of the conference. When the gathering was finished, people returned home to tell, within The Organisation's strict confidentiality code, their families and friends about the outcome of the meeting. A few days later, without any mention of the secret conference, it was simply announced in newspapers that the King and his council had agreed to send a delegation across the Mighty Ocean to negotiate a trade deal with the people of the distant lands. It became a hot topic of conversation in Areho's clubs and taverns. National pride and confidence in the King and his council reached new levels.

Chapter five

Young Jeremy Schemowt, son of James Schemowt, the fourteenth chairman of Schemowt's Bank, was destined to become the fifteenth chairman. He wanted to know every detail of what went on at the secret meeting. James patiently summarized the conference's discussions, emphasising the importance of the proposed venture across the Mighty Ocean. Jeremy listened carefully and when his father had finished he said, 'You know, the thing I don't understand is why there needs to be growth. The country's prosperous, there's plenty of food and people seem to have all they need. I know our industrial friends do all they can to get people to buy things they don't really want. I've often wondered why. Why can't we simply leave things as they are?'

Members of The Organisation were aware of the economic difficulties.

James thought for a while before saying, 'That's a hell of a question, Jeremy, I'll have to think about it. It's not something that's easy to explain. I'll get one of the maids to bring some tea while I'm thinking about it.'

Waiting for the maid and then drinking tea gave James time to work out how he was going to answer Jeremy's question. When he was ready, and the maid had been told that they were not to be disturbed, he said, 'I want you to think about an imaginary country, a little far-away place where people get along without money. They make, catch and grow things, and are quite happy exchanging them for other things. One woman who keeps chickens and often needs firewood agrees with a man who makes tools to exchange some of her eggs for an axe. A fisherman agrees with a woman who is good at baking to exchange freshly caught fish for freshly baked pies; pies she made with fruit from an orchard keeper who'd exchanged it for bread and with flour from a miller who'd exchanged it for scones. Many such exchanges are made every day, and everyone is happy and familiar with the way things are. They don't need money. Can you imagine that?'

To Jeremy, people seemed to have all they needed. He did not understand why growth was essential.

'Yes,' Jeremy answered. 'People swap things they have and don't need for things they need but don't have. Yes, I can imagine that.'

James replied, 'Good. Now imagine that one day a man came along and said he had a brilliant idea. He told the people that he was going to start a bank, and they would then be able to borrow nice colourful pieces of paper called money from it. Money, the wise banker explained, could then be used to make it a lot easier to exchange things. Fish and fruit pies wouldn't need to be exchanged on the day they were fresh. Fresh fish could be exchanged for money, and the fisherman could exchange the money for pies, or whatever else he might fancy, at some time later. The banker gave many other examples of how using money would make exchanging goods and services much easier. When it had been explained in this way, people could see that using money would be very convenient, but they were not convinced it was a good idea. How would we know the value of the pieces of paper, they asked, and how could we be certain they would keep their value?

People in an imaginary land were quite happy exchanging their goods for other things. They did not need money.

'The clever banker said that almost everyone ate potatoes almost every day, and knew the sort, and quantity, of things that could be exchanged for a bag of potatoes. They knew the value of potatoes. For this reason, he said, the bank would promise to exchange its money notes for bags of potatoes, on demand, at any time during working hours. Potatoes would be used to guarantee the value of money. The promise would be printed on every money note. The basic unit of money would be called the *spud*, and a one *spud* note would be redeemable on demand for one bag of potatoes. The bank would also issue ten, twenty and fifty *spud* notes. *Half-spud* notes would also be available, but they would not be redeemable as potatoes because the bank would not be willing to split a bag. Two *half-spud* notes would be needed to redeem a bag of potatoes. Most people agreed that potatoes were always wanted, and their value was reliable and stable, but when the bank opened they were still a bit uncertain about money. They were even more uncertain when they learned that the bank intended to charge 5% annual interest on its loans. They weren't keen on the idea. One woman, however, the one who kept chickens, decided to take out a loan of one thousand *spuds*. It was to be repaid as a single payment, including 5% interest, after one year. She used the money to pay a builder to build her a much bigger chicken house than the one she had, and the builder, knowing that each *spud* note was redeemable as potatoes, accepted them because he knew others, for the same reason, would accept them from him. So, in exchange for *spud* notes, the timber merchants and the hardware store owners provided the builder with the materials he needed to build the chicken house, and they found people from whom they needed things were happy to accept *spud* notes from them. Soon, people happily accepted *spud* notes in their everyday transactions whenever they were offered. The idea of paper money caught on. It made dealings in goods and services much easier than the old system of bartering. People were happy. The woman got her big new chicken house and was able to sell the extra eggs it provided. She saved money from the increased sale of eggs, and perhaps thought she would soon have enough to pay what she owed to the bank. Do you think she'd have been able to save the money she needed?'

Jeremy thought for a while before saying, 'No, it would be impossible. From what you've said, the thousand *spuds* she borrowed was the only money there was, so even if she was able to get all of it back by selling eggs she would only have a thousand *spuds*. When it was time to repay the bank, she would be fifty *spuds* short, for, with interest at 5%, she would owe the bank one thousand and fifty *spuds*.'

The Spud Bank promised to exchange its money notes for bags of potatoes, on demand, at any time during working hours.

'That's right,' James replied. 'It would only be possible for her to repay the bank if other people took out loans and put more money into circulation before it was time to repay her chicken-house loan. Let's say she decided to devote all the money she gained by selling eggs from the new chicken house to paying-off the bank, and until then she would rely on eggs from her original chickens to provide the things needed to live on. At first she'd be no better off than if she'd not bothered to have the new chicken house built, but, provided other people took out loans and put the necessary money into circulation, when her bank loan had been repaid she'd be able to sell many more eggs than before. She'd be much better off. But, before that, she needed to pay one thousand and fifty *spuds* to the bank. For this, she needed other borrowers to put more money into circulation. For simplicity, let's imagine that only one other person took out a loan before she had to repay the bank. Whatever the second loan might have been for, after it had gone into circulation she needed to acquire fifty *spuds* from it. Let's suppose the second borrower's loan was also for one thousand *spuds*, for one year, and, well before the chicken keeper had to repay her loan, it was put into circulation so there was two thousand *spuds* in circulation. Then, provided her chickens laid enough eggs and she was able to sell enough of them, she would be able to repay the bank. But after she's repaid the bank, there would only be nine hundred and fifty *spuds* left in circulation. Would the second borrower be able to acquire the one thousand and fifty *spuds* he would need when it was time to repay his loan?'

Jeremy responded, 'No, of course not. He couldn't acquire one thousand and fifty *spuds* from an economic system with only nine hundred and fifty *spuds* in circulation. He would only be able to repay his loan if other borrowers put more money into circulation.'

James was pleased. 'That's right,' he said. 'Let's suppose that after the first loan had been repaid, but well before the second one had to be settled, a third borrower also borrowed one thousand *spuds,* for one year, and put the money into circulation. There would then be one thousand, nine hundred and fifty *spuds* in circulation. Provided he could sell enough of his goods or services at appropriate prices, the second borrower would then be able to repay the bank one thousand and fifty *spuds* when it was time to do so. But after he had repaid the bank there would only be nine hundred *spuds* in circulation.'

Jeremy responded, 'So the third borrower would only be able to repay his loan if a fourth borrower put more money into circulation!'

James replied, 'That's right, and if the fourth loan was also for one thousand *spuds*, for one year, borrowed after the second loan had been repaid but well before the third had to be repaid, it would, all being well, enable the third loan to be repaid, for there would then be one thousand, nine hundred *spuds* in circulation. But after one thousand and fifty spuds had been repaid to the bank there would only be eight hundred and fifty *spuds* left in circulation.'

Jeremy was pleased he could follow his father's reasoning. He responded, 'So the fourth borrower would need a fifth borrower to put more money into circulation!'

James answered, 'Yes, that's right, and if the fifth loan was also for one thousand *spuds*, for one year, borrowed after the third loan had been repaid but well before the fourth had to be repaid, it would, all being well, enable the fourth loan to be repaid, for there would then be one thousand, eight hundred and fifty *spuds* in circulation. But after it had been repaid there would only be eight hundred *spuds* left in circulation.'

Keen to show he was following the reasoning, Jeremy responded, 'A sixth loan would be required to enable the fifth to be repaid, and a seventh to enable the sixth to be repaid.'

James responded, 'That's right, and there would then need to be an eighth loan, a ninth loan, a tenth loan, and so on. But do you notice something that tells us that this could not go on?'

Jeremy could see what his father was trying to make clear. 'Yes,' he replied, 'the amount of money left in circulation after each loan had been repaid gets less and less. So it couldn't go on and on.'

James was happy he was getting through to Jeremy. 'Yes, that's right,' he said. 'We can now see that if borrowers took out equal loans, at the same frequency as loans were repaid, as we imagined, then the amount of money in circulation would get less and less. It would become increasingly difficult for borrowers to acquire sufficient money to be able to repay their loans, with interest. After not too long it would become impossible.'

Jeremy responded, 'So if all the loans were of equal amounts, the banker, if he wanted to prevent the amount of money in circulation from declining, would need to issue them more frequently, or, if he issued loans at the same frequency he would need to issue increasing amounts. Or, loans of increasing amounts could be issued with increasing frequency.'

James was pleased his explanation was being understood. He said, 'Good. You'll now be able to see that the amount of money in circulation will decrease or increase according to how frequently loans are issued and repaid and how the amounts borrowed vary. In some imaginary situation, therefore, the amount of money in circulation could remain, on average, constant. Let's think about what this would mean, particularly from the point-of-view of the borrowers. Think about the woman who took out a loan so she could have a big chicken house built. Remember, she decided that until she was out of debt she would devote all her increased income to paying-off the bank. She would hoard money until it was time to pay the bank. Then, when her bank loan had been repaid, she expected to be able to sell the extra eggs and keep the extra money for herself. Do you think she would have made the decision to borrow and have a big chicken house built if she knew the amount of money in circulation was to remain, on average, constant?'

Jeremy thought about it. 'I'm not too sure,' he answered.

James replied, 'The woman took a big gamble. She gambled there would be other borrowers. As we've seen, if other people had not taken out loans she'd never have been able to repay her debt. But she didn't only want to repay her loan. After she'd repaid the bank she wanted to increase her income by selling the eggs produced in her new chicken house. If she'd been able to foresee that subsequent borrowers would borrow and repay in ways that, on average, kept the amount of money in circulation constant, she would probably not have taken the risk of borrowing. She would probably have been able to foresee that her ambition of increased income would be practically impossible to fulfil. To be confident of being able to sell all the eggs her new chicken house would produce, she needed to be confident that there would be plenty of readily available money circulating in the economic system. If the amount of money in circulation was, on average, constant, it would be because borrowers were putting money into circulation and, by repaying their loans, were taking it out at the same rate. Borrowers would be behaving as she did until her bank loan had been repaid, they would be hoarding money in order to be able to repay the bank. In such a situation, there would be little money available for buying extra eggs. Egg consumption would, in all probability, remain at roughly the same level as it had been before the new chicken house was built. Building the chicken house would not have been worthwhile.'

Jeremy responded, 'I think I see what you mean. Borrowers will only borrow if they feel confident there will be plenty of money in circulation so they will be able to repay the bank and become better-off, even if this will only be achieved after their loan had been repaid.'

James replied, 'Yes, that's right. People will need to feel confident the amount of circulating money will not decline or remain constant but will increase. In a static or declining system, there would be nothing to gain from borrowing and paying interest. The banker will also need to feel confident that the amount of money in circulation will increase, for if it did not he could not prosper. I asked you to imagine a small, isolated community where people didn't use money. Then, by considering what would happen if a bank was introduced into the community offering to lend money and charge interest, we were able to see that the bank and its borrowers would only flourish if the total amount of money in circulation was, on average, increasing. Essentially, in a greatly simplified way, we looked at the basic functioning of the economic system we operate here in Areho. It cannot function for very long if the amount of circulating money is not increasing. Interest payments act as a drain through which money flows out of the economic system. If it is not replaced by further borrowing, the amount in circulation declines. People would not then regard borrowing to be worthwhile.'

Jeremy replied, 'Yes, I can see that.'

James responded, 'Good. Whether people are aware of it or not, if the money supply failed to increase for a protracted period, the economic system would run into very grave difficulties. This is the economic system's primary defining feature. Growth is a fundamental requirement.'

'Wow!' Jeremy exclaimed. 'I can see it all much better now. The economy has to keep on growing. We can't simply leave things as they are. I used to think growth had something to do with increasing the living standards of ordinary people. I can now see that growth is absolutely necessary for the economic system to function. Any other outcome is incidental.'

Despite the economic situation, members of The Organisation were still able to enjoy themselves.

'That's right,' his father replied. 'I'm glad my little story was useful.'

Both father and son were very pleased their conversation had been satisfying and worthwhile. Jeremy felt he had a better understanding of how adult members of The Organisation thought about economic and political affairs. James went on to emphasize that the need for economic growth was the reason ships were being sent to the people of the distant lands. 'It's essential,' he said, 'that a trade deal is made with them. It's vital for the wellbeing of Areho's economic system.'

Feeling good, they decided they would go together to watch the flotilla of trading ships sail away to the distant lands. As they watched sails filling out in the brisk breeze, Jeremy turned to his father and said, 'There's one thing I don't understand. If growth must go on increasing at an ever increasing rate, as you explained, then when will it end? It surely can't go on increasing forever. There must be a time when it all has to stop.'

James looked at his son and said, 'That's something we try not to think about. Don't worry about it. It's not going to happen in your lifetime.'

Jeremy and James watched the trade ships sail away.

Chapter Six

L ong after the trade ships had sailed, newspaper commentaries sustained the public's interest in the mission. They stressed the economic importance of the venture, and as the time approached when the ships were expected to arrive back their coverage increased. Excitement and anticipation then surged throughout the land, so when it was reported that sails had been observed on the horizon large crowds assembled on Arcue's sea front.

Excitement and anticipation surged throughout the land when it was reported that sails had been observed on the horizon.

As the ships sailed closer, troops were lined up to keep people from the harbour regions. They struggled against the pressure of enthusiastic onlookers as the sea-weary vessels docked. The mood of the crowd was optimistic and cheerful, but this changed shortly after Martin Semsit, the captain of the lead ship, stepped off his gangplank to be greeted by Clive Dilav, the King's Minister of Economic Affairs. After exchanging a few words with the captain, Dilav's expression became noticeably downbeat. Without knowing the reason for his obvious change of outlook the crowd became less buoyant. Something was not right. It could be seen in the Minister's face.

When the crowd could see that nothing more could be gained by hanging about the sea front most of it drifted away, but a few dispirited onlookers remained. Eventually they trickled away but the handful that remained long enough were able to see the reason for the Minister's crestfallen expression. When dock workers started to unload the ships they could be seen transferring packing crates marked *Made in Areho* to the harbour. When this was clear to the remaining spectators they also drifted away. They went away to spread the news that the trade mission had failed. It had been an expensive fiasco.

The captain of the lead ship was greeted by the king's Minister of Economic Affairs.

The following day, the flotilla's principal officers were called before a Board of Inquiry. After formal introductions, the panel's chairman started the proceedings by asking, 'Captain Semsit, in your own words, will you tell us what happened when you reached the distant lands?'

'The people there were very friendly,' Semsit answered. 'Many came out in small boats to greet us, but they were not at all interested in trade. They had factories of their own where they could make all the things they needed; also there was a wide variety of goods for sale in their markets, many we had never seen before.'

'Tell us about these unfamiliar things.'

'Well, there were many strange fruits and vegetables and all sorts of exotic spices they use for flavouring foods. We tried several of their seasoned dishes and found them to be quite delicious. Moreover, there was a wide range of colourful, fancy textiles available, many with intricate woven patterns, the likes of which we had never seen, and all of a very fine quality. Elaborate clothing was commonplace. People could often be seen wearing bright, loose fitting sashes draped over their shoulders. They also wore wide, decorated belts and fancy colourful headwear.'

The people of the distant lands had all the things they needed.

'What about their manufactured goods? Tell us about them.'

'With the exception of useless ornaments and our most sophisticated weapons, all the things we make in Areho are also made in the distant lands, and, although I hesitate to say it, they are of a finer quality than the things we took there to trade. Their crockery in particular is superb.'

A loud muttering quickly filled the room. Representative merchants, bankers and industrialists present at the inquiry as observers had become very annoyed as they listened to Semsit's report. After hearing his comments about the quality of Areho's goods they were unable to remain silent. They simply had to protest at the suggestion that their products were inferior. Their angry voices became louder as the chairman struggled to bring the meeting to order.

Irate and not wanting to hear more, they left the Inquiry and reassembled in The Organisation's favourite city venue. Sitting in one of its luxurious sitting rooms, they continued expressing their displeasure at the contents of Semsit's report. The Inquiry had aroused their deepest dissatisfaction. As seasoned members of The Organisation's secretive elite group they fully understood the economic significance of the failed trade mission. They were demoralized. Their outlook, however, changed radically when one of them, David Nilma, the owner of a nationwide retailing chain, made a few comments that gripped their attention. Their feelings of gloom then ebbed away.

Sitting in groups, members of the Organisation's secretive elite group continued expressing their displeasure at the contents of Semsit's report.

Nilma said, 'The things Semsit said about the goods available in the distant lands made me think that many of them could be sold here in Areho at very good prices. I think we should consider getting some of them over here to see how well they sell.'

The group he was sitting with was silent for a moment before expressing its general approval. His suggestion quickly spread to groups sitting around other tables. A hum of excited agreement then spread around the room, but it quickly subsided when one person, William Adsar, stood up, tapped a glass on the table before him, and said, 'Gentlemen, David's suggestion is clearly worth pursuing, but it's not going to solve the problem of our own factories being unable to sell all the things they produce; the problem, it was hoped, the trade mission would ease.'

His words quietened the room, allowing Nilma to calmly respond, 'If goods from the distant lands start selling well here, by bringing brisk buying activity back to our home markets it may well help our own manufacturing industries. Consumers, as we all know, are creatures of collective habits. Bringing unfamiliar, desirable goods to our shops is, I think, likely to encourage buying in general. Anything that gets customers back in our shops in large numbers can only be helpful. Moreover, novel goods brought here from the distant lands may well inspire our own manufacturers to extend the range and improve the quality of their products. I know industrialists, including their representatives present here, will not like to hear this, but many in the retail business will tell them customers are well aware that many of their products are prone to developing faults. I know this is intentional, a way of ensuring replacement goods will be bought, but when consumers are able to see through the scheme perhaps it's time to realise that it has gone too far. It needs to be less obvious. Goods from the distant lands, therefore, may well serve the interests of our own manufacturers; firstly, by helping them to improve the range and quality of the goods they produce, and secondly, by encouraging consumers to visit shops more frequently.'

The visitors could see there was a wide variety of goods for sale in the distant land's markets.

Industrialists present were eager to respond to Nilma's remarks but were eclipsed by James Schemowt who stood up and said, 'I think David is right. We and the other banks have lowered our interest rates but it has had little effect on consumers. Desirable, novel goods from the distant lands may well be what are needed to revitalize their enthusiasm for borrowing and buying. It may be what is needed to bring new life to our sluggish markets. I suggest that another set of ships be sent across the Mighty Ocean to bring home a supply of the distant land's most attractive goods.'

James' comments brought about an approving round of applause. When it was dying down, George Tegget, a long standing member of the highly secretive Special Intellectual Group, suggested that two or three of The Organisation's most able men should travel with the ships, under the guise of buyers, to find out as much as they could about the people of the distant lands, about their industries, traditions, resources and financial affairs.

Under the guise of buyers, three of The Organisation's most able men volunteered to sail with the ships.

This suggestion also gained enthusiastic applause. The mood of the gathering was no longer gloomy. It was upbeat and keen to proceed. The industrialists present no longer thought it appropriate to respond to the criticisms made earlier about the quality of their products. The discussion continued, but the decision had already been made; a new fleet of ships was to be sent to the distant lands. Its mission would not be to sell, but to buy.

As before, after official announcements by government representatives had been made, newspaper commentaries kept the public's interest in the new venture alive, stepping up the coverage when the ships' return became imminent. Enthusiasm then grew, and, as before, crowds gathered on Arcue's harbour after sails had been seen on the horizon. Again, the crowd saw displeasure spread across the government official's face after meeting the fleet's leader. Later, facing a rapidly assembled Board of Inquiry, Captain Undrel, the fleet's commander, explained that the people of the distant lands had been unwilling to accept their money.

The people of the distant lands lived peaceful lives and seemed to have little experience of violence.

'They simply refused to take our banknotes,' he said. 'We tried to convince them that our money was good and reliable, and we tried persuading them to take cheques, but all to no avail.'

'Don't they have money of their own?' the Board's chairman asked.

'Oh, yes. They have paper banknotes similar to our own, but they are not redeemable in gold, or any other precious commodity. We tried to negotiate an exchange rate but they regarded our banknotes as being worthless so it was impossible. The people do, however, value gold. It's scarce there, and although not used as money it is valued for ornamentation. It was, therefore, something they were willing to exchange their goods for. So, if we want to buy from them we'll need to pay with gold.'

Undrel continued addressing the Inquiry. His report disheartened the business and banking representatives present. After hearing as much as they could endure, they drifted away and headed to The Organisation's city headquarters - regarded by the public as an exclusive gentleman's club - where a more secretive meeting was scheduled to occur soon after the formal public inquiry had finished. Restricted to members of the Special Intellectual Group, the meeting had been planned to hear, in advance of The Organisation's ordinary members, the reports of the men who, under guise, had travelled with the flotilla in order to learn as much as they could about the distant lands. George Tegget chaired the meeting and, after introducing the three travellers to the meeting, asked Alan Efill, their spokesman: 'Alan, tell us what you, David and Jason found. Tell us about the people of the distant lands, about their customs and way of life.'

Alan responded, 'They are indeed friendly people. They live peaceful lives and seem to have little experience of violence.'

'Don't they have an army and guns?'

'Yes, they do, but they seem to be mainly for ceremonial purposes.'

'What about their industries? How do they operate?'

'Well, as we know, they produce high quality, reliable goods. Moreover, the people who work in factories seem to do so without managers. They take a very leisurely attitude to their work and occasionally have meetings to discuss their products and methods. In effect, they run their factories without authoritative supervision.'

'How can that be? How do they keep on working without bosses? There must be some of them that are lazy and don't bother doing what they should be doing.'

'It doesn't seem to work like that. Factories are run by people who own and work in them, and they operate as a team. Their motivation for working, it seems, arises largely from a combination of loyalty to the group and a sense of pride and responsibility for the things they produce. Anyone who didn't do what was expected of him would experience a sense of disapproval from his team-mates, but this, I guess, rarely, if ever, happens. They clearly enjoy making things and seem unable to relax until the products they are working on have been finished. Bear in mind, they produce goods that are very durable and reliable. They have no concept of planned obsolescence as we do here in Areho. They seemed unable to understand the idea of making things that are designed to go wrong after a few years. Their products are designed and made to last indefinitely. Therefore, their work mainly consists of maintaining a stock of products to be used, when necessary, for replacing or repairing ones that have been damaged or lost. Consequently, they work at a relaxed pace, without stress, so anyone so inclined has little incentive for malingering.'

'Don't they ever produce improved products, ones that include new innovations?'

'As I said, from time to time they have meetings to discuss their products and methods, so, I guess, they occasionally might discuss improvements. I can't say for sure. We were only there for a short while, so, although the people were very helpful and keen to answer our questions, we could only get a cursory picture of their methods and traditions. We did, however, learn that new products can be introduced. This is connected to the way in which their society is governed.'

'Tell us about this. How are they governed?'

'Well it may seem alien to us, but they are governed by ordinary people. They seem to manage very well without kings, aristocracy, or any other type of bigwigs. For example, there's a body, a committee if you like, from which any individual or group wanting to introduce a new product, or radically modify an existing one, must seek permission. In deciding whether or not to give permission, the committee is required to consider the advantage the proposed product is likely to confer to society, along with any injury it might bring to local people, the environment, the wildlife or anything else that could be harmed, including existing alternative products. Permission is only granted if the balance is clearly in favour of the advantage. Obviously, anyone gaining permission to produce a new or radically improved product is rewarded with the praise and admiration of the public. This provides a strong incentive to innovators and so enables their civilisation to develop. Members of the committee are chosen and appointed by the operators of existing factories and remain in post indefinitely. Only when one of them dies, decides to leave or retires because of old age is a replacement selected. We asked if individuals could be dismissed if he, or she, proved to be unsatisfactory. We were told that it was possible, but very uncommon. This method of regulation by people working in existing factories ensures that only products that are obviously beneficial and not harmful are introduced. Any that do not meet these requirements are not allowed to be produced. Similar bodies, or committees, regulate almost every aspect of life in the distant lands, including farms, transport, waste disposal, water supply, education, health care and buildings. Personnel in these, and many other fields, select, and replace when necessary, members of regulatory committees for which the overriding decision criterion is the good of their society.'

'And who regulates the committees? Don't they have a proper government?'

'Well, in a way, they do, but it's not like anything we are familiar with. Just as people in the various spheres of activity select and indefinitely appoint members of regulatory committees, members of the regulatory committees select and appoint members of other institutions - ones we would regard as higher authorities - only choosing replacements when necessary. Such bodies we can think of as government departments. One, for example, has the responsibility of regulating the nation's general economic affairs and money. It's essentially a finance committee.'

'You mean it's something like the King's Treasury?'

'In some ways it is, but there are many differences, the most significant being that it doesn't collect tax and it doesn't borrow money.'

'It doesn't collect tax and it doesn't borrow! Where, then, does it get money from?'

'It creates and issues it.'

'You mean it's a bank?'

'No, it's not a bank, it doesn't charge interest and it doesn't seek to make a profit. It simply keeps accounts and issues money whenever it is needed. Printing paper money-notes is done mainly to replace ones that have become damaged, lost or worn-out. It occasionally creates extra money, but not very often. As with the other committees, its overall commitment is to the welfare of society. It fulfils its responsibility mainly by operating offices throughout the country, offices we might call banks, where people can borrow and repay loans and regular allowances are paid to eligible adult citizens. Loans can be credited to personal or business accounts, but no interest is charged. There is little demand for savings accounts, for people can go to these offices and ask for loans whenever they are needed. Their requests can be for some special occasion or some sort of project, such as introducing a new product, and are usually granted if the proposed purpose is harmless and beneficial.

Normally such loans are repaid in regular instalments, although sometimes, if the proposed purpose is likely to be of considerable benefit to society, and of little or no detriment, the money provided can be repaid, either fully or partially, over a very long period, and occasionally need not be repaid at all. Such free or reduced-repayment credits are typically granted for such worthwhile projects as cultivating otherwise unused land, or building a much needed reservoir or service road. The finance committee, in each accounting period, will normally decrease, or increase, the amount it allocates to full repayment loans if the amount it has allocated to reduced-payment loans has increased, or decreased. Repayment-free credits, or grants, are accounted for by creating replacement money. In this way the finance committee seeks to keep the total amount of borrowed money, in circulation and in clients' accounts, constant. When necessary, it will create extra money to ensure stable economic activity - for example to compensate for population increases, or to accommodate any market growth caused by the introduction of new products - but such requirements come about slowly, so money-supply-adjustments are infrequent.'

The chairman paused, absorbing all that Efill had said. When he was ready to hear more, he asked, 'Tell us about the regular allowances for adults you mentioned. What is that all about? How is it paid for? How can the committee continue to issue such money and not flood the economic system with excess currency? How can the finance committee continue issuing money and at the same time keep the system stable?'

Efill replied, 'It has two main sources of income. One is from loan repayments, and the other from another committee, or government department if you wish, that is responsible for running services; services that users pay for. Money received by this committee, in excess of its running costs, is sent to the finance committee.'

'So, in a roundabout way, their government does collect taxes!'

'Well I suppose you could say that, but they are not like the taxes we pay in Areho. Only people who choose to use the services have to pay. Essential services that everyone uses, such as water supply, waste disposal, public amenities and health care, are provided without direct charges. Their costs are part of the services committee's running expenses. Essentially, so far as the general public is concerned, they are free. The optional services for which fees are charged are mainly offered to businesses, although families and individuals can, and sometimes do, use them. The services include building and ground maintenance work, transport facilities and, for farms, supplying workforces and special equipment according to seasonal requirements. The committee, or department, provides many other services, has offices throughout the land and regulates its activities and fees so as to ensure a comprehensive provision of affordable services and to supply the finance committee with sufficient funds to make sure all qualifying adults regularly receive sufficient money to cover their living requirements. Another way of looking at it is to see the services committee as being responsible for taking as much money out of circulation as the finance committee feeds into it by paying eligible adults their regular income payments. In this way it helps to keep the economic system stable.'

'Essential services are free and everyone is provided with an income! How can this be? How can such a system work? Don't the people have to work for their money?'

Young people enjoyed working for the services committee.

'Yes, of course they do. All young people are required to work for the services committee so it can do what it does. They work on farms, they care for grounds surrounding factories, they operate laundry facilities, they look after roads, they transport goods and they provide many other services. Businesses are happy to pay for such services, they find it convenient and efficient, and the young people enjoy doing it. The work they do is not strenuous and many choose from time to time to move from one type of activity to another. As well as being paid for what they do, they also earn points which, when sufficient have been earned, entitles them to the regular payments I mentioned.'

'They get a guaranteed income for life?'

'Yes, that's right. I can see from your faces that many of you are wondering how such a system can work. I wondered about it myself, but I could see it operating usefully and efficiently so I had to stop wondering and try to figure it out. Two things initially came to mind. One was the abundant natural resources the people had easy access to. Their farms are endowed with rich soils and temperate weather and are surrounded by hills, forests and lakes filled with copious sources of natural wealth. The other was the people's relaxed, easy-going way of life. I've told you about the people who work in their manufacturing industries, about them working without management and about the quality of the things they produce. They could never think about producing goods that were likely to develop faults after a few years of use. They make things to last because they have a sense of pride and responsibility in them. They have a secure and adequate income for life from having done their community work for the services committee, so, although they do get additional money from their customers, they work in factories mainly for the satisfaction it brings. As I've already said, they work with commitment and enthusiasm without pressure or stress. This relaxed, tranquil attitude is found in all facets of society; it is a distinctive feature of life in the distant lands. However, when I thought further into it, I realised that abundant natural resources and carefree attitudes to life, although significant, are not sufficient to fully account for the evident wealth, security and serenity they all enjoy. Jason, David and I talked about it. We know many here today will not like to hear this, but the main reason for the success of their civilisation, we found, is that no part of the wealth ordinary people create is sidetracked to support a privileged section of society. Everything they do so cheerfully and enthusiastically is done for the benefit of everyone. There are no people very much richer than others to sustain, so, more or less, their efforts enrich the lives of all in equal measures. No one is poor and no one is much richer than everyone else. Moreover, since everything they make is made to last, the effort required to sustain their way of life is reduced to a minimum. They can afford to rest. They enjoy a level of relaxation only the very rich can here in Areho.'

'But there must be leaders. How do they manage without a king? Are the committees you mentioned the only form of government they have?'

'First let me say again that the committees, or government departments, are groups of men and women chosen by others to manage and make decisions on their behalf. I could think of no equivalent bodies here in Areho, so I called them committees for want of a better word. I've mentioned the finance and services committees, but there are many others. They come together annually to select someone to serve as a ceremonial figurehead, a president if you like, but this person, in office for one year, has no powers over the committees. There's a big national celebration with lots of singing and dancing each time a new one is selected, and thereafter he, or she, fulfils the post's customary duties of office by visiting communities throughout the nation, bringing excitement and goodwill by giving speeches, opening new buildings, praising district committees and generally providing reasons for local festivities.'

There was a big national celebration with lots of singing and dancing each time a new 'president' was selected.

'So what other committees do they have?'

'There are ones for all important components of their civilization, including libraries, schools and colleges, but I think you'll find three in particular are interesting. One is responsible for the army. As I've said, the army's role, it seems, is largely ceremonial, providing frequent public displays of marching, exercise and physical endurance, but it also has the responsibility of being available in the event of natural disasters. It's called to action when necessary to help deal with such events as earthquakes, floods and severe storm damage. There's also a small navy with its own committee. In addition to giving occasional gala displays of seamanship and organising offshore trips with members of the public aboard its ships, it goes into action in the event of disasters at sea. The army and navy are also responsible for upholding customs. This is regarded as being very important, and the origins of their public displays can often be found in historic events. Accordingly, their respective committees work together in close association with the other group I think will be of interest, one we might call the committee for the preservation of traditions, or, more simply, the culture committee.'

'The preservation of traditions? What's that all about?'

'The committee's responsibility is to nourish the spirit that gives meaning to their civilisation, and guard against anything that might threaten it. To try to understand this it's necessary to take a brief look at the distant land's history. As the people were only too pleased to explain, the coastal city we were in is the administrative centre of their country, which is one of several others situated on a huge land mass. Long, long ago, many different tribes occupied this continent, and they didn't always live in peace and harmony. After very many years of conflict, wise men realised that the main reason young men went off to attack and raid other tribes was to capture and take home young women. Tribes that commonly did this tended to prosper and thrive, whereas, for some unknown reason, ones that didn't were scrawny and struggled to survive.

'Eventually, and at a time that is now celebrated by nearly all the distant land's countries, the wise men of the major thriving tribes met and discussed the situation. They came to the conclusion that, over and above satisfying the urges of young men, there were clear advantages in introducing young women from afar into their tribal communities. They agreed that a better way than violence was needed to achieve this and, after long discussions, decided to hold regular festive gatherings in each of their settlements. Young people in neighbouring tribes would be invited, and encouraged by their own elders, to attend. Amidst lots of cheerful singing and dancing, it was hoped, young hopefuls would meet the partners they were looking for in a friendly way, without having to resort to aggression and abduction. After a few initial festivals clouded by doubts and suspicions, the scheme developed into a great success. Tribal conflicts became the stuff of distant memories. Intermingling brought peace and prosperity, and, for some still unexplained reason, the peoples of the formerly struggling tribes enjoyed improved vitality and vigour. As goodwill spread throughout the continent the tribes flourished and, in time, developed into nations. In doing this many tribes combined, and the countries so formed cooperated in agreeing territorial boundaries, choosing natural features such as rivers, forests and mountain ranges as borders. They still have regular meetings to ensure continued peace, interaction and stability.'

'This is all very interesting, Alan, but what does the committee for the preservation of traditions do?'

'Well, as I said, it works closely with the army and navy to uphold traditions. Accordingly, in many of their public displays, soldiers and sailors symbolize and celebrate important events in the history I've briefly described. But the committee does other things, including providing venues for public meetings and promoting participation. In a way somewhat similar to the way people in Areho go to churches, people attend these gatherings with enthusiasm. They talk, sing and dance, and many of their most popular songs are about stories of the past, about events and people that have shaped their civilisation. They also sing in praise of the way things are now, about their prosperity, freedom and security. They also have songs and poems celebrating occasions when tough decisions had to be made about proposals of unsure advantage. They sing, read poems and talk about many other issues, including how everyone needs to be watchful for any threat to their carefree way of life.'

'What do you mean by proposals of unsure advantage?'

'It seems that in the past certain important businesses made proposals to change in some way, perhaps by changing their prices or products, and their suggestions were not clearly advantageous to society. They were borderline cases in this respect, so tough decisions were needed to determine if the proposals were to be allowed. Such determinations involved lengthy discussions and are remembered, and talked about, because they helped to set standards by which proposal assessments are now made. They set precedents.'

'You said these meetings are in some ways like church services. Do they include religious worship? Are the people religious?'

'When I said they were like church congregations I was thinking about the way the people all sing together, enthusiastically giving voice to songs they all know and enjoy. Also, the meetings seem to have a similar effect on people as church attendance has on worshipers in Areho. After singing, dancing and talking with others about life, love and morality, they go home feeling uplifted and confident. However, although a representative of the culture committee is usually present, mainly to listen and sometimes to contribute, there is no one with a role similar to that of a priest, although many of the songs and poems are about gods. It seems that long ago, when tribal wars were common, each tribe had its own god or set of gods, usually associated with local mountains or forests. Many of these deities are remembered and, although no longer thought of as divine beings with real existence, they are still regarded with respect. They feature in many well-liked songs. I think this is a legacy of the time when the tribes decided to cooperate and avoid war. They knew that if their plans were to succeed it was important to respect each other's religions.'

'Don't they believe in a god; a modern one?'

'I don't think they do. We never heard them talk of one. They do, however, talk about the mysteries of life and the religions of their ancestors. They find it interesting to wonder how prehistoric tribes came to believe in their various gods.'

'You mean they are atheists?'

'Well, I suppose you could say that.'

Joe Muroff, the meeting's chairman, could see that the people listening to his dialogue with Alan were restive. They had been noticeably uneasy and restless after hearing Alan's comments about the distant lands' people not having to support a privileged section of society. Muroff, therefore, judged it to be a suitable time to adjourn the meeting. He said, 'Thank you, Alan. You've been very helpful. Thank you also, Jason and David. I know you both worked hard along with Alan to bring us so much interesting information.'

Turning to the others present, he said, 'Gentlemen, I think we should finish for today. I suggest we all meet again in a few days' time to hear more from Alan, Jason and David. Having had time to absorb and consider all we've heard today, we'll be able to discuss it and ask questions.'

James Schemowt, the leading figure of the group, addressed everyone saying, 'You'll all be welcome to come to Schemowt Hall to spend an interesting and rewarding weekend there.'

'Thank you, James,' Muroff replied. 'I think we all agree, that'll be very enjoyable and convenient.' He went on to say, 'Tomorrow Jason will be giving an account of his experiences in the distant lands to the elite section. Alan will be able to sit back and take a rest. I hope you'll all be there; we don't want anyone to suspect from our absence that our special exclusive group exists. You'll not have to listen again to all you've heard today for, and I think you'll all agree with this, I am going to ask Jason to cut out a lot of what we've just heard. Using a need-to-know principle, I want him to put less stress on the peaceful contentment of the distant lands' people, completely omit that they work without a portion of their earned income being deducted to support a wealthy section of society, and put some emphasis on them being atheists. Afterwards, perhaps with further amendments, we can put out a pamphlet for circulation amongst ordinary members of The Organisation. Thank you, gentlemen and I look forward to seeing you all again tomorrow.'

James Schemowt inconspicuously attended the following day's meeting and, when the dialogue between Joe and Jason was finished, slipped away unobtrusively. He left the elite group discussing Jason's censored version of the three undercover agents' report and returned home to give instructions to his staff. Schemowt Hall, a far more lavish and spacious mansion than the one built several centuries earlier by James' ancestor, was prepared to cater for around twenty guests. In the course of the weekend gathering, the three spies mingled with other members of the Special Intellectual Group giving more details of the people they'd been sent to investigate. Many questions were asked. How did young people acquire the skills needed for their manufacturing industries? The answer being that those who were interested, during their final years of working for the services committee, elected to spend time in factories where they could learn how things were made. Other questions were not so easily answered. They were versions of: how is it that influential, able and ambitious individuals don't rise to prominence and amass personal riches, how are decisions made about what is advantageous to society and how do they make moral judgments without guidance from religious beliefs?

Of the three spies, Alan was the most forthcoming in trying to provide answers. He said he thought answers to such questions were to be found in the distant land's history, and went on to say: 'I think that since the whole continent was so well endowed with natural resources, tribal conflicts were not territorial disputes inspired by persuasive megalomaniacs, but were mainly about access to young women. Consequentially, the peace treaties that followed, involving friendly intermingling arrangements, laid the foundations for continent-wide peaceful co-existence. Thereafter, generation after generation lived in harmonious communities, and knew of violence only from cautionary tales of ancient times when bloody conflict was rife. So, as time passed, a culture of communal concord evolved. In such a cooperative, friendly environment any individual who tried to rise to prominence would have been incongruous and without support, and moral guidance from gods would have been unnecessary.'

The weekend conference continued with many lively discussions focused on the spies' assessments of the distant land's people and culture. It culminated with a formal banquet in Schemowt Hall's grand dining room. After the ladies had retired to sitting rooms and the men were smoking and drinking more wine, James stood up and said, 'Gentlemen, we've had a very enjoyable and productive meeting and learned a lot about the distant lands, but we've not found time to discuss what it means to us. Remember, the two voyages across the Mighty Ocean were intended to help relieve some of the economic difficulties we are experiencing here in Areho. Those difficulties are still here and we need to talk about them. I suggest we meet again here next weekend to decide what needs to be done.'

James' suggestion was met with unanimous approval, qualified only with the agreement that, in the interests of secrecy, their arrivals and departures to and from Schemowt Hall needed to be random and inconspicuous.

Chapter Seven

When the guests had left and the staff had cleared away all traces of their stay, and before it was time to prepare for the following conference, James found time to sit and talk with his son. In view of his youth, Jeremy had been excluded from the formal proceedings of the conference. He wanted to know all that had been said and decided. He listened carefully as James summarised the report given by Alan and the other spies and became particularly interested in their comments about working people not having to support a wealthy elite. 'What does it mean?' he asked. 'I don't think I fully understand it.'

'It simply means there are no fabulously rich people, and no extremely poor ones.'

'But doesn't it also mean that people who are rich are rich because they are supported by working people? That's what it sounds like to me.'

'Well, yes it does. That's how it is in Areho, but in the distant lands things are different. People here work in factories, mines, farms and other places of employment and they produce things that are sold, but only part of the money so obtained is given to them. The rest goes to the owners of the factories, mines, farms and other facilities. It goes to providing them with profit. That is why it was said that working people support their employers.'

'But their employers have expenses to pay such as taxes, rents and interest on loans.'

'Yes, that's right. I should have explained that by profit I mean the money that the employers have left for themselves after all their expenses, including their workers' wages, had been paid.

'So working people don't only support their employers, they also support the recipients of the other expenses?'

'Yes, they do. One or two of the friends we had here at the weekend employ many thousands of workers and each one helps to support their prosperity. They, and the receivers of monies they have to shell out, are, therefore, supported by working people. I should mention that in many small businesses the owners also work and are paid wages in addition to their profits, but they usually take on less strenuous tasks than the other workers, and are able to evade manual work altogether if their profits are sufficiently high. They become business managers, or bosses, fulfilling roles remote from physical effort. There are other situations, such as in shops, warehouses and offices, where no physical products are made but working people still have to do things so their employers can acquire money, only part of which is paid to them as wages.'

'You said owners of small businesses might become business managers, but can they become very wealthy and thereby considered to be members of the elite?'

'It's possible for them to become very wealthy, but it's very rare. However, unless they are part of our secret Organisation they can never be regarded as belonging to the elite. Most of the owners of very large firms were very wealthy before entering the world of business and belonged to The Organisation from birth. We need to understand the phrase *the elite* to mean people who are extremely rich and, by virtue of their great wealth, are able to clandestinely exercise far-reaching political power. In other words, being part of *the elite* essentially means belonging to our Organisation.'

'I understand what you've said, and as you spelt it out I could see that I had known it all along, but it was the notion of working people supporting a wealthy elite that I found a little puzzling.'

'I can appreciate that; it's not something we'd normally say. I believe Alan used the expression in order make clear the differences between the economic system on the other side of the Mighty Ocean and the one we have here in Areho.'

'Life in the distant lands seems so strange. How is it possible for it to be so different from how things are here?'

'To understand this I think we'll need to go back several months, to a time just before the first fleet of trade ships sailed off to the distant lands. You asked me why there has to be growth. We talked about an imaginary place where people conducted their affairs without money and then considered what might happen if someone opened a bank and persuaded them to borrow and pay interest. Do you remember?'

'Yes, you explained why economic growth is essential. Interest payments drain money out of circulation, therefore on average the growth rate has to be greater than the interest rate. Without sufficient growth, money in circulation would decline, bank loans could never be repaid and the economic system would collapse.'

'Yes, that's right. I'm impressed that you understand and remember it so well. It's perhaps important to make clear that growth here means the annual growth in the supply of money, which, more or less, is the same as the annual growth in the sale of goods and services. I said *more or less* because one or two factors such as inflation and savings should be considered, but let's not be concerned with them, they don't significantly change how our economic system compares with the one in the distant lands.'

'So growth is important when comparing the two economic systems?'

'Yes, very much so, it's at the very core of how the two systems differ. Interest, as you clearly understand, makes growth absolutely essential. In the distant lands there is no interest. Their government, which itself is very different from the one we have here, controls the issue of money and charges no interest on any loans it provides. Therefore growth is not absolutely necessary as it is here. This is the fundamental difference between their system and ours. All the other differences follow from this basic reality. Any growth they do have arises largely from population increases and innovations, which are only implemented if they are clearly advantageous and give rise to few, if any, unwanted consequences. Here in Areho, since economic growth is absolutely vital for the well-being of our financial system, our industrial friends have to continuously churn out products that are used for a while before being discarded. Their marketing colleagues have to incessantly persuade consumers to buy new products, and to help them in their quest many products are deliberately, or indifferently, made with limited life-spans. Latent defects mean they go wrong after a while and, intentionally, are difficult, or impossible, to repair. Short product usefulness and persuasive, incessant advertising are the main means by which relentlessly increasing consumer spending is sustained. Without these measures the endlessly increasing supply of money, so necessary for bank loan repayments, cannot be maintained. Moreover, since economic growth is absolutely imperative, our industrial friends cannot allow concerns for the natural environment or local communities to obstruct their activities. Growth to them means increasing profits. To ensure they have their way, The Organisation makes sure that sufficient politicians are compliant. In the distant lands things are very different. Since economic growth is not vital, they don't need to make things with limited lifetimes, and they don't need to forsake concerns for communities and the natural world. Also, since the things they make are made to last indefinitely, they don't need to have long working days and nights producing things that will soon need replacing. They can afford to take a relaxed attitude to manufacturing. Moreover, they don't need to manage problems of disposing of ever increasing mountains of discarded goods that have ended their short lives of usefulness. Growth is an option they can choose, not a fundamentally essential feature of economic life, not something they have to endlessly chase after. For individuals, many benefits follow from this basic reality, including the option of enjoying ample leisure time. This, no doubt, is the reason many people in the distant lands seem to enjoy lots of singing and dancing.'

'I understand what you've told me, that the differences between the two economic systems all hinge on interest.'

'Yes, and never forget that all the wealth, comforts and luxuries we enjoy also hinge on interest.'

The conversation continued. Jeremy asked if working people in Areho knew they were supporting their wealthy employers.

'Yes, I think many of them do,' answered James. 'They don't know about the existence of our Organisation - we have ways of ensuring that - but many will know that they are paid a fraction of the money accrued by their employers as a result of the work they do. Some with sufficient determination and tenacity occasionally try to persuade their fellow workers to collectively campaign for a larger fraction of the accrued money, but we have ways of averting their efforts.'

Some workers occasionally tried to persuade their fellow workers to campaign for fairer wages, but there were ways of averting their efforts.

'The people in the distant lands seem able to avoid such difficulties. How do you think they do that?'

'Well, as Alan said, businesses are owned by the people who work in them so they get to keep all the profits. Also, largely for historical reasons, they have a culture in which the accumulation of massive amounts of personal wealth is strongly opposed. Here in Areho things are very different. The Organisation ensures that very wealthy people remain firmly in control of the government. The people of the distant lands have their own form of organisation, which, in a way, is an inversion of ours. If we carefully examine the things we were told by Alan we can see that their organisation exists to ensure that no individual or special-interest group can take control of how they are governed. He called it the *committee for the preservation of traditions*.'

Jeremy had many more questions, and his father answered them as well as he could, but eventually, as midnight approached, both felt too tired to continue. It was time for bed.

Some factories had to close because there was insufficient demand for the goods they produced.

The scheduled weekend gathering of the Special Intellectual Group at Schemowt Hall commenced soon after everyone had arrived and been able to refresh themselves after their journeys. James Schemowt took on the role of chairman and principal spokesman, and, after welcoming his guests, he started the meeting by saying, 'I think you'll all agree, we cannot simply ignore what we now know about the distant lands and its people. Many of our factories have had to reduce production and are now in a worse state than before we dispatched the first fleet of trade ships. They simply need more consumers, and the only place we can hope to find them is in the distant lands.'

An unmistakable murmur of general agreement filled the room. When it subsided, James continued, 'As for buying goods from them, as we've heard, they are unwilling to accept our money. Perhaps we should have been able to foresee this for, without places where our banknotes could be redeemed, the promise of redemption on demand would have been meaningless. I talked with Alan and Jason about this. They told me they tried to get them to accept our money by telling them that it could be used to buy goods from us, but, as they had seen the things we had to offer, they were not persuaded.'

Again, James had to pause while sounds of murmuring came from his audience, sounds this time of indignation. When appropriate, he continued, 'I know many of you don't like to hear criticisms of the goods we produce here in Areho, but if that's the way the distant foreigners feel about them there's nothing we can do about it. We can't make them buy things they don't want. Furthermore, if we want to buy goods from them we will have to pay for them with gold, but, as I'm sure you are all aware, if we were to do that we'd soon be in far greater difficulties than we are now. It wouldn't take long before the general public was asking, "If all our gold is being sent to the other side of the Mighty Ocean what's going to be left to support our currency?" I'll not bother to suggest what might happen then; you've all got good imaginations. Consequently, we simply cannot send large amounts of gold to the distant lands. So, that's the situation. They won't buy from us, we can't buy from them, and we can't simply ignore them. What are we to do? I'm going to open up the meeting to general discussion.'

James knew what the answer would be, as did everyone else at the meeting, but they also knew it was necessary to discuss the situation further before announcing any conclusion. It was a matter of decorum. Accordingly, they talked. After a short while George stood up and said, 'Something we need to consider is if by some means we were able to come to some sort of trade agreement with them we would be risking the spread of dangerous ideas amongst the public. Sailors would inevitably bring back tales of how people live in the distant lands. Such stories would soon infect our populace with unwanted notions. They would undermine the popular beliefs we have so carefully crafted: that spending generates happiness; that an individual's income is determined by his, or her, contribution to the economy; that thoughts of ideal societies are the unrealistic ideas of starry-eyed dreamers; and that, providing it is free to function without government interference, our economic system is the best of all possible economic systems.'

Alan responded, 'I agree. We considered the risk of domestic-ideology corruption while we were in the distant lands. We had the captain of each ship warn his crew against talking about how things are over there when they arrived back in Areho. We made the captains believe our concerns were about the obliging way young women there welcomed their crews and that if accounts of this were to become known by young ladies back home it might corrupt their maidenly virtues. The captains understood our expressed concerns, or made out that they did, and warned their crews accordingly, making each sailor and ship's officer aware that if they ever said anything more than the stories they were told to use they would never again work in the shipping industry.'

Jason added, 'I think we all agree with George and Alan – thinking about a possible trade deal is pointless. Even if some sort of arrangement could be made, it would be too dangerous. It would be too much of a risk. There's something else I think we must consider. The distant lands, we've been told, are full of natural riches, especially in the mountains, rivers and forests. It would be unfair of the people there to keep them all to themselves. We surely should have a share of the natural bounty God has provided.'

David added, 'I agree, and there's something else we need to consider. From what we've been told, it seems the people of the distant lands could very easily be persuaded to work for very low wages. This is something we cannot ignore.'

The discussion continued for a little while longer. Before arriving at Schemowt Hall everyone had known what the outcome of the meeting would be, but they also knew they needed to go through a semblance of debate before declaring it. When James could see that everyone who wanted to speak had been able to, he stood up and asked, 'Gentlemen, are we all agreed?'

'Yes,' they all answered with one voice.

'What's it to be then?' he asked.

Still in unison, they cried out the answer, 'War.'

Chapter Eight

The King, Thomas IV, was unaware of The Organisation's existence; nevertheless he was influenced by it in many ways. Knowing of their academic reputations, and influenced by the recommendations of people he trusted, he had appointed several members of the Special Intellectual Group to his Council of Ministers. Other Organisation members were highly regarded advisors to the Council. However, the issue of war was not put before him until the mood of the country had been suitably prepared. Shortly after a modified version of the spies' account of life in the distant lands had been told to The Organisation's elite section, a modified version was told to ordinary members. From them, as intended, appropriately embroidered stories of life on the other side of the Mighty Ocean were leaked to the press. With profuse journalistic embellishments, newspapers, whose editors were either members of The Organisation or were answerable to proprietors who were, reported to the public accordingly. To add seeming credence to their stories, reporters interviewed sailors still mindful of their voyages across the Mighty Ocean. Knowing that the warning of being excluded from employment in the world of shipping was real, and most likely the least of what was being threatened, crews stuck firmly to their skippers' instructions. They stuck to the approved narrative. The press then had all the material it needed to spin on. After swallowing the news media's stories, the general public was left with a firmly fixed belief that the distant lands were populated by undisciplined, anarchistic atheists.

When newspaper stories about the people of the distant lands no longer warranted front page headlines, and it was thought the time was right, Dennis Heram, The Organisation's top man in the Royal Council, approached the King and said, 'Your majesty, there's going to be many difficulties ahead and I'm afraid war is the only way of averting them.'

'War!' the King retorted. 'What are you talking about? Who do you think we should have a war with?'

'The people of the distant lands.'

'Why? What have they done?'

'They've insulted Areho, your majesty. Our friendly proposals of establishing a trading agreement with them were summarily rejected. First they slated the quality of the goods we offered by way of trade, they then discredited our currency, claiming it was not worth the paper it was printed on. They have snubbed us, and at a time when we are desperately in need of increased foreign trade. Moreover, the country is governed by ungodly tyrants. They control the people's thoughts, and won't allow them the freedom to worship God and use the abilities He gave them to achieve happiness in their own ways. Their suffering is intense. Accordingly, humanitarian concern alone is sufficient to justify military intervention.'

'Yes, I'm fully aware of what the newspapers have been saying. They keep calling this place you want to have a war with *the distant lands*. Doesn't it have a name? If it's a country it should have a proper name. You can't go to war with a country with no name.'

'It's called Yevad, your majesty.'

'Then why on earth do you keep calling it *the distant lands?*'

'I'm not sure, your majesty. It's been called that since it was first discovered. I think it's simply become a habit.'

'Then get rid of it. It's not a habit I like. As for war, you've not given any good reasons for sending our sailors and soldiers across the Mighty Ocean. We can't go to war with the people of Yevad simply because they don't want to trade with us and we don't like their religious views. I've no serious reasons for being angry with Yevad, and I don't see why there should be war.'

'But, your majesty, some of our factories have had to close because there's insufficient demand for the goods they produce. Without increased trade things can only get worse. More factories will have to shut down, people who worked in them will become unemployed, they will become very angry, they will protest in the streets and might even riot.'

'I don't like the idea of riots, but I like the idea of unjustified war with a faraway country even less. I can't see how the people of Yevad can be blamed for factories in Areho making too many things. I don't want war. Do I make myself clear, Doctor Heram?'

'Yes, your majesty, you do.'

Members of The Organisation's inner circles were extremely dismayed by the King's attitude. Many others felt the same way. Industrialists in the business of manufacturing guns and ammunition were particularly displeased. War would have been very good for their companies. They would have made lots of profit. Their lobbyists approached the King and tried to persuade him to change his mind by emphasizing the financial advantages of war. They told him, 'Work would be found for thousands of unemployed victims of the industrial situation. Their wages would feed into the economic system, thus providing jobs for many more idle workers. The economic crisis would be solved, and it wouldn't place any strain on your Treasury. The banks will provide all the money needed for the war, and national debt increases can easily be repaid in years to come by modestly adjusting the income tax rate.'

The King was not convinced. 'We can't wage war on innocent people in a foreign land just because our own economic system is in a mess. What sort of a country would we be if we did that? What would other kingdoms think of us? Now let's hear no more of your worthless arguments. Gentlemen, I bid you good day.'

The Special Intellectual Group was infuriated by the King's attitude. Many high ranking army officers felt the same way. They had been very keen to have a war. As part of their normal military duties several leading generals, all members of The Organisation, regularly conferred with the King. When an opportunity occurred they also tried to persuade him to change his mind. 'From all we've been told, your majesty, Yevad's army is little more than a bunch of circus clowns. They're no better than schoolboys playing at being soldiers. Our best estimate is that war with them will be over in a matter of days.'

'That's not the point. We can't go about starting wars with other countries just because they're weak. It would be disgraceful and dishonourable.'

'But, your majesty, too much marching up and down in nice colourful uniforms is not good for soldiers, they are meant to fight and they need to do it from time to time. Soldiers need to do more than parade about in cute uniforms; they need to gain experience of fighting in wars.'

'Are you all mad? What are you thinking about? It seems to me that you are not thinking at all. You can't start wars simply because your soldiers need practice. Get them out on manoeuvres if you think they need more training. Get them out on the shooting ranges. Give them some bullets to practise with, and try not to let them kill anyone while they're at it. Now good day, gentlemen, and next time you come to see me try to think of something sensible to say.'

The King's refusal to authorize war aroused intense irritation. Members of The Organisation were infuriated. To discuss the situation, the Special Intellectual Group met at Indolder Hall, the country home of Gordon Indolder, chairman of the Indolder Banking Empire. Acting as chairman, Gordon welcomed his guests and started the proceedings by saying, 'Gentlemen, it seems that King Thomas has put a serious obstacle before us. If he has his way our plans will be scuppered. We can't allow this, but the question is what are we to do about it? Or, more to the point, what can we do about it?'

Edward Erten suggested, 'A nice fatal accident could be arranged.'

'That would do us no good,' Alan answered. 'He'd quickly be replaced by that hopeless Prince David and he'd be no more use than his pathetic father.'

'That's the trouble,' George responded, 'we have no influence over who sits on the throne. We can choose who gets to be head of the church, commander in chief of the army, leading high court judges and holders of many other powerful posts, for we hold sway over their appointments, but we have no control over the monarchy. We're up against hereditary succession and there's nothing we can do about it.'

The King told everyone he didn't want war.

'Let's not be too sure of that,' James Schemowt responded.

'Why?' asked Jason. 'Do you have something in mind?'

'Just leave it all to me. I don't like King Thomas. He's patronising; too full of his own self-importance. It's no good arranging advisors for him if he won't take their advice. It will be a pleasure to get rid of him.'

'Why, what do you have in mind?' Alan asked.

'As I said, just leave it all to me,' James replied.

When James was able to speak privately with the owners of the other banks he told them what he had in mind. Within days, along with new atrocity stories about Yevad, newspapers announced that the banks, in a further attempt to tackle the economic crisis, were to drastically cut interest rates. When people approached the banks seeking low-interest loans, they also found the criteria by which would-be-borrowers were assessed had been significantly relaxed. News of the banks' new easy-money policy spread quickly. Large loans were readily made available to customers the banks wouldn't normally regard as suitable borrowers. It didn't take long for the economic system to respond. New factories opened, old ones were re-equipped, unemployed people found jobs, production increased and eager customers flocked to the shops with full purses, enthused by enticing advertisements telling them that new things were fashionable, old things outdated and that shopping was trendy, leisurely and therapeutic. The economic crisis soon became a barely remembered issue of the past.

Without any mention of war, the King's refusal to back the army was reported in newspapers.

As the bankers expected, prices started to increase. There was no shortage of things regularly bought by ordinary working people - basic foods and things that went wrong after a while and were very difficult to repair - so their prices

125

increased only a little more than usual. Prices increased because bank loans were easily available, so it was the prices of business premises, houses and other things people took out large bank loans to buy, things known as assets, that started to rise; and because their prices were increasing, people, thinking prices would increase further and they would thereby become richer, started buying them enthusiastically. Buyers acting in this way became plentiful. This caused asset prices to increase even faster. Escalating house prices in particular aroused the attention of newspaper columnists. They were keen to keep their readers fully informed of the extraordinary behaviour of the housing market. Prices continued increasing dramatically until the day came when the bankers, in great secrecy, told appropriate members of The Organisation that it was time to sell their assets. Owners of newspapers, magazines and other opinion shaping concerns, however, were advised to ignore the instruction and retain control of their businesses. Other people, still able to easily take out low interest loans, and still expecting prices to go on increasing, were keen to buy, so the bankers' friends had no difficulty in doing as they'd been advised. They were able to make very large profits by selling assets they'd bought when prices were much lower.

The economic crisis soon became a barely remembered issue of the past.

Individuals who saw what wealthy, well-connected people were doing, and grasped just a little of what was happening, also started to sell. Others, who could see what was happening but had no idea why, decided they should also sell. Soon enthusiastic sellers became plentiful and prices quickly stopped increasing. Some people, ones who in earlier times would not have been considered by bankers to be suitable borrowers, had borrowed heavily to buy premises so they could run businesses that generated sufficient income to service their bank loans, but little more. They had not expected to make much money by running their enterprises, but had expected the prices their premises could be sold for to go on increasing, so that, in years to come, they would have been able to sell and make large profits. When it became clear that this was not going to happen, many decided to sell. However, without increasing prices, once the main reason for purchasing assets, very few people wanted to buy. Sellers had to lower the prices at which they were willing to sell, but the expectation of further price reductions made prospective purchasers even more reluctant to buy. Very soon prices were falling far faster than, only a short while earlier, they had been rising. They were said to have crashed.

Businesses were being offered for sale and once again the economic system was running into difficulties.

Collapsing prices produced the results the bankers expected. Businesses were being offered for sale and very few were finding buyers, so ordinary people could see that the economic system was, once again, running into difficulties. The resulting uncertainty focused minds. People cut back on unnecessary buying. They started to see that they didn't really need many of the things powerful advertisements urged them to buy. This added to the difficulties. Unable to sell sufficient goods or services, business owners who'd borrowed heavily became unable to continue re-paying their debts, and the bankers, as they said they would, and as the law allowed, took their businesses, and often their homes, from them. The bankers were particularly keen to take possession of newspaper businesses that were not already owned by members of The Organisation. Compliant newspapers had been printing articles about dreadful atrocities committed by the people of Yevad. Designed to arouse powerful public feelings of anger and disgust, the campaign used fabricated stories of horrendous rituals, and the bankers did not want unrestrained journalists revealing that they were untrue.

Business owners wanting to sell had to lower their prices.

The economic system continued declining dramatically and showed no signs that it might easily recover. People who'd worked in failed industries became unemployed, and ones who'd borrowed heavily to buy their homes became unable to service their debts. They became homeless. People in general started to feel gloomy and anxious. Many became seriously depressed. People asked why it had happened and who was responsible. Newspaper commentators provided answers. They repeatedly claimed that it had all been caused by reckless borrowers. When this explanation had been widely accepted by the public, the banks, as if in agreement, announced that interest rates were to be increased and stricter criteria were to be used when considering prospective borrowers. The bankers knew this would bring a deep and dire depression to the floundering economic system.

Unemployed people became very unhappy.

Ruined hopes, dreams and ambitions drove normally quiet people onto the streets to protest. Riots often flared up, and in several places, when tempers cracked, angry mobs attacked empty factories and left them burning. The situation deteriorated and, as more and more people became unemployed and more and more businesses and homes were taken from insolvent borrowers, the protests became angrier and the riots more frequent. By then the bankers, or their very close friends, owned virtually all the news supply and delivery businesses, and journalists knew what they had to write, or to keep quiet about, if they were to remain employed. Very few outside journalism knew this. Most people believed everything they read in newspapers. Columnists previously respectful to royalty blamed the King. He was supposed to be in charge of the country, yet he had been the most reckless of the reckless borrowers. Journalists who earlier had praised the King for the wisdom of his public works programme held him responsible for the economic crisis. He was accused of excessively increasing the national debt, so bringing doom and despondency to his kingdom. Some journalists criticised the King so frequently, and so convincingly, that they started to believe the things they wrote. Others decided not to think too much about it, or to keep their thoughts to themselves. Editors had been assured there was no reason to fear legal consequences. High court judges who were members of The Organisation backed the newspapers, and ones who were not, with the aid of suitable financial inducements, and other forms of influence when necessary, had been persuaded to agree with them. So comments about the King's management of the country became increasingly caustic.

Ruined hopes, dreams and ambitions drove normally quiet people onto the streets to protest.

Newspaper reports produced the intended results. Angry crowds became increasingly critical of the King. Violent incidents occurred frequently. People were not thinking clearly. They were anxious and confused. They were concerned about their homes and jobs. The King's stupidity and incompetence was proclaimed so frequently by the press that people simply accepted it as being indisputable. They did not ask how it could be that the King was responsible. They needed someone to blame and, without thinking about it, allowed journalists to shape their opinions. They had little alternative. They had no other sources of information.

Angry mobs filled the streets and the King's situation became perilous. Accordingly, he ordered his trusted generals to use soldiers to control the crowds and protect his palaces. He did not know, however, that the generals concerned knew of plans to depose him and put in his place someone who would be more compliant to the needs of the economic system. They had been assured that the intended replacement was from a regal family and had legitimate claims to the throne. They also knew that the proposed new monarch favoured wars of economic conquest and large armed forces with plenty of new weapons. Encouraged by such prospects, the colluding generals told soldiers not to fire their guns at crowds of protestors. Soldiers were to use minimum necessary force to stop people who were trying to invade the King's palace, but to go no further. So all day and all night angry mobs surrounded the royal palace chanting insulting taunts, and when the King complained the generals told him soldiers would mutiny if they were ordered to use military force against ordinary people. They would not fire their guns at crowds in which their hungry and homeless brothers and sisters might be protesting. The King was furious when he heard the generals saying this for he fully understood what they were really saying. He knew that ordinary soldiers would be far too fearful of the consequences to disobey orders, so he knew the generals no longer supported him. And he knew he was powerless without their support.

Chapter Nine

The Special Intellectual Group had been keeping a close watch as the bankers' plans unfolded. It had also been working closely with its lawyers to ensure Prince David's right to succeed would be forfeited in the event of his father's abdication. When it was confident that compliant judges would negate every possible objection the Prince might make to the loss of his hereditary rights, and it had heard from the generals that their implied message to the King had been delivered, it was ready to proceed to the next stage of its scheme. Accordingly, newspaper editorials unleashed two new campaigns with the same level of persistence and persuasiveness they'd used to make people believe the King was responsible for the economic crisis.

One campaign, emphasised by one group of newspapers, at first suggested, and later advocated, that, in the interests of the monarchy's well-being and the country's economic stability, the King should be replaced by a royal personage with superior capabilities. Once familiarized with this prospect, readers were informed of the existence of a suitable royal replacement and persuaded of the desirability of his prompt enthronement. The aspiring usurper, they were told, could trace his lineage back through the centuries to King Arnold, then reigning from his palace in Arvin. Where necessary, history books and official records had been suitably adjusted in advance of the newspaper reports. King Arnold, readers were told, had been deposed by armed forces and replaced by an impostor, King Walter II, King Thomas' distant ancestor. Once the public had been so misinformed, editorials interlaced harsh criticisms of the existing hard-pressed King with flattering appraisals of the pretender's qualities of judgement, wisdom and fair-mindedness. Newspapers so editorially inclined appealed to readers predisposed to unfaltering belief in monarchy but convinced that the current King's incompetence was responsible for the prevailing economic situation.

The other campaign, promoted by a different set of newspapers, advocated the rejection of monarchy and its replacement by a radical alternative form of government called democracy. Democracy, readers were told, featured in a fairy tale about an imaginary ancient city called Athens. Mythical people known as Greeks lived in Athens during a prosperous period, a golden age, and democracy was the name they gave to the method by which they were governed. Brief but positive descriptions of Athenian customs, as told in the fable, were given, after which readers were told that, while admirable, they were not, without modifications, ways that could be fruitfully employed in Areho. Editorial writers then skilfully introduced their readers to the basic ideas of a form of democracy in which local communities, known as constituencies, elected representatives. For a fixed period, after which there would be fresh elections, the representatives discussed and, if satisfactorily persuaded, approved policy decisions made by a group chosen by representatives with similar views, a group known as the government. Democracy, readers were persuasively told, was therefore a method by which ordinary people could effectively influence the way in which their lives were governed. It was an essential prerequisite of freedom, for it was a system by which elected representatives were answerable to the collective will of the people. This suggestion of a close association between democracy and freedom was very heavily promoted. Columnists supporting the campaign frequently used democracy and freedom as seemingly inseparable words. After a while many readers started to think of them as being equivalent and interchangeable.

The editorial writers' efforts soon produced the desired results. As the economic situation deteriorated and feelings of hopelessness and despondency became entrenched, the opinions of ordinary people became more and more divided. Two distinct blocs with roughly equal numbers of supporters emerged, each led by zealous enthusiasts. Monarchists, eagerly awaiting the coronation of their champion, the pretender, passionately opposed democrats who looked forward to the end of monarchy and the onset of freedom. Without thinking about it, people believed newspapers had accurately reported statistics and other relevant information, including quotations from learned authorities, in support of their respective campaigns. So believing, they never suspected their passionately held views had been gently fashioned by skilful persuaders. Their opinions, freely formed and objectively supported, were their own. They never doubted this. They did not suspect concealed influences had been behind the newspaper crusades for they had no reasons for thinking such things. The Organisation kept its affairs very, very secret. The general public knew nothing of its activities for such matters were never reported by the news media. The vast majority of people did not even faintly suspect that a government-controlling secret society existed. Some individuals, more astute than the rest, were able to see that the newspaper campaigns had not been conducted without bias, but did not think there was anything sinister about it. Editorial writers, they felt, were entitled to express their own sincerely held views. A few who did think a little more about it, wondering if all the recent fateful events could have been caused by some unseen, evil factor, did not speak of it. They risked being laughed at and called fools if they spoke openly of such thoughts. So the monarchists and democrats continued to argue passionately in support of their respective causes.

When the two blocs had become firmly fixed in their views, each no longer able to produce fresh points of view, a proclamation by the royal pretender appeared on the front pages of all newspapers. He announced that if he was chosen by popular consent to be the new King he would stand aside from all political activities and wholeheartedly support a democratic form of government. He recognized that professional politicians, chosen by the people, were needed to govern the economically developed country into which the kingdom had been transformed. As King, he would regard his role as that of a ceremonial head of state. The age of old-fashioned monarchy had passed. It was time for a new democratic version in which the collective will of the people prevailed. People were initially astonished by the proclamation. However, guided by the approval expressed unanimously by editorial writers, they soon became enthusiastic supporters of the pretender. The passionately held principles that had divided the people into two fervently opposed blocs simply evaporated. The public's openly expressed approval of the proclamation was heartfelt and extensive; accordingly, four days after its publication the pretender was able to appear in the main square of Arcue and address huge crowds of enthusiastic supporters. The King, a virtual prisoner in his own palace, could only look out on the events occurring in his kingdom and feel the reality of his powerlessness.

Surreptitiously, members of the Royal Council approached the King and, with feigned regret, advised that abdication was the only way he could survive the unfolding events with dignity. The King, as ignorant as the general public of The Organisation's role in the breakdown of his kingdom, still trusted the reliability of their wisdom. Accordingly, he announced his abdication in a short and dignified public statement and unceremoniously retreated to live with relatives in a neighbouring kingdom. The public, guided as usual by seemingly credible columnists, showed little concern for the fate of the

King and focused its attention on the person destined to be his replacement. Excitement and hopeful anticipation spread quickly. When it was announced that the pretender, assuming the role of King, was to make an important statement from the palace balcony, every place from which the balcony could be observed became tightly packed with enthusiastic supporters. When he appeared, the crowd started chanting *"Long Live The King"* over and over again, only becoming silent after being urged to do so, after a carefully considered period, by hand gestures given by the would-be King. When the crowd was ready to listen, the pretender asserted his right to claim the throne in view of the old King's abdication. When enthusiastic cheering had abated, after declaring the date of his planned coronation and giving brief details of the proposed ceremonial arrangements, he went on to announce particulars of the proposed transition to democracy.

The King was furious when he knew the generals no longer supported him.

In view of its novelty, a public holiday was declared for the day of the first elections. It was to be two months after the coronation. As Election Day approached, newspapers, after months of informing the public of every detail of the crowning ceremony, obligingly provided readers with step-by-step guides to the proposed democratic system. All adults would be eligible to vote. They were to go about getting their names on electoral registers and were to cast their votes secretly on Election Day at designated places called polling stations. Also, as readers were repeatedly informed, all adults able to show they had a significant number of supporters, and able to pay a deposit designed to deter frivolous candidates, were eligible to seek election. Many such adults did put themselves forward as candidates, but as Election Day approached it became clear in most constituencies that two candidates, with nearly equal numbers of supporters, were outstandingly more popular than all the others. In the remaining constituencies, although they did not have roughly equal support, there were also two candidates with significantly greater popularity than all the others. Moreover, soon after details of the election process had been announced, groups of people with similar ideas of how the country should be governed formed throughout the land. The groups became known as political parties, and although there were quite a few of them only two became outstandingly popular. What is more, in each constituency, the two outstandingly popular candidates were members, one from each, of the two outstandingly popular political parties. No one, it seemed, asked why. The formation of two outstanding parties, each with outstanding candidates, seemed to happen quite naturally. No one, apparently, suspected that unseen influences might have caused it to happen.

Abdication was the only way the King could survive the unfolding events with dignity.

Although the two popular parties had very similar policies with regard to the economic crisis, by emphasizing their differences they were able to make it seem otherwise. One stressed the importance of reducing the national debt by cutting back on the public works programme. The other, while acknowledging that the size of the national debt was a serious problem, argued that cutting back on public works too drastically would seriously harm the prospects of economic recovery. The public works programme, it said, was essential to the working of the economic system in two important ways: it maintained and expanded the vital network of public utilities on which commerce and industry relied, and, by safeguarding jobs, it ensured money essential for economic recovery flowed into the economic system. It was, they said, a policy for growth. Their opponents disagreed. They told prospective voters that the proposals suggested by the other party were inadvisable because they did not focus on the crucial need to reduce the national debt. It was a policy of making the same mistakes that had caused the economic crisis in the first place. Their policy, they claimed, would restore the economic system to health in a fundamentally different way. By making drastic cut-backs in government spending it would reduce the national debt and so reduce the burden of taxation. This, they claimed, would provide the spending that was necessary for economic recovery in the most efficient way. By allowing consumers to spend their hard-earned money as they wished it would allow the economic system to operate freely and efficiently, unburdened by the deadening effects of government spending. It would cure the system permanently. With such policies, in the period prior to Election Day, each of the two outstandingly popular parties tried to persuade people to vote for their respective candidates. They argued incessantly about the virtues of their own policies and the flaws of their opponents.

The Organisation's obedient and resourceful minions in the news media had served their financial masters well. Soon after the economic crisis had started to take hold, long before the old King's abdication and the pretender's proclamation, several academics, with only slightly differing emphases, had propounded the basic ideas behind the policies advocated by the two outstandingly popular parties. Seeing the advantages of such ideas, the Special Intellectual Group clandestinely used their cronies in the media to ensure they were well promoted. Accordingly, newspapers and magazines favourably reviewed books written by the chosen academics and provided simplified summaries of their ideas. Profuse articles also provided information in harmony with their ideas. While seemingly reporting events fairly and accurately, the media skilfully moulded the general public's opinions and beliefs about how the economic crisis might be resolved. One group of newspapers examined and praised the works of thinkers who recommended that the national debt should be drastically reduced, while the works of those who stressed the importance of public works were promoted in a similar way by a different group. So it was that as people were being informed of the procedures, and persuaded of the virtues, of the proposed democracy, they were also familiarized with two seemingly different sets of ideas about managing the economic crisis.

The new King's right to the throne was celebrated by his supporters.

Creating celebrities was one of the media's most resourceful and persuasive techniques for moulding public beliefs. Of the promoted academics, ones with a flair for communicating effectively with the public were interviewed supportively, and frequently asked to write lengthy articles for publication. They became widely known and admired personalities, unaware that their rise to fame had been secretly orchestrated. Another effective opinion-shaping technique was information exclusion. Thinkers who proposed alternative ways of dealing with the economic crisis, including ones who critically examined the fundamental structure of the financial system and recommended far-reaching public inquiries into the ways in which money was created and used, were ignored by the media. Their ideas threatened the well-being of The Organisation, so the general public was told nothing about them or their suggestions.

The media was instructed to give roughly equal attention to the two political parties that were to be made outstandingly popular, for, provided it was won by one of them, the outcome of the election would be of little concern to The Organisation. Although much was made of differences between the policies of the two parties, after the elections there would be very little scope for either of them to significantly modify the economic system. Whichever formed a government would find its ability to fulfil its promises to the electorate was seriously restricted. The bankers knew and understood this. Whether the elected government wanted to stress the importance of public works or the national debt it would still have to use taxpayers' money to pay what was owed. The government would only be able to slant the relative importance it gave to public utilities or the national debt. Sustaining the public works programme would involve increasing the national debt and continuing to pay high levels of interest, whereas attempting to reduce the debt would divert taxpayers' money away from the nation's public utilities. Either way, taxpayers' money would find its way to the bankers' coffers.

So it was that two seemingly opposing sets of ideas of how the economic crisis should be managed became widely known by the general public, while alternative ideas that critically examined the structure of the system and recommended fundamental changes were largely overlooked. With the coming of democracy, politicians seeking election were treated in the same way as the thinkers. Those proposing policies based on ideas advocated by well promoted thinkers were highly praised by the media, while any proposing policies based on ideas suggested by ignored thinkers were ignored. So, as political parties were forming, and the public was being familiarized with the basic concepts of democracy, members of the general public were made to believe that the apparently conflicting policies of the well promoted parties were about fundamental issues that determined the quality of their lives. When the news media published the names of candidates seeking election, as it was expected to, the other parties were briefly mentioned. Had they not been, the media's bias would have been obvious. However, brief statements made about the other parties usually included contemptuous and trivializing comments, especially when individual candidates or parties were seen by the press as easy targets for mockery. Moreover, candidates and their parties needed money to publicize themselves and their policies, so, while doing all it could to prevent money going to other parties, The Organisation clandestinely ensured that the two parties it favoured received all they needed. So, as Election Day approached, the general public, because it was uninformed or misinformed about alternatives, regarded the two well-publicised parties as being the only two they could sensibly choose from.

As Election Day approached, interest in democracy gained momentum.

When Election Day came one of the outstandingly popular parties had more successful candidates than the other and, as planned, its leader was asked by the new King to be his prime minister and to take on the responsibility of governing the kingdom. The prime minister, according to plan, then chose other successfully elected members of his party to support him and be known as ministers. In this way a group known collectively as the government took on the task of running the country. The kingdom was under new management. Or so it seemed. Members of The Organisation were very pleased. The King had been replaced by one from a family with long standing connections with the banking business, and the new government consisted of individuals with amenable political views. They referred to the outcome of their scheme as the *magnificent revolution*. Long after the elections, members of the two outstandingly popular parties continued arguing publicly about the faults of their opponents' opinions and the merits of their own. It was just as The Organisation had intended. As crafted, democracy proved to be a very effective way of distracting the public's attention away from matters the bankers did not want examined. They didn't want people asking where money came from. Democracy had been introduced exactly as they wanted, and no one suspected that its formation, and all that had led to it, had been secretly planned.

The election was won by the party that wanted to cut spending on public utilities and use taxpayers' money to reduce the national debt. But the new government soon found the extent to which this could be done without causing very serious difficulties was very limited. The spending reductions it was able to make intensified the economic crisis. More businesses failed, the number of people who were unemployed increased and, as required by law, insolvent individuals and businesses relinquished possession of property to the banks.

Although interest payments the bankers received from the government was slightly reduced, they benefited from being handed large amounts of taxpayers' money as national debt re-payments and by gaining possession of valuable property. If the party favouring public works had won, the national debt would have increased or remained unchanged and the bankers would have gained less confiscated property, but would have continued receiving high levels of interest payments. But this was of little importance to the bankers. They had been able to ensure the election was won by one of the two parties they had secretly backed, and very few votes had gone to other parties. This was very important. It showed that The Organisation had comprehensive control of what people thought and believed. Its members were very pleased.

Chapter Ten

The Special Intellectual Group, although delighted by the success of its *magnificent revolution*, knew it needed to weigh up the situation and carefully plan its next moves. Accordingly, once the new government had settled in and its style of action could be seen, another weekend conference was arranged. The chosen venue - Telslow Hall, home of Dennis Telslow, the owner of the Telslow Banking Empire - provided splendid facilities in a discreetly secluded country estate, situated far from prying onlookers. As before, in the interests of security, members arrived individually and randomly.

Telslow Hall.

Dennis assumed the role of chairman and opened the proceedings by saying, 'Welcome everybody, it's a delight to see you all looking well and satisfied, and satisfied you may well feel, for the investiture of King James and the introduction of democracy was a glorious achievement. I think we need to start the meeting by saying a few words about democracy. It has now been running long enough for us to be able to assess some of its characteristics. One of its main features, you've probably noticed, is that it mollifies people. Expenditure on public services has been cut back, more businesses are failing and unemployment continues to rise, but, compared with how they were before, there's been fewer political demonstrations and the riots that have occurred have been smaller and less violent. Democracy, it seems, pacifies people. They were told *free speech*, the right to criticise the government openly, is one of the most important features of democracy. Accordingly, they've been appeased, I think, largely by being able to explicitly disapprove of their political leaders without fear of consequences.'

With democracy, desperate people were more inclined to begging than to protesting.

Alan interrupted to say, 'Have you noticed that a child's desire for a toy is often lessened after it has gained possession of the toy? I think grown-up people are the same in many ways. Once it's permitted, the attraction of criticising authority loses a lot of its appeal.'

'Yes, I think you're right,' Dennis responded. 'The government, or so it seems to the public, is responsible for the worsening economic situation, but it's a government that was elected to office by the people. Accordingly, in a way probably not found in alternative political systems, people feel in some small way responsible for the behaviour of their political leaders. They argue publicly, often ardently, but only a minority denounce the government. More than half of the adults who took part in the election voted for the government's party, so they can't easily criticise, and people who didn't bother to vote are similarly constrained. Only people who voted for other parties will feel they have a right to criticise, and their carping, it seems, is curbed since they believe they were given a choice. Nevertheless, many people, thinking democracy and free speech make their opinions count, take part in heated political discussions. This, I think, eases tensions and makes many people less inclined to participate in mass demonstrations and violent riots. They are placated by democracy, unaware that their political opinions are largely bounded by horizons set by our friends in scholarly institutions and news media. Their discussions, therefore, remain focused on the policies of the two political parties they've been conditioned to believe are the only ones with feasible policies. It's probably too soon to draw any firm conclusions, but it seems to me that democracy's pacifying qualities are pronounced and very advantageous. It makes people more manageable, more malleable.'

Unemployed people looking for work were more likely to find abuse.

'I agree,' George commented. 'And while we have that in mind there's something else I think we need to consider. The government, if only with an eye on the next elections, will need to respond to issues people get excited about, so we'll need to continue carefully creating, shaping, amplifying or suppressing public concerns. We learned a lot about manipulating public opinions in the course of getting rid of King Thomas and introducing democracy. With help from our friends in the news media, we determined which politicians formed the government, and we manipulated the beliefs, values and policies they supported and the public concerns they responded to. People think the government has control of the country and has trustworthy reasons for its policies, so we've clearly refined our techniques, but I think there's still a lot more to learn. If we are to maintain clandestine control of both the government's and the people's thoughts I suggest we consider establishing a new scholarly institution, or university department, dedicated to studying mass opinion management. Of course, we can't call it anything like that. In the eyes of the public it will need to be called something like *The Institute of Personal Relations*. I think there's a wide range of issues it could examine, including the influence of distress on mass susceptibility to propaganda. It seems to me that, in addition to democracy, the harrowing reversals of economic outlook we engineered made people easily persuaded to see things as we wanted them to. I think it's something we could get a team of suitable, compliant thinkers to look into. It may well be something we'll be able to use in the years ahead.'

George's suggestion gained unanimous approval. It led Colin to say, 'As I'm sure you are all aware, our learned institutions are now commonly known as *think tanks*. It's an interesting development, and it's remarkable that no one, it seems, has ever asked how they are financed. No matter, I think there are a few issues we could get one or two of them to look into. Our predecessors provided generous donations to establish foundations, masquerading as charitable institutions, where intellectuals they approved of could formulate ideas. Initially, their real purposes were to ensure Kings received advice our forerunners wanted them to hear, and to formulate notions that would furnish the economic system with apparent credibility. To fulfil their public relations commitments, they simply churned out, by way of the media, points of view subtly advantageous to the image of banks and big businesses, and aphorisms supporting the belief that the economic system is the best of all possible economic systems. One of their best obfuscations, and my favourite, is that by accepting deposits banks transfer surplus money from one part of the country to other parts where it can be usefully employed in economic activity. Later they promoted the ideas that were used by the two main political parties.

But now we need them to come up with something different, something very specific.'

'What have you in mind?' George asked.

'Things are going well,' Colin replied, 'but there are some difficulties we'll need to overcome before we can proceed with our plan to invade and conquer Yevad. Introducing democracy was an ingenious move. As we've found, it has many advantages, but it isn't perfect. We've not been able to completely suppress discussions outside the boundaries set by the thinkers we supported, and free speech has allowed unwelcome ideas about the workings of the economic system to circulate amongst an uncomfortably large number of people. Several insightful individuals realized the old King's extravagance was not the only reason the economic system ran into difficulties. Banks that supplied him with loans, they said, were also responsible. The notion was not too difficult for less insightful people to understand and, by the agency of public discussion, it quickly spread. Now, more people than we can be comfortable with have started talking about the role banks play in the economic system. People are publicly discussing interest rates and lending criteria, and how both influence national economic performance. From such discussions a new idea has emerged that we need to take very seriously. It is that banks should be regulated by the government.'

Unemployed people were urged to start their own small businesses.

'That's preposterous,' Dennis responded angrily. 'We must quash such ideas decisively before they get out of hand.'

'I agree,' Colin responded. 'It's very dangerous. Banks being regulated by anyone outside The Organisation is totally unacceptable. Some of us have talked to friends in the newspaper business, to editors and journalists who keep a close watch on public concerns, and they think the idea is now too widespread to ignore. Initially they avoided drawing attention to it, thinking it unwise to give it publicity, but now, with our approval, they plan to publish editorials pooh-poohing the idea. They intend to try to persuade readers that the banking system is far too complex to be regulated by people who are not experienced bankers. However, and we agreed, they don't think their arguments will be sufficient to curb the idea's growing popularity. Far too many people think the idea is good for them to be easily persuaded against it. Accordingly, I think our scholarly institutions should be asked to come up with some powerful new ideas; ideas able to counter the looming menace of government bank regulation.'

After unanimously agreeing that the task of finding a solution to their dilemma should be given to academic institutions with expertise in economic matters they were about to adjourn the meeting when Alan stood up and said, 'Before we finish there's another suggestion I think we should consider. After we've dealt with the bank regulation problem there'll be other issues we'll need to settle before we can go ahead and start a war. It's likely that some time will pass before we'll be ready; time that will be sufficient for another voyage to Yevad and back. I suggest a single ship with a stash of gold coins be sent there to obtain samples of their manufactured goods. From the samples our own manufacturers may well glean useful ideas, but that is incidental. The proposed voyage to Yevad will have other objectives. Firstly, by letting the Yevadians believe we are still interested in trade, and the ship's purpose is to obtain examples of their merchandise in advance of more gold-bearing ships seeking business, they'll think they are seeing trade ships when our war fleet appears on the horizon. This, I think, is not too important, for they were not alarmed by our previous visits to their shores, but it's possible they were prepared for hostilities but kept it hidden so as not to appear distrustful of their foreign visitors. No matter, the main aim of the ship's visit will be more important. It will be to learn more about the Yevadians, about how they are likely to react to a hostile invasion. We'll need to know more about their army. Is it just a bunch of theatrical performers, as it seems, or is it a well-equipped and highly trained fighting force? Are its soldiers efficient? Are they fighters we should not underestimate? These are the sort of questions we'll need answered. I'll be happy to go back to Yevad, and I'm sure David and Jason will want to sail with me once again, but I think a few more wise heads should accompany us. I'm sure there'll be no shortage of volunteers. I propose we ask Martin Semsit, the commander of the first trade mission, to captain the ship, and to choose his crew from dependable officers and men who sailed with him.'

Alan's suggestion was approved by everyone present. After a brief discussion about details they'd need to decide before the proposed voyage could be started, the next meeting of the group was planned. It was to be shortly after suggestions had been made as to how the bank regulation dilemma should be handled. Any proposals would need to be carefully considered. They were right in thinking this. The academic institutions chosen to look into the problem cooperated in seeking answers, and after several months of intense study they came up with far reaching recommendations. At the heart of their proposals was the establishment of an autonomous institution to be called *The Central Bank*. It was to be managed by experienced bankers, free from government involvement, and dedicated to overseeing the banking system. Its operations were to include overall administration of the nation's financial system and management of the government's banking needs. The King's personal account was to remain with The Royal Bank of Areho. Supplementary recommendations concerned banknotes and the introduction of new financial commodities called bonds.

Banknotes issued by the four banks were to remain in use for a while, after which they would be taken out of circulation. They were to be replaced during this period by new banknotes issued by The Central Bank. Although the new notes would show promises to their bearers regarding their values, they would not be promises of redemption in gold, or any other valuable commodity. Instead, their values would depend on legislation. In accordance with laws the government would be required to introduce, the new banknotes were to be known as *Legal Tender*, meaning their values were guaranteed by law. Accordingly, it would be unlawful to refuse to accept them in settlement of a debt.

The idea of The Central Bank was welcomed, mainly because experienced bankers, all members of the Special Intellectual Group, would be in charge of its management. It was to be the only institution authorised to issue banknotes.

Bankers were happy about this. They had no love for their banknotes. The originators of their business may have found printing them to be satisfying, but to current practitioners it was tedious and costly. The nuisance of printing and handling banknotes, it will be remembered, was the main reason cheques were introduced. The bankers were also delighted they would still be able to create money by crediting borrowers' accounts, albeit according to rules set by The Central Bank. Creating money out of nothing more than book-keeping was part of their business the bankers feared they might lose, for rumours had suggested that if the government decided to regulate banks it would make itself the only institution legally authorised to create money. Creating money, by nothing more than strokes of a pen, was at the profitable heart of banking. Accordingly, the bankers regarded The Central Bank suggestion to be a blessing. They couldn't have done better if they'd planned it all themselves. The *'Legal Tender'* proposal was particularly appreciated since it would mean it was no longer possible for banknote holders to demand redemption in gold, so eliminating the fear that hordes of anxious customers would calamitously demand their promised metal if it became commonly known that banks had insufficient bullion to back all the banknotes they had issued.

Areho's Central Bank, the only one in fairy-tale world, was soon up and running.

The rules banks would have to follow were also welcomed. They would make the business of banking much easier to manage. Each bank would be required to hold reserve funds in an account with The Central Bank. The lowest acceptable level of a bank's reserves would be determined by its responsibilities to its depositors and would govern the extent of its lending operations. It was proposed that initially each bank's reserves were to be at least ten percent of its deposit liabilities. Accordingly, for every thousand arets deposited, for which the bank would be legally responsible to its clients, the bank would be allowed to create nine hundred arets by way of lending. And since the newly created money would, by way of transactions in the economy, give rise to new deposits, more money creation would thereby be allowed. More depositing and lending would subsequently follow. In this way, after numerous successions of transactions, deposits and lending, the initial one thousand aret deposit would allow the creation of around ten thousand arets. For all practical purposes, The Central Bank's rules would place no unwelcome money-creation-restrictions on the banks. Moreover, the required fraction didn't have to be ten percent; it could be changed according to economic circumstances by The Central Bank's governors, all of which were to be experienced bankers. Also, since each bank would be required to have an account with The Central Bank, debts between banks, the inevitable consequences of using cheques, would be conveniently cleared by means of transfers between their respective accounts. Furthermore, if needed, as, for example, when many depositors were making large withdrawals at around the same time, banks would be able to borrow from The Central Bank. To lend money to a bank The Central Bank would simply credit the bank's account with the required amount, thereby creating money in much the same way as banks create money when they make loans to their clients; and since there was to be no obligation to back its money with gold, or any other physical commodity, there was to be no limit to the amount of money The Central Bank could create. When banks borrowed from The Central Bank they would have to pay interest at a rate to be known as the *bank rate*. It was reasoned that this interest rate, in conjunction with another of the institutions' recommendations - pieces of paper known as bonds - would influence the interest rates banks would charge their borrowers and pay their depositors.

According to the proposals, the government should no longer take loans directly from banks. Instead, it should obtain money from would-be lenders by printing government bonds - certificates bearing the government's guarantees of both repayment of borrowed money at the end of a specified period and regular payments of fixed interest during this period. Bonds were to be sold by auction and any individual or business wanting to lend money according to their terms would simply buy them. After their initial auction sale by the government, bonds were to be exchangeable at negotiable prices, buyers thereby becoming new beneficiaries of the government's loan guarantees. If necessary, the government could sell bonds directly to The Central Bank, the holder of its account. This, it was suggested, should initially be the main method of government borrowing. In order to buy government bonds, The Central Bank would simply create the amount required by crediting the government's account accordingly. In this way, without any need for gold, or any other valuable commodity, the government would have access to virtually unlimited amounts of borrowed money. It would, of course, have to honour its obligations to bond holders - to pay interest periodically and return borrowed money when the bonds expired. To do this it would need to use part of its income from future taxpayers. With this in mind, the government would need to think carefully about its level of borrowing. It would need to avoid overburdening the national debt. It would also need to be mindful of the possibility of causing unwanted inflation.

The news media, as directed by its financial overlords, ardently promoted The Central Bank suggestion. It easily persuaded its readers that the idea had many merits, and, as intended, popular ideas of banks being regulated by the government soon faded away. However, politicians at first seemed unconvinced by The Central Bank idea. They had been unsure of how the government could effectively regulate banks, and now they were uncertain as to why the suggested new institution was needed. Before voting in favour of the idea they required something more than public and media enthusiasm to convince them that the country needed a Central Bank. They wanted the prime minister, Harold Lalutum, to show them leadership. He had been told that experienced bankers would take care of all that would be required in setting-up The Central Bank. Nevertheless, like his fellow politicians, he remained undecided. He needed to be swayed. He needed inducement. The required prompt came from King James. In accordance with the terms of his proclamation and coronation, the new King was expected to leave management of the kingdom to the elected government. However, he did express his views on important issues during regular confidential meetings with the prime minister; and the views he expressed were invariably the views of The Organisation, for, although formally excluded from the elected government, he was fully included in the clandestine group that really governed the country from behind the scenes. As a member of The Organisation's inner circle he had far more control of the kingdom that the old King ever had, and he knew how to use it effectively. He knew of the political uncertainty about the proposed Central Bank, and he knew how to handle the prime minister. Cashing in on his royal mystique, he simply told the indecisive prime minister, in confidence, that he thought the idea of a Central Bank was splendid. It was all that was needed. Encouraged by the prime minister's new-found confidence in the scheme, politicians readily voted in favour of the new institution. Areho's Central Bank, the only one in fairy-tale world, was soon up and running. Members of the Special Intellectual Group were very pleased. They had control of The Central Bank, and The Central Bank had control of the rate at which new money was created. Little had changed. They could still make the economic system operate as quickly or as slowly as they wanted it to, so causing economic expansions or recessions as they wished.

Members tried to be inconspicuous as they travelled to the meeting, but they didn't want to be late.

With the threat of government bank regulation dispelled, the bankers and their friends were free to turn their attention to their primary ambition, to arranging that there would be a war with the people of Yevad. Accordingly, it was decided that another secretive conference was to be held in Schemowt Hall. In the interests of confidentiality, members tried to be inconspicuous as they travelled to the meeting. They arrived sporadically and chatted as they waited for latecomers. They talked mainly about The Central Bank, about its convenience and about how the dreadful threat of government bank regulation had been so cleverly evaded.

James Schemowt, seeing that everyone was present, eventually called the meeting to order. 'Welcome everyone,' he started. 'It's good to see you all once again, and yes, I agree, the inauguration of The Central Bank was a magnificent achievement. Now, however, we must move on. First I'm going to ask Alan to tell you about his visit, along with David, Jason, Colin and George, to Yevad. You'll remember, the primary reason for their voyage was to learn more about the Yevadians, about their fighting capabilities. So, without further ado, I'll hand you over to Alan.'

'Thank you, James,' Alan said as he stood up. Facing his audience, he went on to say, 'We learned a lot while we were in Yevad, and, I'm afraid, it's not good. As before, the Yevadians were very friendly and cooperative. They seemed to trust us unreservedly, but we still felt we had to be very careful when trying to find out about their military capabilities. We didn't want them to suspect that we might have had more than commerce in mind. As it happened, we were lucky to be there when they were having one of their spectacular public displays of military proficiency. It allowed us to casually chat with our helpful guides about the soldierly talents on display without revealing clues to our warlike intentions. By making flattering comments about the dexterity and proficiency of the performers we were able to learn that the display teams were only part of a sizable army. Many more soldiers, trained to the same level of physical attainment and commitment, were available to defend Yevad if necessary. Clearly we couldn't ask too many questions about their weaponry, but we did learn that they do have some experience of fighting. It seems that beyond the civilised regions of the distant lands, the parts occupied by Yevad and its peaceful neighbours, there are remote areas inhabited by barbaric savages. Yevad is occasionally raided from these wild places by gangs of brutish bandits with rape, looting and destruction in mind, and it's the army's job to drive them out. And, by all accounts, it's highly effective in getting rid of the unwanted marauders. So, you see, our intended invasion will not be opposed as ineffectively as we first imagined. Accordingly, it will be necessary to send a much larger force than we initially planned. However, overthrowing the Yevadian army may turn out to be the least of our difficulties.'

The visitors were able to learn that the display teams were only part of a sizable army.

Alan's words caused his listeners to become edgy so he paused before continuing. When he felt they were ready he went on to say, 'I guess I'm right in thinking that most of you assumed, as I did, that after Yevad had been conquered we would be able to take clandestine political control there by means of manipulation and misinformation, just as we've done here in Areho, and then, with all the mollifying advantages of democracy, we would be able to transform their economic system so that it could easily coalesce with our own. I have to tell you that this is not going to be accomplished without a great deal of difficulty. The people of Yevad are smart and sophisticated, and they are deeply committed to their way of life. It would be very wrong of us to underestimate them. If we are to entertain any thoughts of winning them over to doing things as we do, we'll need to accept that it will not be easy. By using overpowering physical force it would, of course, be possible to turn them into slaves, but, as I'm sure you'll all agree, that is not what we want. Slave labour would be ideal if we simply wanted to have things made, crops harvested or minerals mined, but our requirement, as you all know, is quite the opposite. Our problem is the need to grow the economy. It's not Yevadian slaves that we need; it's an overseas extension of what we have here. We need extra tame, working, voting consumers. Without many more customers our economy cannot grow, and, as you all know, without growth our financial system will collapse. So, it's not the bodies of the Yevadians that we'll need to enslave, it's their minds. As I've said, that's not going to be easy, for they are profoundly devoted to their existing way of life. At an earlier meeting I said their societal commitment has many of the features to be found in religions. We'll need to be fully aware of this when we take on the task of converting them to our customs and beliefs. We'll be attempting to replace a well-worn, easy going and deeply rewarding faith by one that, to them, will be unfamiliar, taxing and altogether alien. Invading their country may not be too difficult, but invading their minds will be a far more challenging undertaking. It will stretch our powers of deception and persuasion to the full.'

After a pause, he went on to say, 'Incidentally, for anyone interested, examples of Yevadian goods we brought back with us can now be seen in the Ranty Museum on Arcue's waterfront. They are going on display to the public in two weeks' time, so if you want to see them without the hassle of mingling with the masses you'll need to do it soon. Also, as I'm sure most of you have already heard, seven Yevadians - a past successful participant of their *president-for-a- year* scheme, his wife, two children and three voluntary helpers - came to Areho with us with the intention of establishing an embassy here. At first we were not sure of the wisdom of the idea, but they were insistent so, thinking it would do no harm, we agreed to let them sail with us on our voyage home. A suitable property has been found for them in Arcue, and they are now busy turning it into an embassy. So, without wanting one, we now have a Yevadian ambassador living here in our capital.'

Alan had said all he had to say but could sense that more was expected. James Schemowt, seeing his difficulty, stood up and said, 'Thank you, Alan. That was very interesting. You've given us many things to think about. You are absolutely right, although it will be difficult, we'll need to take effective political control of Yevad. Then, with many more people and far greater resources at our disposal we'll be able to operate our debt-fuelled economic system on a much larger scale. No longer restricted to operating in one country, we'll be able to continue creating money without running into such problems as overproduction and excessive inflation. But first we'll need to take control of the minds and souls of the Yevadians, and, as Alan has made very clear, doing this will not be easy. Nevertheless, it will have to be done. It will, no doubt, require a lot of careful planning, but I'm sure we'll be able to come up with suitable means of persuasion, deception, propaganda and pretext. They are measures we are good at, and, as we speak, carefully selected experts at the newly established *Institute of Personal Relations* are already looking into the problem. However, before we'll need to face up to the challenge there are two major obstacles we'll have to confront.

The Yevadian Embassy.

'First of all, we'll need a substantial proportion of the general public to want to go to war with the people of Yevad. No important members of the government are unaware of their dependence on the covert financial backing we provide. They know we own the political system, and that they are required to see to it that there is a war. Nevertheless, if there is insufficient public hostility to the intended enemy they'll be unable to convince sufficient numbers of elected representatives that there's a need for military action. With help from our friends in the media, we'll be able to overcome this obstacle without too much difficulty. The second difficulty, however, is a little trickier. Even if the government could convince enough elected politicians that we needed to go to war, it would not be able to mobilise the required armed forces without spending a lot of money. It's committed to stabilising the national debt, not to increasing it. We could easily create sufficient money, as we do, but, regardless of any problems it would bring to the government, it could not be done without causing serious inflationary difficulties. Restricted as it is to the limitations of the country, the economic system can't sustain a further significant increase in the national debt. I suggest we hand over the task of formulating a solution that will be acceptable by the public and government to our loyal think tanks. They'll know what needs to be done, and will be able to dress it up with copious academic terminology so it can be easily swallowed by the government and the masses.'

It did not take long for the think tanks to come up with a suitable scheme. They suggested that national assets could be sold. Many parts of the country's public utility systems, their proposals suggested, could be sold by the government to the people. Since the people, or their predecessors, had already paid for them by way of taxes, they would first need to be convinced that privatisation, as the scheme was dubbed, was highly recommended by economics experts. Presenting themselves as the required experts, think tanks' spokespersons, with help from the news media, set in motion the first stage of their programme of persuasion. Using suitably reassuring language, peppered liberally with economic jargon, they set about convincing people that national assets such as dockyards, highways, bridges, canals, tunnels, sewers and water supply systems would all function far more efficiently if they were operated as profit-making companies. When the message had been exhaustively repeated in a wide range of pedestrian styles, so it had convincingly infused the consciousness of a sizable section of the population, the second stage of the grooming plan was put into action. It was to persuade people to use their savings to buy shares in such companies. Potential investors were told the values of their shares were likely to increase and they would also receive regular payments, called dividends, out of profits the companies would make. Members of the Special Intellectual Group loved the idea. They had mulled over such a scheme many times, and now their obliging think tank minions had ironed out practical problems so that it could be realized. The Group was delighted. People buying shares in resources they already owned. It was brilliant. It was as good as any other scam The Organisation had ever devised.

After an approving nudge to the prime minister from the King, the government, with intense encouragement from the news media, launched the privatisation scheme. People with sufficient savings bought shares in companies supplying vital services formerly provided by nationally owned facilities. In addition to losing interest from their savings accounts, shareholders soon found bills and fees for essential services were higher than before, and steadily increasing. If, however, they had been able to buy sufficient shares, the dividends to some extent off-set their lost interest and increased services costs, for the companies' dividends were more fruitful than savings accounts. People who were rich enough to buy very many shares, therefore, were able to more than off-set the increased costs and lost interest. The privatised companies were able to pay such dividends, and pay very substantial salaries and bonuses to their directors, because very many people with little or no savings with which to buy shares, and better-off ones who had chosen not to buy any, were still required to pay the increased bills and fees. Members of The Organisation were very pleased. The companies took high and increasing payments from all utility users, but only paid dividends, high salaries and generous bonuses to relatively few. Privatisation was a brilliant scam.

From opinions expressed by the news media and think tanks, and the King's suggestions to the Prime Minister, the government knew what it had to do with the funds provided by the privatisation scheme. The money was allocated, as The Organisation required, to the construction of new warships, the manufacture of guns and ammunition, and the recruitment and training of extra men for service in the armed forces.

Chapter Eleven

Expanding the armed forces took some time; time in which James Schemowt took the opportunity to sit with his son, Jeremy, and answer his numerous questions. Jeremy wanted to know about the recent meeting, about all the issues discussed. He was particularly interested in the services The Central Bank planned to provide for the business of banking. After being told of the topics discussed at the meeting, he asked his father, 'Why do we need a Central Bank?'

Privatisation money was allocated to the manufacture of guns and ammunition.

James replied, 'There are many answers to that. To try to understand them I think we'll need to go back to the early days of banking. When our predecessors found they could create money out of pieces of paper linked to gold in their vaults, they soon realised very few customers ever wanted to redeem their banknotes. Accordingly, they knew they could print extra banknotes; only a fraction needed to be backed by gold. The system became known as fractional reserve banking. It allowed the creation of lots of extra money. This would have caused serious problems of inflation had manufacturers not been encouraged to produce many more things consumers could spend their money on. Our ancestors found they could keep prices stable by matching the creation of new money to the production of goods and services. They had given birth to a system that initially resulted in brisk economic expansion, but as the years passed the growth became increasingly sluggish. Consumers became gradually less inclined to go out and buy new things. For a while we were able to counter this trend by allowing the creation of money to slightly exceed the production of goods and services, thereby causing prices to steadily increase. Other methods of encouraging consumers to go out and spend were also tried. They were effective for a while, but recently it's become virtually impossible to get people to buy all the things industry is able to produce. Do you remember some time ago you asked why there had to be growth?'

Privatisation money was allocated to building new warships.

'Yes, I do. You explained how interest charged on loans makes growth imperative.'

'Yes, that's right. A little while later you asked when will the growth end?'

'Yes, I remember. It was while we watched ships sailing away to the distant lands. You told me not to worry about it.'

'I did, and there's still nothing for you to worry about, but I think I should tell you a little more about it. The economic growth we talked about is called exponential growth, and while many people correctly understand this to mean a type of growth that quickly becomes more and more pronounced, few know that it occurs when, whatever it is that is growing, keeps on regularly doubling. This means exponential growth can start off in an unspectacular way but can very quickly become very dramatic. There's a story from the other world that describes this in a surprising way.'

'You mean it's from fantasy-land, just like the story of Greece and democracy?'

Privatisation money was allocated to increasing the size of the army.

'Yes, that's right, but I think that even in fantasy-land this story is a fable, or legend. There are several versions of it, but I think this one gives the basics of the story: A wealthy emperor wants to reward a man who has provided him with a much appreciated service and asks what he would like. The man asks for rice, and seeing a chessboard beside the emperor says he would like one grain of rice for the first square, two for the second, four for the third, eight for the fourth, sixteen for the fifth, and so on for all sixty-four squares, each time doubling the number of grains given for the previous square. The Emperor agrees, thinking the man's request was very modest, but soon found the amount of rice required was increasing beyond his expectations. It was outside the scope of his supplies. There was not enough rice in his empire to enable him to fulfil his promise.'

'I was able to work out in my head that the last square on the first row would require one hundred and twenty eight grains, and the first square of the next row would require two hundred and fifty six, but I lost count after that.'

'That's very good. You should easily be able to see that the next square would require over five hundred grains, and more than a thousand would be needed for the next one. It's nearly thirty-three thousand for the last square of the second row. Do you see how exponential growth, starting from very small numbers, very soon produces very large ones?'

Army practice intensified.

'Yes, I do. Two rows on the chessboard and the number of rice grains increases from one to nearly thirty-three thousand. With six more rows to go I can see why the emperor wouldn't have enough rice to keep his promise to the man.'

'That's right. He'd need very many tons of rice. The point I want you to understand is that with a fixed interest rate and stable economic conditions the money supply, just like the grains of rice on the emperor's chessboard, will keep on regularly doubling. The period in which the amount of money will double will change if interest rates change and the economy has periods of unsteadiness, as it had when we engineered the overthrow of the old King, but this doesn't significantly change the way in which the supply of money grows, it remains essentially exponential.'

'When you explained why there has to be growth, you said, in a roundabout way, interest payments on loans is only possible if there is an ever increasing supply of borrowed money. I asked when the growth will end. You told me not to worry about it; it was not going to happen in the foreseeable future. I'm not worried, but I am curious. If it must end, what will happen then?'

'I don't know, and I don't think anyone does. There might be a catastrophic collapse of our civilization, or perhaps Areho will survive and there'll be a peaceful transition to some alternative economic system. We just don't know. Anyway, let's not be distracted by what might happen in the distant future. The point I want to make is that without fractional reserve banking we and our sister banks would not have been able to continue lending money and charging interest as we have done for several centuries. It allowed the amount of money in the economy, either as paper money in circulation or as deposits in clients' accounts, to go on increasing more or less exponentially while the amount of gold in our vaults remained fixed. This inevitably meant that the paper money for which there was redeemable gold became a smaller and smaller fraction of the total amount. Which brings us back to your question: why do we need a Central Bank?'

'I was wondering when you were going to get round to it.'

'I thought I needed to tell you about exponential growth and fractional reserve banking so you would understand that we, and our three sister banking corporations, can no longer go on conducting our business as we have done. It would be unsafe. The amount of gold in our vaults has barely changed since our ancestors first started the business of money lending, but in that time the amount of currency we have created has increased astronomically. It's increased exponentially! This means we can no longer risk being held to the promise on our banknotes, that they can be exchanged for gold. The uncertain political conditions following the overthrow of the old King caused too many people to ask awkward questions about the role banks play in the economic conditions of the country, thereby raising the possibility of government interference in our affairs and magnifying the risk that large numbers of people might want to redeem their banknotes. The Central Bank gets rid of these risks. Under the legislation that introduced The Central Bank there was the requirement that paper money was no longer to be backed by gold, or any other valuable commodity, it was to be backed by the law and was to be known as legal tender. This means that the amount of money we can create is theoretically unlimited.'

'Does that mean we can create as much as we like?'

'Not exactly, the amount we can create is constrained by the need to maintain its value. If we create too much it will lose its value.'

'That's called inflation.'

'That's right.'

'I understand we have to be careful about creating too much money, but what about creating too little? Can there be a shortage of money?'

Large amounts of food were needed for the enlarged army.

'The thing for you to keep in mind is that in the course of our business we create money and we annul it. When a customer takes out a loan we create the money he, or she, asked for, and when it's is paid back it's annulled.'

'You mean it's destroyed?'

'Yes, it is, but we prefer to say it's annulled.'

'So, money is being created and annulled all the time, and the amount grows when the rate of creation exceeds that of annulment. Is that how I should see it?'

'Yes, and you should now see the answer to your question about a money shortage. If loans are restricted and annulments take place as intended the amount of active money will not increase as quickly as it does when loans are issued more liberally. Such a situation can be regarded as a shortage of money, although it would normally be called a recession or slump.'

'From what you told me about the need for growth, if there is such a shortage some people will become unable to repay their loans.'

Excited by the prospect of imminent war, generals were keen
to discuss their ideas of strategy and tactics.

'That's right, and we then have to take possession of their property. This is why we lend to people who intend to buy durable assets such as houses or business properties. It would be unwise to lend money to someone wanting to start a business such as a hairdressing salon operating from rented property. If such a business failed there'd be little to gain by repossessing scissors, combs and hairdresser's chairs.'

'I understand about it not being realistic to promise to redeem all our banknotes for gold, and why The Central Bank's notes are called legal tender, and I see how having an account with The Central Bank is useful to our bank, but there are still a couple of things I'm not too sure about. I know that introducing The Central Bank forestalled the risk of the government taking control of banking, but I've a feeling that somehow there's a deeper political rationale involved. Am I right to feel this way?'

'You're right; there is more to The Central Bank. Democracy, as we introduced it, placated the masses by ostensibly offering them a choice between two parties that seemed to have opposing programmes, whereas the policies they offered can have no significant influence on the way the country really operates. Democracy allows the people to openly criticise the government and, if enough are dissatisfied, to throw it out and replace it with an alternative one at the next election. It seems to be working well at the moment, although it may become necessary to limit the scope of free speech. We can't have people asking too many awkward questions about where money comes from, about our secret meetings or where the origins of real power are to be found. To overcome such difficulties it may become necessary to introduce laws that, while seeming reasonable and limited, can be applied to almost any situation, such as offending vulnerable individuals or groups, or publishing information we can claim to be false. However, as it is, people seem appeased by being able to ardently discuss the provision of public parks, the availability of health care, the times taverns are allowed to stay open, whether a person's sexual inclinations should be of interest to the law, how long shops should stay open on Sundays, when school holidays should start and end, and many other issues of trivial consequence. Voters and unimportant politicians, unaware of the nation's real centres of political power, argue passionately about such matters. The Central Bank has command of the nation's money and holds this power regardless of what the government's treasury may think or do. Indeed, the laws that founded The Central Bank made it independent of government control, and prohibited politicians from inquiring too deeply into its affairs, whereas it is paradoxically expected to advise and guide the government. Our Organisation secretly brought about its existence, and it operates according to our directions. It controls the financial affairs of the country and the government, and we control it. It's not at all likely, for we have effective control of the political parties, but if it seems that measures detrimental to our interests might be introduced, the country's economic system can easily be made to wobble so the government will be overthrown by the voting public. As coached by our friends in the news media, the public firmly believes The Central Bank is a benign, politically-neutral institution that operates in the public's best interests, so any blame for economic failure will be directed at the government. So you were right in thinking there is a deeper, unseen political side to The Central Bank.'

'That's brilliant. The Central Bank seems to be an excellent invention. One thing that puzzles me is what is to happen to the gold in our vault? Who will it belong to when our banknotes are taken out of circulation?'

'The law that introduced The Central Bank included a clause that effectively negated the promise on our banknotes. It stated that anyone wishing to redeem their old banknotes would have six months to do so after the cut-off date for their use as currency, and from the time when the new laws were announced would only be able to redeem them for Central Bank banknotes unless they could show evidence of specific amounts of gold having been deposited by themselves or their relatives. The assertion supporting this clause was that only people who had actually deposited gold should be able to claim gold; those who came into possession of banknotes by other means should only be able to redeem them for Central Bank banknotes. This, of course, means that no one will be able to ask for gold that is not in a bank vault. Only individuals in possession of vouchers that were used many centuries ago will be able to claim gold, and there are not many of them about. It means that when the time limits have elapsed we will become the legal owners of the gold in our vault.'

'What will we do with it?'

'It will depend on the price it can be sold for. Some people might want it for making jewellery and ornaments, foreign countries that still use it as money might want it and some individuals might want it thinking there may come a time when it will be used as currency once again. If it can't be sold for a better price, we'll transfer it to The Central Bank and our account there will be credited accordingly, at the old value ascribed to gold when it was used to back banknotes.'

'I like it. It seems we can't lose. But why does The Central Bank want gold?'

'Foreign countries we trade with find it convenient and reassuring to keep a stock of our currency. They'll probably be a little suspicious of our legal tender laws and will feel more secure knowing our Central Bank has a good stock of gold in its vaults.'

'I see. Tell me more about the bonds you mentioned earlier. I don't understand how they will influence interest rates. I know the bank rate is the interest rate we'll have to pay if we borrow from The Central Bank, but what will the new bonds have to do with it?'

'The bank rate will be used by The Central Bank to regulate borrowing if its directors think there is a need to ease or tighten the availability of bank loans, and since its directors will all be experienced bankers, their decisions will always be in the best interests of banking. If the bank rate is increased, or decreased, in general the interest we charge or pay our clients will also be increased, or decreased in the same direction, but not necessarily by the same amount or at the same time. However, the bank rate is not the only way The Central Bank will seek to control borrowing. When the government wants to borrow it will print certificates, known as bonds, and sell them to banks and other lenders. Each bond will bear the government's promise that the money it was sold for will be repaid at a specific time in the future, and regular, fixed interest payments will be paid to the bond holder until that specified time had been reached. Many bonds will be sold at each government issue, and thereafter they may be sold on to others at whatever price the buyers are willing to pay; the buyers being entitled to any outstanding interest payments and the money that is to be repaid when the bonds reach their terminal date.'

'Can the government borrow directly from The Central Bank?'

'Yes, by selling bonds and it will do so for a while until the new system is operating as intended for The Central Bank will need to hold a stock of bonds. Afterwards it will only buy bonds directly from the government in exceptional circumstances, for example, when for whatever reasons lenders, including banks, are unable or unwilling to meet the government's borrowing requirements.'

'So we and our sister banks will lend money to the government by buying bonds from it?'

'Yes, but so might others, such as big companies or wealthy individuals. Large companies in need of money will sometimes offer to sell bonds of their own, with similar terms as the government's, instead of borrowing from banks in the usual way. Many companies will also offer to sell dividend-paying shares to acquire extra money, particularly after the privatisation scheme. But let's not go into such details right now. When the system is operating as intended, a variety of bonds will have been printed, issued and sold. They will be held by banks, other businesses and wealthy persons, and if the price they can be sold for is attractive they might be transferred to others. When everything is operational, The Central Bank will buy and sell bonds in order to influence the level of borrowing. Although others may well become involved, to make things simple, let's initially say that only banks such as ours will be involved when The Central Bank offers to buy or sell bonds. If The Central Bank buys bonds from us new money it has created will come to us and, assuming we had already lent out as much as we were allowed to by the minimum reserve rule, we will be able to issue more loans. Effectively, The Central Bank will have eased borrowing. Whereas, if it wanted to tighten borrowing, it would offer to sell bonds at prices attractive to us, and by selling them it would take money from us, so restricting the loans we were able to issue.'

'That seems straightforward, but what has the bank rate to do with this?'

'If buying bonds causes our reserves to fall below the minimum level we are obliged to maintain, we will have to borrow from The Central Bank.'

'So, in order to buy from The Central Bank we'd have to borrow from The Central Bank. That doesn't seem very sensible.'

'Bear in mind that we will not be forced to buy bonds, and, after considering the possible cost of borrowing from The Central Bank at the bank rate, we will only do so if it is to our advantage. Remember, The Central Bank is there to keep a watch over the business of banking in the service of banking. There's something else we need to consider. In order to sell bonds, The Central Bank will reduce their prices. This will increase the value of their fixed interest payments relative to their prices. Effectively, their buyers will be paid a higher interest rate. Wealthy individuals or companies might then buy bonds instead of investing their money with us. This will mean that, in addition to our reduced ability to make loans, we will have to increase the interest rates we charge and pay our customers. When the new system is operational, if it thinks it is necessary, The Central Bank will seek to reduce bank lending by a combination of selling bonds, thereby taking money out of the banking system, and by increasing the bank rate thereby making it less likely that banks will borrow. Similarly, if The Central Bank wants to encourage borrowing it will buy bonds and reduce the bank rate.'

'I think I have a vague idea of how it will work.'

'In that case you know as much as anybody. We won't have a good understanding of how the new system will perform until it's been running for a while. Hopefully, that will not be too long.'

'You said difficulties that might arise in Yevad after the invasion were discussed at the meeting. Tell me more about them. What sorts of difficulties are expected?'

'The Yevadians, it seems, are very firmly set in their ways, which are very different from ours. So it's likely that persuading them to behave as we want them to will be a long and difficult task. We'll simply have to be flexible in our approach and not expect too much too soon.'

'What will we want them to do? Will we want them to be just like us?'

'We'll just have to wait and see what can be done with them, but we do have a clear idea of how we will want them to behave in order to serve our interests. We don't want them to become just like us. We want them to become more like the people of Areho's neighbouring kingdoms.'

'Why is that?'

'As you know, by persuading neighbouring kingdoms to join together in a trading bloc we were able to find extra borrowers and buyers, as well as useful providers of basic materials and other goods.'

'I remember you telling me about it. The other kingdoms had to surrender their national sovereignty. They had to follow laws of the community.'

'Yes, they did, and we, the most powerful country in the community, made the laws. We persuaded them to borrow on our terms, fix their exchange rates and impose no restrictions on trade within the bloc. Although very beneficial to us for a while, eventually the economic community became insufficient to meet our needs. It did not allow our financial system to continue growing as it needed to, which is why we had to cross the Mighty Ocean looking for additional trade deals. But the obstinate people of Yevad were reluctant to trade with us. Accordingly, we need to send warships and troops to persuade them to see things our way. Although it might take some time, if at all possible, Yevad will eventually become a member of our economic community. That is why I said we want them to become like the people of the kingdoms near to Areho. We want them to become part of an expanding trading bloc, part of a growing economic and political union. Moreover, building warships and making guns and ammunition is in itself a useful activity – it provides the economic system with a purpose without any direct need for consumers.

However, it does need enemies. There's no point in making weapons if there are no enemies. Also, there are other reasons why Yevad must be conquered.'

'What other reasons?'

'Their current way of doing things, both politically and economically, is based on some very dangerous ideas which must never be allowed to infect the people of Areho and nearby kingdoms. Many years have been spent conditioning Arehoians to believe they are special, and their economic system is the best of all possible economic systems. If Yevadian ideas and beliefs ever found their way here this sense of Arehoian exceptionalism could be seriously undermined. It must never be allowed to happen.'

'I understand, we can't allow our economic system to be upset by unwelcome ideas. When you told me about the issues discussed at the meeting you said in order for politicians to agree to war it will be necessary to make people hate Yevadians. How is that to be done? How will we make people hate Yevadians?'

'That has not yet been decided, so I'm afraid you'll just have to wait and see. Now it's late, so I think it's time for you to go upstairs to bed.'

'Yes, I agree.'

'Goodnight, Jeremy.'

'Goodnight, Dad. I'll think about the things you've told me for a while, but I don't think it'll be too long before I'm fast asleep.'

Chapter Twelve

For some time the news media, with steadily increasing frequency, had been publishing accounts of dreadful atrocities committed by the people of Yevad. The concocted stories, presented as factual reporting, were intended to arouse powerful public feelings of anger and disgust. The campaign reached a high point when it was reported, with abundant measures of journalistic cant, that the old King, Thomas IV, had been assassinated. King James, the prime minister and other significant personages expressed their deepest sadness. The following day the media announced, with profuse helpings of feigned anger, that there was irrefutable evidence that the King's assassins had been acting for the Yevadian government. The ambassador denied his country's involvement, and demanded that the so-called irrefutable evidence be shown, but the media was able to misinterpret his words and make him seem insincere and devious.

It was reported that the old King, Thomas IV, had been assassinated.

No credible evidence was produced, no explanation of the presence of Yevadians at the location of the killing given and no possible motives were suggested, but people believed what the newspapers told them. Hostility against Yevad soared. After an additional media campaign designed to make people fearful of Yevad's alleged aggressive intentions against Areho, the government, urged by enthusiastic editorials and King James' recommendation, directed money to a further expansion of the armed forces. The generals and admirals were delighted. They knew what dreadful weapons they wanted added to their arsenals. The public, totally unaware of the secret intention of going to war with Yevad, fully supported the supposed defensive arms build-up.

With suitably sombre and extensive media coverage, King Thomas' body was reverently returned from his foreign sanctuary, the place of his assassination, and honoured with a full ceremonial royal funeral. It produced the required effect. Public hostility to Yevad soared to a peak when the archbishop, using grim words of an ancient language, ushered the royal coffin to chambers beneath the capital's cathedral. A huge crowd had gathered in the nearby market square. It became silent when, accompanied by solemn sounding ceremonial horns, the archbishop stepped outside the cathedral's main doors and announced that King Thomas had been laid to rest and was deservedly destined to eternal heavenly peace. After a suitably respectful pause, the crowd, slowly and quietly at first, but soon gathering pace, volume and passion, started singing the national anthem.

With public sentiments suitably prepared, the Special Intellectual Group, as previously planned, assembled inconspicuously at Schemowt Hall. After welcoming his assembled guests, James Schemowt announced that he had just received news from a courier that the Yevadian Embassy had been attacked and ransacked by angry crowds. The ambassador and his family had been taken into protective custody, and two diplomatic assistants had fled and their whereabouts were unknown. Other than this the courier had no further details. Schemowt added, 'I've sent messages to loyal editors with suggestions as to how the events should be reported.'

The group, familiar with protocol, knew that comments would be inappropriate and silently awaited the chairman's expected address. When he felt his audience was ready and settled, Schemowt went on to say, 'Gentlemen, I feel certain you'll give your full approval to certain proposals I'm going to put before you. I've been having lengthy discussions with Alan, David,

Jason, Colin and George about the difficulties we expect to find in gaining the cooperation we require from the people of Yevad. As the scouting party has reported, Yevadians are proudly and staunchly committed to their way of life. After an aggressive invasion and forceful occupation of their lands we would have to expect prolonged hostility and resentment. We had to conclude that a satisfactory outcome of a straightforward invasion was far too much to hope for. It will not be enough that we desperately need to expand our economic and financial systems into new territories; we need the people swallowed up by our spreading out to accept our ways. In the absence of events able to shatter Yevad's existing cultural and economic traditions, this will be too much to expect of its people. Moreover, we looked into the problems we would encounter in providing convincing stories for our own public. It's easy enough to secretly arrange atrocities attributable to intended opponents so that people are enraged and ready to support retaliatory military action, but it will be more difficult to provide them with convincing reasons for continued occupation of a defeated nation. From such considerations we decided we needed a new plan for tackling the problem of Yevad. We've devised an alternative to direct military action I think you'll all support. I'm going to ask Alan to tell you about it.'

Schemowt Hall.

Alan stood and said, 'Thank you, James, I think you've clearly outlined the problems an invasion would give rise to. It would not bring about the outcome we require. We discussed the difficulties during the last meeting and, although we fully appreciated their complexity, we thought they were not insurmountable. Mulling over the situation I realised we were being far too optimistic. Much as we would like it to be possible, invading and occupying Yevad will not enable us to exploit its people and resources as we would like to. Thinking about the situation, I kept recalling accounts we were told of barbaric savages who raid and plunder Yevad from time-to-time. I discussed it with David, Jason, Colin and George and we felt we had a good idea of how we could go about finding the bandits. The wild regions they come from were described to us several times with gestured indications of their location. If we were to return to the distant lands we would have little difficulty in finding them. When we told James of this, after several lengthy discussions, we came up with an alternative to direct invasion. The new plan is to get the barbarians to attack and invade Yevad. We'll secretly provide them with all the arms and support they'll need, and then let them go ahead and fight the Yevadians on our behalf. The war, of course, will be entirely unaccountable to us. We'll get the result we want with little risk to the government's domestic and international reputation.'

The plan was to offer a generous selection of gifts to the bandits.

'You propose attacking Yevad with surrogates?' Dennis Telslow asked rhetorically.

'Yes, that's exactly what is being proposed,' Alan replied.

'How do you know the barbarians will be willing to go along with your plans?'

'We can't be absolutely certain, Dennis,' Alan replied. 'But from what we've been told by the Yevadians, although they are always violently driven back to their wild regions, the savages never get tired of returning. They seem to find rape, plunder and destruction irresistible. If they are provided with copious supplies of arms and ammunition, and other inducements, I think they'll be more than keen to launch a new offensive against their old antagonists.'

'What *other inducements* do you have in mind?'

'To ease our first encounter, and show our non-aggressive intentions, we thought it would be prudent to offer a generous selection of gifts to our intended collaborators. The choice of gifts is yet to be decided. Also, when we reach the stage of sitting down with our proposed allies to discuss our respective objectives, we thought it sensible to let them believe we want their leaders to become the new rulers of Yevad. We'll tell them we've recently been trying to establish friendly relations with Yevad but all we got was abusive rejection. We can elaborate the story so as to make them believe we would like there to be a coup d'état, and will be willing to help them bring one about. In addition to providing all the arms and ammunition they will need, we will be happy to provide them with all the help they'll need in establishing a new government. All we will want from them in return will be the trading cooperation and friendship we were unable to obtain from the ousted government.'

'And you think they'll go along with such a scheme?'

'Yes, I do. From what we've been told about the bandits, they are unsophisticated, inclined to aggression and envious or resentful of Yevad's prosperity and social order. We can be certain its young men are eager for respect and adventure and, like feral youth everywhere, will know only violence as a means of achieving it. We talked about it and concluded that with encouragement and support the bandits' gang of energetic, adventure-starved young men will provide us with the fighting force we'll need. We'll be able to sit back and watch a proxy army attack and disrupt Yevad.'

'Do you have details of how all this is to be accomplished?'

'We've worked out a provisional plan but will welcome and take into consideration any suggestions made here today. Clearly, of course, how negotiations with the bandits proceed will have to be handled at the time by the team we send out there to talk with them. However, conditional as it may be, here's an outline of the plan we've come up with. Jason, David and I will sail to the distant lands in two or three ships with a sizeable detachment of capable and trustworthy men handpicked from the army's Special Forces. The ships' cargo holds will be filled to capacity with arms and ammunition, including consignments of the new field guns. These recently developed light cannons run on two large spoked wheels and can easily be pulled quickly over large distances by a single horse and managed swiftly into firing positions by two men. Moreover, by means of the latest design feature in artillery, they can be loaded by way of the breech, making it possible for them to be fired far more rapidly than earlier cannons. Another advantage is that lots of them can be packed into the hold of a ship in parts and quickly and easily assembled after being unloaded. They will give the bandits a distinct advantage over the Yevadian army, which, as far as we've been able to observe, only have large cumbersome cannons which can't easily be moved from place to place. The bandits will be able to act as a fast moving, hard-hitting fighting force.'

Ships were to be filled to capacity with arms and ammunition, including new field guns.

'I think we'll need to give them a name,' William Adass commented. 'When fighting starts in Yevad, news of it will inevitably reach Areho and before too long newspapers will want to tell the public about it. I know we have good control of the media, but I think we need to consider in advance how we will want it to deal with the situation. If we want it to express some knowledge of the rebels fighting in Yevad, as I imagine we will, it will need to have a name for them. It won't be appropriate to call them bandits or barbarians. It will want a name for them, and perhaps we should provide one.'

The plan was to provide the bandits with all the arms and support they'd need.

'I agree,' Alan replied. 'Perhaps someone can suggest one. We did consider how we will want the media to deal with the fighting and I was just about to get round to it. If everything goes as planned, or as near to it as can be managed, our information to the media will be that civil war has erupted in Yevad. Earlier, newspapers will have reported that ships, with soldiers aboard in case of hostilities, had been sent to Yevad to investigate the assassination of King Thomas, to find out why our dearly loved retired monarch had been killed. When people are told that a ship had returned with news of serious civil warfare occurring in Yevad, the assassination and all the atrocities reported earlier will become clear to them. Bad feelings harboured by people opposed to their government had been gathering force for some time, and extremists amongst them had been responsible for all the terrible things the Yevadians had allegedly been committing. The situation had finally resulted in civil war. People will swallow the story without question, and will discuss it heartily in clubs and taverns for it will have all the answers they've been wanting since first reading about appalling events occurring on the other side of the Mighty Ocean. As long as they can see the civil war as a battle between good and evil, with easily identified righteous and wicked sides, they'll believe everything they're told.'

'You plan to hand two or three ship-loads of our latest weapons over to the brigands?' Dennis asked. 'Don't you think that might be a little reckless?'

Guns were to be fired from a ship to reveal their power and accuracy, and to show the bandits what could be used against them if they became hostile.

'Initially only one ship will approach the region where we believe we'll find the barbarians, the others will remain anchored offshore and out of sight. Highly trained Special Forces will go ashore and, after gaining rapport with the bandit leaders with the aid of gifts, will put our proposals to them. If all goes as we expect it to, samples of our armaments will be taken ashore and demonstrated to our intended accomplices. Only sufficient ammunition for the demonstrations will be taken ashore. Guns will also be fired from the ship at appropriate shore-based targets - isolated trees for example - to reveal their power and accuracy, and to show the savages what could be used against them if they became hostile. Then, provided all goes well, when the size of the rebel force we'll be able to assemble has been assessed, an appropriate quantity of arms and men will be taken ashore. The Special Forces will train the proxy army to use their new weapons and advise it as to how an offensive against Yevad could be accomplished most effectively. Then it will be a matter of leaving it to the bandits to launch an attack against the unsuspecting Yevadians.'

Dennis asked, 'Do you think the contents of one ship will be sufficient?'

'From what we've been able to learn about the Yevadian army we think less than that will be enough to enable the rebels to get a war started. The remains of the shipment can be unloaded when and if required.'

'What about the other two ships anchored out of sight? I'm assuming you'll decide on taking three ships out there rather than two.'

People were to be told that a ship had returned with news of serious civil warfare occurring in Yevad.

'Yes, on reflection, I think three ships will be the best option,' Alan replied. 'Our aim will be to keep supplying the rebels with enough weapons and other resources so the war will keep on going until both sides are totally depleted. We want a war of attrition. Accordingly, we'll bring the other ships into play, one at a time, as necessary. When extra equipment is needed we'll simply tell the rebels that we need to return to our own country to re-stock our ship. A short time later another ship will arrive back with extra supplies. The naive rebels will deduce from this that we come from not too far away and that we can provide an endless supply of the things they require. It might be useful for them to think this; it might encourage them to continue fighting when otherwise they would want to call it a day.'

'How long after the ships have put to sea do you think it will be before we get to know how well the mission is going?'

'It shouldn't take too long. The first ship to become fully unloaded will return home with news of the war, and, if necessary, will go back with extra equipment. If for some reason it takes longer than anticipated to get the war started, the first ship to deliver equipment to the rebels will return home with news after transferring any remaining cargo to the other ships. So we should get news after a time not very much longer than is needed to sail across the Mighty Ocean and back.'

The bandits were to be shown how to operate the field guns.

'What will happen when the rebels and Yevadians no longer have any fight left in them? What will happen then?'

'Then, with our flags flying high, we'll go in as peace-makers. The plan is to keep sending our speediest ships to the war zone and back, taking extra equipment for the rebels if necessary, so we can be kept informed of the action out there. When we are able to judge the fighting is starting to decline we'll send out a full fleet of manned warships, the invasion force we'd originally planned to send there. When close to the battlegrounds, the fleet will remain anchored out of sight, but, by means of small boats, will receive news of the fighting from the Special Forces working with the rebels behind the scenes. When the time seems right, when the fighting has dwindled into insignificance, any rebels left standing will be told to return to their wild regions and our soldiers will go into Yevad with the pretext of being saviours. They will appear to be driving the rebels back to their lairs in the wilderness. Yevad will be ours, and to its people we will be their redeemers. Obviously, if necessary, we'll need to be prepared to amend our plans as events over there unfold. For this reason we'll need to have capable men out there able to make critical decisions. The Special Forces commanders entrusted with this task will be fully cognisant of our overall objectives and will be able to guide events accordingly. This, then, is the provisional plan we've devised. I'm now going to open up the meeting for general discussion. So, are there any questions or suggestions?'

It was expected there would be opposition to intervention in a foreign civil war.

Dennis, knowing the answer, but wanting to hear it expressed, asked, 'What will happen in Yevad after we've taken control?'

Alan answered, 'We expect it to be devastated after the war. Its economic system will be wrecked. Its towns, cities, villages and farms will be ruined. They will all need to be rebuilt or restored. Accordingly, Yevad will become an ideal marketplace for all the goods and services we produce. Our prestige as saviours and providers will spiral upwards. Moreover, its cultural and political structures will be shattered. Consequently, there will be a widespread ideological vacuum. The country's philosophy will have been swept aside leaving a wide open vacancy ready to soak up ours. So, in addition to our goods and services, we'll be able to provide them with ideas, policies and values. We'll be able to introduce them to our system of banking, borrowing, debt and democracy.'

'It seems an excellent plan. I particularly like to think it will consign their system of creating interest-free money to obscurity. It's a very dangerous practice. If it became widely known that it's possible to create money without any need for borrowers willing to pay interest, it could threaten the very core of our livelihoods. It must never be allowed to happen. So let's get on with it. Let's send ships filled with guns and mercenaries to the distant lands without delay. Let's rid the world of such treacherous ideas.'

Colin responded, 'I fully agree, Dennis, as I'm sure we all do, but there's something we need to consider before we inform the government of our plans and thereby put them into practice. As the old king was being interred, public hostility to Yevad soared to a peak, but, like any other media-managed mass sentiment, public anger soon subsides. When we are ready to send a full fleet of warships out to Yevad public hostility will have abated. People will know of the civil war, they will have consumed newspaper reports of its progress with great interest, but such interest will not stretch to supporting a full scale overseas military operation. They will ask, why are we sending our men over there? If they're having a civil war, let them get on with it. It's got nothing to do with us. Why should our soldiers risk their lives over there when there's no reason for us to be involved? This is how people will react, and without powerful public support for military intervention the government will not get the votes it will need from elected politicians. This is one of the drawbacks of democracy. With the old monarchy it was only necessary to convince the King that we needed to go to war; with democracy the masses have to be persuaded. Accordingly, renewed public outrage will be needed when we are ready to send out the warships. Public fury will have to be re-ignited.'

'You're absolutely right,' James Schemowt responded. 'And we have thought about it. I can tell you that after the old King's funeral, the burial chambers beneath the cathedral were bricked up with very frail mortar by undercover agents dressed inconspicuously as workmen. If required, the chambers can very easily be re-opened. Let's leave it at that. Now, are there any other questions or suggestions?'

'Going back to the question of finding a name for the rebels,' William responded. 'I suggest we call them Esehems.'

'Esehems? Where did that come from?' Dennis asked. 'I've not heard it before. What does it mean?'

'It's a word my mother used whenever anything untoward happened. If something became inexplicably missing or damaged she'd say, *"It must be the Esehems."* So it was just a word she used for imaginary sprites she could blame for annoying events she couldn't account for in any other way. I've not heard anyone else use it, I've not been able to find it in any dictionary and my mother couldn't tell me where she got it from, so I thought it might be a suitable name for the proposed band of revolutionaries. As we agreed earlier, when news of civil war hits the headlines the media will need a name for the rebels. In order for our narrative to be convincing it will need to be able to describe them as a coherent group with a plausible political motivation, not simply as an assortment of violent, undisciplined bandits from the wilderness. Our proxy army will need to have a semblance of unity and purpose, and for this it will need a name.'

'I agree, and Esehems seems as good as any,' James replied. 'So, unless anyone has an alternative suggestion or objection, we'll call our surrogate fighters Esehems.'

The meeting continued with no further queries or proposals, only favourable and enthusiastic comments. The group became eager for action and the plans were approved unanimously. When everyone had said all he wanted to say, measures were taken to put the proposals into action. Within days, the government authorised the dispatch of an overseas expedition to investigate Yevad's alleged involvement in the old King's assassination. Newspapers reported that three ships, carrying a small detachment of armed soldiers in case of hostilities, were to take a team of expert emissaries to Yevad to find the culprits responsible for the assassination. However, in conditions of strict secrecy, the ships were loaded with arms and ammunition, and manned by Special Forces squads. No spaces able to carry military equipment were left empty. The latest field guns, dismantled and shrouded by packing materials, were compactly stacked deep in the vessels' holds. When ready, the ships sailed off to cross the Mighty Ocean with a minimum of ceremony. Newspapers, as instructed, reported the event with due professionalism but without going into too many details.

Chapter Thirteen

With the ships underway there was little for the Special Intellectual Group to do but wait for one of them to return with news and talk about possible modifications they might have to make as their plans unfolded. James Schemowt took the opportunity to sit with his son in an isolated wing of his mansion where he knew they would not be disturbed. He knew Jeremy, in addition to being his successor as head of the Schemowt Banking Corporation, was destined to play a valuable role within the innermost circles of The Organisation and was coaching him accordingly. Jeremy, as usual, wanted to know every detail of what had been discussed at the meeting, and James obliged without restrictions.

James Schemowt took the opportunity to be with his son, Jeremy, and answer his many questions.

After listening to his father's account of the conference, Jeremy asked, 'If Yevad is devastated after the war, as you expect it to be, how will its people be able to pay for all the goods and services we'll be wanting them to buy from us?'

'That's easy,' James answered. 'We'll let them borrow. By we, of course, I mean Areho's four banking corporations.'

'But if their country is in ruins how will they be able to pay us back?'

'We'll tell them not to worry about it. We'll point out that the only realistic way they'll be able to recover from war is by borrowing, and that we'll make it easy for them. We'll tell them they won't have to start paying us back until they are able to. They'll not be able to come up with a better plan.'

'But if they are ruined, if they have nothing, how will they be able to start paying us back? You've always taught me about the dangers of making bad loans, about how we must always be wary of borrowers with little prospect of being able to service their debts. Now you're telling me we plan to lend money to a country in ruins. I can see that after a while, when Yevad has started to recover, it will be able to begin to pay-off its debts in a small way, but by then, with interest, it will owe more than it borrowed. It seems to me that unless it recovers a great deal very quickly it's possible it will never be able repay its loans. Its debt will go on increasing faster than its ability to pay.'

Jeremy expected Yevad would be in ruins after the war.

'I'm glad you remember what I've told you about bad loans, but lending money to the people of Yevad will not be the same as dealing with risky companies or individuals. Until they are able to establish a new government we'll be over there running their country. We'll decide how they are to recover, how much they'll need to borrow, how they are to repay it and when they'll be able to govern themselves. I can appreciate why you think they may never be able to repay their loans, but since we'll be over there governing their country, in effect we'll be lending to ourselves. We'll be spending money in our own interests, money we'll create out of nothing, money they'll eventually have to repay. We'll not hand Yevad back to its people until they are able to welcome our version of democracy and service their debts.'

'Do you think they'll agree with this? Will they go along with it?'

'Remember, we'll be there in great force in the guise of peace-makers and peace-keepers. They'll see us as saviours, so they'll trust us; they'll go along with us. Moreover, they'll have no viable option. At the first sign of any opposition to our plans we'll simply let them know we can easily leave and thereby allow the Esehems to return. They'll soon see things our way.'

'I understand what you've said, but I still find it difficult to imagine how a country left in ruins after a prolonged war, no matter who is there to govern it, will be able to recover quickly enough to make a start at repaying money it needed to begin its restoration.'

'I'm glad you're thinking as a banker, always looking ahead and judging the risks involved in loans, just as I've taught you, but let me try to put your mind at rest. During the war our Special Forces will be out there supervising the Esehems, and one of the things they'll be trying to ensure is that economic facilities we'll find useful when the fighting is over are not unduly harmed. Yevad's economic recovery, and its ability to repay loans, will not then be appreciably delayed. If we are successful, and I feel confident we will be, goods and resources we'll want back here in Areho will be produced very soon after we've taken control. I'll say more about this later, but first let me tell you if Yevad's economic capabilities are so severely damaged that it's not possible to recover quickly enough to start repaying its loans before accrued interest makes it impossible for them ever to be repaid, as you suggested, we'll have to instruct the government that it needs to give money to Yevad. We'll tell the Prime Minister that he needs to introduce a scheme of *overseas aid* to help Yevad recover, a policy that will inevitably become known as the *Lalutum Plan*. Since the money will be provided by the government it will be paid for by taxpayers, or, if necessary, by government borrowing, in which case it will be paid for by future taxpayers.'

'Won't people ask questions? Won't they think the government is using taxpayers' money inappropriately?'

'No, most people don't think that way. Unlike us, they allow sentimental and ethical feelings to cloud their judgements. Their ideas of self-interest are muddled by notions of right and wrong, and being concerned about the tragedies of others. So when the news media starts telling them heartbreaking stories about post-war Yevad, about children left without parents, about shortages of food and clean water, about severely injured people having to cope without medical aid and about all the other misfortunes of war, enough will willingly support a policy of overseas aid. Many will even want to make their own donations to help the distressed people of Yevad.'

'Don't you think some will oppose giving aid because of the atrocities they believe were committed by Yevadians?'

'Yes, some might think that way, but not many. The news media will have emphasised that it was Esehem rebels that committed the atrocities, not peaceful Yevadians. The aid will be for the victims of violence and aggression, not the perpetrators.'

It was expected that people would make donations to help the distressed people of Yevad.

'If some people oppose overseas aid despite what the media tells them, do you think it will be because they don't believe newspapers?'

'Well, it could be because they believe the government has no mandate to give taxpayers' money to foreign countries, or that the money should be used here in Areho, but I don't think many will oppose overseas aid because they don't believe newspapers. What made you think they might?'

'We are going to furtively arrange a war in Yevad, have it fought by a proxy army, go in as peace-keepers when the country's in ruins and the fighting is virtually over, and, if necessary, use taxpayers' money to rebuild it so it can serve our own interests. It's a brilliant scheme, but I couldn't help thinking about the difficulties that will be involved in keeping it secret. It seemed to me that some smart individuals might become a little suspicious; they may perhaps think there are too many anomalies, omissions or coincidences in the stories told by the media, as I think there will be. They might then suspect that newspapers cannot always be relied on to tell the truth. I was thinking about all the snags we'll have to avoid if our narrative to the public is to be believable. We'll need to ensure there are no anomalies or obvious omissions. I couldn't help thinking this will not be easy.'

'I see what you mean, but I don't think you need to be concerned. The public has been conditioned over the centuries to believe Areho is honourable and righteous, in the main its political leaders, as they keep promising, have its best interests at heart and are guided by well-founded moral principles. These beliefs have been deeply ingrained into the public consciousness by slanted and selected versions of historical events presented as factual narratives. Legends of Areho's glorious past, tales of its courageous heroes in times of conflict, and its wise and noble statesmen in times of crisis, along with countless fictional stories based on such themes, have helped to shape the way people see their country, its leaders and themselves. Along with tales of wrongdoers whose evil deeds were inevitably exposed, such stories create a backdrop of deep-seated patriotic beliefs against which people form their opinions. Accordingly, provided it fits easily within this framework of convictions, most people will believe the story of Yevad as told by the news media irrespective of any abnormalities. We needn't be too concerned about omissions, contradictions or coincidences, for they will be overlooked. If they imply that Areho is not behaving honourably they will be rejected. Most people will not even see them. Those that do will look for ways of explaining them away, for they will be unable to allow them to threaten their ingrained framework of jingoistic convictions, their tightly knitted structure of patriotic beliefs, the foundations of their notions of good and evil.'

'But what if some of the contradictions are too obvious to be overlooked or explained away? I don't think we'll be able to pull off a scam as elaborate and prolonged as the proposed Yevad project without glaring inconsistencies or ambiguities occurring in the stories we tell the public. Some astute individuals, surely, will notice them and be unable to explain them without questioning the integrity of the government.'

'I'm impressed by your reasoning. I think you'll become a very useful member of The Organisation's innermost circle but there are still a few things you need to learn. You correctly said the Yevad War will be prolonged. It might go on for several years, and during this time anomalies may well crop up in the media's account of it. It could be that events reported when the war is well underway conflict with statements made when it started. It's impossible to foresee such difficulties, but this is not something we need to be too concerned with. You see, very many people do not relate recent affairs with what went before. They forget or overlook past events and fail to connect them with present ones, especially if it enables them to avoid threats to their cherished patriotic beliefs. This is one of the reasons we don't need to worry too much about contradictions in the stories we tell the public, even very obvious ones. Yesterday's news, as they say, is soon forgotten. No matter how nonsensical the stories may be, provided they are consistent with deep-seated, comfortable, patriotic beliefs and acknowledged by prominent personalities, they'll be believed.

'You are correct in thinking there will be one or two smart individuals able to notice flaws in the media's narratives, there always are, and some will want to make a fuss about them. However, we know how to deal with such nuisances. In the main we ignore them, but if for some reason this is not possible we call them *intrigue fantasists*. Most people understand this phrase to mean crazy paranoiacs who unreasonably see the influence of wicked conspiracies when reasonable people do not. We successfully introduced it into the public's lexicon by having friends in the media use it in a derogatory manner when talking about individuals who proposed ideas we wanted discredited. Several celebrities, particularly popular comedians and others who are listened to by large audiences quickly picked it up and used it in their routines, as we knew they would. Before long it came to be widely understood to mean deluded idiots whose views should be ignored or dismissed. Now, most people regard anyone branded an *intrigue fantasist* as someone they should not be associated with for fear of themselves being thought of as being one. Of the few who are willing to listen to what they have to say, most will know it is wise to keep quiet about it. Now we can tell the public transparently nonsensical tales, clearly at odds with the facts, with the advantage of being able to call any smart alecks making a fuss about them *intrigue fantasists*. Their contentions will then be regarded as the confused ramblings of deranged fools and automatically dismissed without thought. So, you see, you've no need to be concerned about inquisitive individuals with wide-reaching imaginations, or Yevad's post-war debts, or about anything else.'

'Yes, I understand.'

'I can see by the look on your face that you have many more questions. Am I right?'

'Yes, but I need to think about them. I need to consider all the things you've told me. There's a lot for me to mull over.'

Continental Union Headquarters.

'I appreciate that, so let me try to help you. Let's first consider the alliance of Areho's neighbouring kingdoms, or the Continental Union as it's now known. I know you are familiar with how and why we encouraged and developed it, but taking a second look from a slightly different perspective might help you appreciate our plans for Yevad. As our industrial and financial capabilities developed it eventually became clear we were able to produce more goods and offer more services than our own people, with the wages we were willing to pay, were able, or wanted, to consume. Moreover, our factories required ever increasing supplies of basic raw materials. Many of these could be obtained from our own resources, but some soon became seriously depleted, and it was clear that eventually others would do the same. Also, as some of the goods we produced became more complex, materials were needed that could only be obtained from other countries. So trade with our neighbours, which for centuries had been operating on a steady but relatively low level, started to increase. At first this was just a consequence of our increasing prosperity. We started to import luxury goods and desirable things easily available in other countries, such as wine and unfamiliar foods.

'However, our need for raw materials from our neighbours increased as our industries developed, so we had to take our financial and technical knowledge into their lands, particularly in the business of transportation. I know you are familiar with the story of our canal building traditions, but we also became skilled in road making. We encouraged them to borrow from us and thereby employ our capabilities to develop their infrastructure, making it easy to import the goods we needed and export to them the things we produced in abundance. It was a very lucrative scheme. We benefited from interest payments, cheap imports and from having a market for our surplus goods. They benefited, although to a much lesser extent, from the employment provided and the goods they were able to buy from us as a result.

'At roughly the same time we convinced them of the advantages of tariff-free trade, fixed exchange rates and the folly of trying to compete with well-developed industries in other countries. This, of course, protected our industries from foreign competition. Inevitably, steered by borrowed money and economic arguments based on notions of free trade, their financial and business systems became manifestly intertwined with ours. Above all, they became heavily indebted, and this gave us a powerful means of influencing their political opinions. After they had had time to digest the changes, operating stealthily we persuaded them of the need for common rules, regulations and laws. Of such measures, being able to recruit workers from any of the countries of the Union, particularly the poorer ones, was particularly welcomed by business owners in Areho and its wealthier neighbours. It helped with the problem of local workers incessantly campaigning for higher wages. This had been made manageable by laws designed to restrict workers from combining, and media campaigns designed to undermine the credibility of any attempting such tactics, but the ability to hire workers from low-wage regions of the Union reduced it further. 'Naturally, this policy was not popular with poorly paid employees in wealthy countries, above all Areho, but this was more than offset for most people by overblown propaganda praising the virtues of the Union. Even many low-paid workers were persuaded by this misinformation, particularly the frequently repeated claim that the formation of the Union had eliminated the fear of war between neighbouring countries. Our policy of curbing warfare between countries with which we did profitable business by means of low-profile interventions designed to equalise the military strengths of potential adversaries was, and is, largely unknown, so convincing the public that the creation of the CU reduced the threat of war was not too difficult.'

Jeremy already knew many of the things his father was telling him and was keen to learn something new. He asked, 'How is all this connected to the proposed Yevad project?'

'I was just about to get round to it, but I wanted to go over the formation of the CU to show you what we have in mind for Yevad and the rest on the distant lands. I'll try to be brief. Without being seen or suspected by the masses in any of its countries, with the possible exception of a few *intrigue fantasists,* our Organisation now controls the social, political and economic affairs of the CU. Effectively, the Union is a collection of subordinate, or vassal, states. Areho, although the most prominent, wealthy and powerful state, is no more than a vassal itself. It is true that most of the CU's extremely powerful families and corporations are based in Areho, but equally influential people and businesses can be found in other wealthy states. They comprise The Organisation's membership. Principal executives of the most powerful multinational corporations, the elite core of The Organisation, are the Union's invisible overlords. They secretly govern every country of the CU without sentimental allegiance to any one in particular. Areho might seem to be an exception, but its predominance arises principally from its unrivalled military strength, a consequence of its concentration of extreme wealth. As a necessary and inevitable result Areho is, by far, the most compliant vassal. Its military might is a matter of vital importance.'

'I've not seen Areho that way before. It's not the way most Arehoians see it. It gives me a new way of understanding its importance. How do you think other people in the Union regard their own countries?'

'While recognizing that CU rules and regulations involves some loss of sovereignty, and judging this is acceptable in view of the perceived advantages of belonging to the Union, the people of each country, with the exception of senior Organisation members and their subservient lackeys, and a few *intrigue fantasists,* believe their government has control of their vital concerns. They are unaware of the concealed forces guiding their leading politicians. And of the giant enterprises behind these forces none has more political clout than Areho's banking corporations, for they, operating through their Central Bank, have ultimate control of the national debts of each state of the Union. Any one of them can be destabilised whenever we think it would be useful. So, I want you to see the CU as a guide to what we hope to achieve in Yevad.'

'But we expect to find Yevad devastated by war, whereas when the Union was formed its countries had not been involved in warfare for many years. Do you think this is significant? Is it important?'

'No, it's not important. You see, we'd been involved with the countries of the Union - lending money, building roads, harbours and canals, curtailing wars and developing trade - long before the Union was formally established. Until we became involved they did have a long history of warfare, but not of a kind that left them devastated. They were underdeveloped in the sense of not being industrialised, but did have well-organized farming estates, and wars were fought for possession of valuable agricultural land. Although the fortified homes of enemy barons were attacked occasionally, armies typically confronted each other in open spaces away from cultivated regions their lords wanted captured or defended. Consequently, before we started to take a commercial interest, the countries that eventually became the CU were accustomed to intermittent warfare, but were not ruined as a result. They had simply not benefited from long enough periods of peace to allow the development of manufacturing industries. They did, therefore, have some similarities with how we expect to find Yevad and - when it's their turn to be attacked and absorbed - the other countries of the distant lands. But there are differences. When we became interested we acted to circumvent their militaristic tendencies, whereas we intend to secretively incite and supervise Yevad's. Other differences concern issues that are important to us with regard to Yevad, but didn't apply to the countries that eventually formed the CU.

'Yevad has well-developed manufacturing facilities we want preserved, it also has deep-rooted ideologies we want destroyed. As I mentioned earlier, our Special Forces working covertly with the Esehem rebels will try to ensure that certain factories are not harmed while others are reduced to rubble. Ones that make products we expect to be sought-after in Areho and other states of the CU, especially fine pottery and delicate, intricately-patterned textiles, are to be spared. We expect their goods to sell at very worthwhile prices. But factories that produce things we manufacture in abundance are to be destroyed. Farms where foods we expect to be popular in Areho are produced are also, if at all possible, to be spared the devastation of war. Then, when the fighting is over, all being well, we'll be able to benefit from a scheme somewhat similar to the one we pulled off in the early days of the CU. Yevad will be able to supply desirable, low-import-cost goods and much needed raw materials, and at the same time import our surplus manufactured goods. Just like the poorer countries of the CU, its balance of trade will substantially favour Areho. It will, therefore, be able to repay, with interest, its post-war debts.'

Special Forces will ensure that useful economic facilities are not unduly harmed.

'Yes, I can see how it will work. Apart from the war, it's basically the same racket as the CU scam. Yevad is to become another vassal state.'

'Yes, but we don't like to call it a racket, we prefer to call it free trade. You are right about their similarities, but their experiences of warfare, or lack of it, and their differing manufacturing capabilities, make them quite distinct. Also, Yevad is far away on the other side of the Mighty Ocean, whereas the CU countries are Areho's continental neighbours. But there's another difference, one of even greater significance. Between Yevad and Areho there's a wide cultural disparity. It didn't arise as a significant problem with the CU countries, but with Yevad it's an issue we'll have to deal with. While protecting economic facilities we want preserved, and obliterating any we don't, the Special Forces will also encourage Esehems to destroy all gathering places where Yevadian customs and values are taught, promoted, respected, protected and cherished. These places, which have been likened to churches, harbour beliefs which, to us, are subversive and offensive. They give credence and support to ideals which put concerns for public amenities and natural facilities above business interests. They promote and defend ideas of social welfare and cost-free leisure activities. They uphold and endorse a tradition of manufacturing goods with unlimited life spans. But most seditious of all is their odious practice of creating interest-free-money. The thinking behind these values and customs is very dangerous. It makes industrial and financial interests subordinate to social wellbeing and environmental concerns. It's loathsome. It must never be allowed to cross the Mighty Ocean and permeate into the public's consciousness. Yevadian culture must be totally destroyed so debt-fuelled consumerism and propaganda-controlled democracy can be introduced in its place.

The Esehems will be instructed to destroy all gathering places where Yevadian customs and values are promoted and cherished.

'Now, Jeremy, I've talked a lot and told you all I can about our plans for Yevad. Only time will tell if they can be realised. We'll have to wait until one of the ships returns with news before we can judge how well our plans are unfolding. So I think we should finish with international trade and politics for today, especially since I understand the chefs are creating something special for dinner.'

'Alright, let's go and see what there is to eat, but before we do I've one more question.'

'What's that?'

'You said it was mentioned at the conference that it will be necessary to arouse intense public anger before a fleet of warships can be sent to Yevad. How will this be done?'

'That is something we don't talk about. Occasionally, in the affairs of The Organisation, it's necessary to arrange events that must remain known only by those directly involved. It might be an assassination, a bombing outrage, a disappearance or any other occurrence that must remain untraceable to us. There needs to be credible refutability for such actions. We don't want to provide *intrigue fantasists* with plausible arguments unnecessarily. Accordingly, whenever any such act is planned only those who will be directly involved in its implementation are told of it. All others must remain uninformed. In this way the possibility of incriminating remarks being made inadvertently is reduced to a minimum. Sometimes, however, a carefully measured snippet of information is disclosed to selected individuals who will not be directly involved. This will be done if they will need to know what to do when, or just before, the planned event occurs. It might be because there may be doubt as to who is responsible and they will need to know who is, or they will need to act in a specific way in order to avoid being harmed or implicated. Whatever it is, they will not be told any more than they need.

'In the case of the incident designed to arouse public fury in advance of the planned military mission to Yevad, members at the recent meeting were told it will involve Arcue Cathedral. That is all they need to know. They will now avoid visits to the Cathedral, or to any place near to it, or mentioning it in conversations, when it is known that fighting in Yevad is waning. Also, when the event occurs, they will know the army and navy expedition to Yevad is standing by waiting for orders to go. There'll be no need to call everyone to another conference.'

'Why do you sometimes refer to guests at conferences as the Special Intellectual Group?'

'Many, many years ago, in the early days of The Organisation, an elite section of highly intelligent specialists was set up to secretly formulate and inconspicuously float ideas designed to shape and direct the thinking of other members. To the few who knew of its existence it became known as the Special Intellectual Group, and within The Organisation's innermost circles the name is still used. No one has ever questioned it or suggested an alternative. Why did you ask about it?'

'You said the Group was not told what will happen, only that the Cathedral will be involved. I just thought they might be a little annoyed. If they are highly secretive members of a special elite group won't they think they should be fully informed? Won't they feel excluded?'

'No, they won't think that at all. They fully understand they've been told as much as they need to know and are not to ask for more details. It's a protocol they all appreciate and follow, and it applies to you, so don't ask any more questions about it.'

'I won't, but I do have just one more question about something else.'
'You've asked three or four questions since the last time you said you wanted to ask just one more. I'm hungry, so let's make this one the last.'

'You said you hoped propaganda-controlled democracy can be introduced in Yevad. I understand how it operates in Areho and the rest of the CU. You told me it depends on having concealed control of news and history. I can see how we'll be able to take control of the news media just as we've done here in Areho. It churns out relentless propaganda masquerading as accurate, objective news. But control of history is quite different. As you've explained, people here in Areho are tutored from birth to see the world, their country and their lives from the perspective of an ongoing jingoistic narrative of commonly held beliefs constructed by selected, shaped and slanted stories from the past. This makes me wonder how Arehoian-style democracy can be introduced in Yevad. The people there have been coached from birth to see the world from a different perspective, a Yevadian perspective. We'll be able to select and shape the news in much the same way as we do here in Areho, but how will it be possible to make it harmonise with deep-seated, patriotic notions of Yevadian history? We'll be trying to impose an alien way of seeing the world that is fundamentally at odds with their ancient traditions. Can we really expect to be able to introduce propaganda-controlled democracy in Yevad as easily as we've been able to here in Areho?'

'That's a very big question, Jeremy, and a lot of careful consideration has been directed at it. You are absolutely right: deep-rooted beliefs and values will probably obstruct our plans for Yevad, although, hopefully, not too seriously. It's thought that many Yevadian traditions will be drastically undermined by being taken to the very brink of total defeat and destruction in war, thereby making it easier for new ones, Arehoian ones, to take their place, especially if they offer promises of recovery. The planned destruction of their cultural meeting places should prove to be very helpful in achieving this. However, it is also thought that traditional beliefs will be so deeply ingrained in some Yevadians, especially older ones, that it will be too difficult for them to adapt to new ways. If there are too many of them and they present difficulties it may be necessary to relocate them away from the rest of the population in reservation enclaves. So that their customs and beliefs will die with them, any children they have will need to be taken far away, handed over to new guardians and taught how to work, vote, borrow, consume and be part of the new Yevad. However, this is all speculation. We won't know exactly what we'll need to do until we've taken control of the country and started to set up a new regime. Now, Jeremy, we're going to be late for dinner, so if you've any more questions you'll have to ask them later. You know what your mother's like when I'm late at meal-times.'

'Yes, let's go and see what the chefs have prepared. You've given me many things to think about, so in a while I'll probably have many more questions.'

'Well, if you wish, and provided your mother has no objection, we can continue our little chat later.'

After they had finished dinner, and remained in the dining room long enough to satisfy the requirements of good manners, James and Jeremy withdrew in order to continue their conversation. When they were settled once again beside a roaring fire, Jeremy asked, 'Some time ago you compared our Organisation with the arrangements they have in Yevad. You said their system of safeguarding their interests is in some ways an inversion of ours. I think I understood what you were telling me, but I'm not too sure. Can you say a little more about it?'

'Yes, I remember saying something like that. Let me think about it for a while. As we talked about earlier, over the centuries, by controlling the ideas and information the masses have had access to, The Organisation has fashioned the public's consciousness. It's crafted the public's collective perception of the world and its ways.'

'The view of reality the masses have been conditioned to believe is true?'

'Yes, that's right. All the ideas, information and opinions held by the general population are permitted, directed, shaped and promoted by The Organisation.'

'What about Yevad?'

'Over the years, ordinary members of the public there have developed a different lifestyle. Many people, with the commitment and enthusiasm commonly found here in religious gatherings, regularly meet in groups to promote, celebrate, sustain, venerate and affirm their faith in their way of life. The pride and patriotism they generate finds its way to the general public. In this way their thinking is protected from disruptive internal influences. Any persuasive, ambitious individuals wanting to shape society in their own interests are thwarted by the people. Their society is, therefore, largely immune from unwanted political corruption. That is why I said the system in Yevad is in some ways an inversion of ours. Their system protects the masses from being controlled by a powerful upper class, while ours protects a powerful upper class from being controlled by the masses. Here, we have structured society so that our privileged way of life is protected from any disruption that could arise from manipulation by the masses. In Yevad, society has been structured so that ordinary people are protected from any disruption that could arise from manipulation by ambitious power seekers.'

Jeremy and James preferred to sit and talk in an isolated wing of the mansion where they knew they would not be disturbed.

'That's what I thought you meant, but I wasn't fully sure. As you were explaining it I kept thinking about democracy, about how the masses here were told it would put them in command of the government. It seems that the people in Yevad really are in command of their government - they are the government - but here in Areho people only think they are.'

'Yes, that just about summarizes it.'

'What was the thinking behind the introduction of democracy? I could appreciate the need to get rid of King Thomas, but I don't think I fully understood the need to bring in democracy at roughly the same time. I know it makes the masses more manageable, but did it have to be introduced just as the old King was being forced to abdicate?'

'It was the best time for it. In order to create the circumstances in which King Thomas had no realistic alternative to abdication it was necessary to plunge the economic system into a turmoil in which the people were seriously agitated. The intention was to arouse popular rage and direct it at the King, but it quickly became clear that replacing him by an alternative monarch, no matter how popular he might be, would not be sufficient to curtail the powerful feelings of anger and hopelessness we'd aroused. Too many smart individuals were asking too many awkward questions. Democracy provided a way of dealing with the problem. By giving the masses something to focus their attention on, something that seemed to promise them a say in how their country was governed, we diverted them away from issues we didn't want them to be concerned with. Now they are less angry. Their minds are occupied. They are distracted. We gave them two political sides to choose from, two alternative ideas to focus on. Distraction is one of the most powerful tools of propaganda, and democracy provides a very effective distraction.'

'Provided The Organisation controls what the masses believe and what their options are.'

'Of course.'

'I remember the election and the two main political parties that competed for votes. Both told voters that the national debt was an important issue the government needed to take care of. If I remember it correctly, one party argued that the debt was far too large and needed to be quickly reduced by cutting back on government spending, while the other argued that very drastic reductions of government spending should not be used to reduce the debt too rapidly, it would injure the economic system too deeply. How did that situation occur? What made people think reducing the national debt was important?'

'Soon after we'd set about upsetting the economic system, several thinkers started writing books and articles about the situation. Of course, they didn't know the real reason for the economic difficulties. However, we found those who argued that the economic problems were caused by the size of the national debt to be interesting and useful. Basically, they claimed the King's public works programme had cost more than the country had been able to afford. The national debt, they said, had increased beyond the level the economic system was able to easily support. Some claimed the government should not go into debt; it should not spend more than it received from taxation. We found their lines of reasoning to be interesting for two main reasons. Firstly, they were simple arguments the general public could easily swallow. People understood that if they continued spending more than they could afford, and went deeper into debt, they would soon run into difficulties. So they could easily be convinced that the same reasoning applied to the government. Secondly, promoters of the national debt reduction argument were obviously divided into two factions: one advocating drastic cuts in government spending, the other arguing for a more cautious approach. We could see, therefore, that their opinions provided ideal foundational issues for the version of democracy we wanted to introduce. The argument was available in two clearly distinct versions and both could be easily digested by the general public. Accordingly, with help from our friends in the news media, we promoted both sets of debt-reduction thinkers, and ignored or discredited others. In this way we made people believe that reducing the national debt was very important.'

'I understand what you've said, that it was ideal for the introduction of democracy, but what about the argument itself? Is reducing the national debt important?'

'To adequately answer that question I think we'll need to go back to the time when you asked me why economic growth was important. If you remember, we were able to see that if interest is charged on loans, the amount of money active in the economy, on average, has to keep on increasing.'

'Yes, I remember it well.'

'We were able to understand the importance of growth by first talking about an imaginary tiny country that didn't use money and then looking into what would happen if its people were persuaded to borrow cash from a bank and pay interest. The point I want to make is that we never said anything about the imaginary country having a government. It was not necessary. There was no need to talk about a national debt. All the money put into circulation was borrowed by the people. It was all owed to the bank. It literally was the national debt.'

'Anyone in possession of money was in possession of part of that debt.'

'Yes, that's right. Now the important point you need to appreciate is that nothing of any significance would change if the imaginary country had a government. If the government borrowed, perhaps the only change needed would be in finding a name for its debt. If the phrase *national debt* was used, as it is here in Areho, to mean the debt owed by the government, then a different name would be needed for the debt owed by the people - perhaps it could be called the *private debt*, as it is here. Other than this, nothing of any importance would change. For the economic system to function smoothly, so that the total debt, both *national* and *private*, could be serviced, the total amount of money active in the economy, on average, would need to keep on increasing.'

'Yes, I can see that. The argument about the need for growth would be just the same. The total debt would need to keep on increasing.'

'We can now take a look at the government's decision to reduce the national debt. Here in Areho, since the introduction of The Central Bank, the situation differs significantly from that of the tiny country we imagined. However, irrespective of the circumstances, provided governments are not willing to default on their loans, borrowed money has to be repaid, with interest, from tax income. Borrowing simply spreads out the burden of taxation into the future. Here, if it wishes, the government can borrow directly from The Central Bank or any other bank, thereby involving the creation of new money, but once the new arrangements had settled down it has avoided doing so and instead has borrowed by selling bonds to businesses and wealthy individuals. So, by asking if the government's decision to reduce the national debt was a good one, essentially we are asking if it was a good idea for the government to reduce, or stop, the sale of bonds, and to repay existing ones, as required, at the appropriate times.

'At the time of the election, as I'm sure you'll remember, the economic system was functioning very badly and the two main political parties seeking votes, in addition to promising to reduce the national debt, with differing levels of commitment, also promised to provide financial aid to unemployed people and struggling small businesses and regional councils, again with differing levels of commitment. So the government, once elected, had two conflicting promises to fulfil. It had promised to reduce the national debt, but it had also promised to spend money on struggling people, councils and businesses. It decided to scale back its spending promises and concentrate on reducing its borrowing by selling fewer bonds and, as required, returning money to existing bond holders when their bonds expired. From this there was no change in the amount of money in existence. All that happened was bond investors had more to spend and the government had less. It had less to spend on the promises it had made to unemployed people and struggling businesses and councils.'

'What did the investors do with their money?'

'Since they were unable to buy equivalent replacement bonds, they looked for alternative investments, pushing up the relevant prices. This did nothing helpful to the ailing economy.'

'It's starting to seem that trying to reduce the national debt was not such a good idea. It returned money to people who didn't need it at the expense of people who did. What happened?'

'People reacted to the government cut-backs. Many needed to spend their savings and/or increase their borrowing in order to try to keep the amount of active money in the economy as it had been. Of course, they didn't think of it in that way. Businesses with reduced or cancelled orders, or reduced support from the government, and government employees with reduced or terminated wages, and those who, in one way or another, depended upon them, simply tried to sustain the state of affairs they had become used to. Businesses tried to uphold their levels of economic activity and profitability, and individuals and families tried to maintain their established lifestyles. They didn't want to cut back on their customary activities or forsake their cherished ambitions. Whatever way they thought about it, since the government was spending less, businesses and the people had to spend more. Spending savings helped some for a while, but for many maintaining their familiar economic activities soon depended on borrowing.'

'Did borrowing solve their problems?'

'It did for a while, but public borrowing could not go on indefinitely. Debts kept on increasing. Before long we had to say we couldn't let them continue borrowing. They were trying to sustain their usual economic activities, but their usual means of servicing their debts were no longer available. Because of the government cuts, their incomes, either as employers or employees, were no longer as they had been. They had to accept that they could no longer go on spending as they had been and instead endeavour to reduce their debts. Money was returned to banks and, as you know, it was then annulled. It no longer existed. Consequently, the economic system's difficulties became exacerbated. The total amount of money in existence decreased. You asked about reducing the national debt by means of government cutbacks. There's the answer. The consequence of reducing the national debt causes economic activity to decline.'

'Yes, I understand, but it makes me wonder why those writers you told me about thought reducing the national debt was important. Did they have any good reasons to support their thinking?'

'I think we'll need to look at that question in a little more detail. When a government plans to spend more than it receives from taxes there is said to be a deficit, and in order to fulfil its spending plans, it borrows. The national debt arises from the build-up, with interest, of successive yearly amounts of outstanding government borrowing, and it can be increased, kept as it is, or it can be reduced. We've seen the economic consequences of it being reduced. Let's see how it can be kept as it is.

'Let's imagine the government wanted to leave its spending commitments unchanged and keep the size of the national debt, relative to the size of the economy, unchanged. That is, it wanted to keep the proportionate amount of debt constant without cutting its spending plans. Each year, from its tax income and usual level of borrowing, it can keep to its spending plans. However, the national debt will increase each year because of the interest payments owed to bond holders, but, if all is well, growth will also occur. If the growth rate, after allowing for inflation, exceeds the interest rate, it is possible for the proportionate level of national debt to remain constant. The increased tax revenue associated with real growth will be sufficient to provide for the interest payments. The debt, relative to the size of the economy, can then remain unchanged. Only if the real growth rate is lower than the interest rate will the proportionate size of the debt increase with the undesirable consequences the writers feared. They disregarded the very low interest rates introduced because of the poor state of the economy and that prudently spent government borrowing can increase the rate of growth. They feared that if the national debt became too high, relative to the size of the economy, the interest the government would need to pay to bond holders would become an unsustainable burden on taxpayers. They were particularly worried that investors would become reluctant to buy bonds because of the possibility of the government being forced to default on the interest payments. Wealthy businesses and individuals, fearing the thinkers were right and the government's spending promises would push the national debt up to unsustainable levels, became less inclined to buy government bonds.'

'Weren't the government's advisors aware of this?'

'They were, but many elected representatives were reluctant to shirk the promises made to voters. They knew it would cause a lot of hardship for the masses. However, enough were persuaded to change their minds by the government and its advisors who were thinking about the tax needed to service the national debt. To their way of thinking, if the debt was reduced, the tax needed to service it would be reduced, and the economy would correspondingly benefit from tax cuts.'

'So they were thinking about tax cuts, not government cuts for their own sake?'

'They thought the economic system would function most efficiently if the government interfered with it as little as possible, and tax was one form of interference they particularly disliked.'

'Was that because they didn't like paying tax?'

'Yes, although they didn't say so openly. They argued that the economic system needed to operate without regulation. They said it needed to be free, and it couldn't be free if it was constrained by taxation. They said they wanted a small, ineffectual government that wouldn't try to regulate the economy. They said if the economy was left to its own devices it would function efficiently.'

'Does The Organisation agree?'

'It appointed the government's advisors, so yes, it does agree. Their job was to make the government and the masses believe cut-backs were vitally important so the deficit could be drastically reduced. The real aim, of course, was to reduce government regulation of the economic system, to get uncooperative elected representatives out of the affairs of The Organisation.

'Soon, however, everything will change. When military activities in Yevad get underway the government will need lots of new money. It will need to sell lots of bonds to The Central Bank and the national debt will soar. In times of military conflict, when its vital interests are at stake, The Organisation will argue for a large, powerful government; one able and willing to support the armed forces, although this variance with previous thinking will necessarily remain obscured.'

'If The Central Bank has to create lots of new money won't it cause inflation?'

'It will, but it won't affect the bulk of the masses. We've blocked all the ways in which workers can seek to increase their incomes, so the prices of things they customarily buy will be effectively limited by what they are able to pay. The extra money will go to high ranking individuals involved in the production of war materials, and they will direct it into investments. That will take care of inflation. Along with other assets likely to appreciate, they will buy pieces of paper bearing, or implying, the promise of worthwhile future returns on their investments. The prices at which they'll be able to sell their paper certificates and other assets will soar because of all the extra wealthy investors.'

'Won't they eventually want to realize the fruits of their investments?'

'They probably will, but when they do they will only buy more assets and investments. People with plenty of money to spare will probably then turn their attention to tangible assets such as land and big fine houses; and, for us, mortgages will become very interesting. If interest in houses regains momentum, we'll encourage many more people to take out mortgages, even ones we wouldn't normally consider to be reliable borrowers. We'll then be able to sell mortgage-based financial products to other investors looking for new ways of parting with their money. They'll be attracted to investments linked to real assets such as houses, and think they'll be able to enjoy steady income streams from homeowners servicing their mortgages. They'll probably end up being very disappointed, but that will not be of any concern to us.'

'That's clever. What about the national debt? Will it just go on increasing?'

'It will, but that's nothing you need to worry about. Remember, The Central Bank can create as much money as it likes. Its capacity is unlimited. If it makes loans to the government it's not going to worry about them being paid back, with or without interest. As we keep on arranging wars on the other side of the Mighty Ocean, and rebuilding defeated countries, the government debt will keep on growing to astronomical levels, and ideas of it being repaid as if it was an ordinary bank loan will simply fade away. Making people believe reducing the national debt was important was just a bit of political theatre. It gave the government an excuse for evading all the promises made to voters. It told them the country could not afford to provide all the things they wanted. It needed to cut-back on government spending.'

'I understand, but it might take me a while to get used to it. I'll have to get out of the habit of thinking the national debt will eventually need to be repaid.'

'Just think about private debt. What would happen if it, along with the national debt, was repaid?'

'There'd be no money left. It would all be annulled.'

'That's right. All the paper money and deposits in bank accounts would no longer exist. The only money left would be metal coins, and they comprise only a tiny fraction of the money now in existence.'

'That makes me remember a question I've asked you a few times. If interest on loans means debt must go on increasing exponentially, when will it all end? You told me no one knew, it was not going to happen in my lifetime and I was not to worry about it. I'm not worried, but I am curious. From the things you've been telling me, I'm even more curious.'

'The basic answer is that the economic system we now benefit from will come to an end when it's no longer possible for real, tangible economic activities to keep on growing in line with the growth of money. In other words, when it's no longer possible to produce and sell things in step with the exponentially increasing quantity of created money. As I said, no one knows when it will happen, but it's nothing you need to be concerned about. Planned obsolescence, war, weapons, investment inflation and foreign conquests will extend it well beyond your lifetime.'

'That's good to know.'

'We'll have to finish now. It's getting late and your mother will want us back.'

'Yes, you're right.'

The conversation had given Jeremy many things to think about. James' thoughts were also aroused. He felt he wanted to examine some of the issues he'd been discussing with Jeremy with one or two of his colleagues. He decided he would pay a visit to Harold Amme, the director of the new Institute of Personal Relations.

Chapter fourteen

During James' visit to Harold Amme the two decided to convene another conference of the Special Intellectual Group at Schemowt Hall. Harold had intended to call a meeting to give his report on the proceedings of the Institute of Personal Relations once it was clear that events in Yevad were unfolding as intended, but in view of his conversations with James and of there being no sign of ships returning with news, it was decided to hold it earlier. James opened the meeting by welcoming everyone and then asking them to approve of his son's presence. He addressed his audience saying, 'You've all met Jeremy many times during your visits here, but, because of his youthful years, until now I've always excluded him from our formal meetings. However, confident that in due course he will become a very useful member of our Group, in recent years I've kept him fully informed of the gist of our discussions. Accordingly, he fully grasps our aims and ways. He's here to refine and extend his understanding of The Organisation's philosophy, to deepen his appreciation of its underlying principles. Accordingly, gentlemen, I ask you all to make him feel welcome and wanted at this meeting.'

In response the members present stood and applauded. Jeremy walked confidently to the stage, stepped up to the speaker's podium, thanked everyone for making him feel welcome and assured them of his intention of becoming a credit to the Group. Enthusiastic applause filled the room as he returned to his seat, during which James returned to the podium. After thanking everyone for giving his son such a warm reception, he went on to say, 'In fact we owe our thanks to Jeremy for our meeting here today, for after a day of doing my best to answer his many searching and thought provoking questions I decided to pay a visit to the Institute, to find out if it's come up with anything I should know about, and it was there that Harold and I decided to call this conference. A few lengthy conversations made us conclude that we should take the opportunity to hold another meeting while we wait for a ship to arrive back from Yevad. We thought there were a few ideas we wanted to discuss with you, ideas you'll later be able to casually communicate to The Organisation's general membership. I'll say no more about them for

213

I understand Harold has a full presentation to put before you. So, without further ado, I'll simply ask you to welcome Harold to the podium.'

Enthusiastic applause arose as Harold walked up to the stage and James returned to his seat in the audience. After thanking everyone for their cordial welcome Harold started his address by saying, 'There's one or two things I want to draw your attention to, and a few more general issues you may find interesting. To me they all seem interrelated, and it's not easy to know how to describe them so you will also appreciate this. Hopefully things will become clearer when we move on to a general discussion after my talk.

Harold told his audience he had one or two things to say.

'I'm going to start by telling you how we proceeded, and what we found, after being given the task of founding a new institution with the broad assignment of inquiring into the nature of human affairs. Our initial step was to conduct a wide ranging survey of Areho's universities and other learned institutions to compile a resource of related material and references to work with. We wanted to be fully acquainted with what was already known about the issues we'd been asked to inquire into. I'm not going to overburden my talk by acknowledging the various sources we looked at, but for anyone interested a list of references is available on the table in the lobby. In my conversations with James he expressed an interest in the national story, the collection of beliefs our Organisation has led the general population to accept as being beyond doubt; an interest revitalized by his efforts to answer Jeremy's many questions. He wanted to know if there was anything he might have missed, anything more we could tell him about the topic. I have to say that there was nothing of any significance we could add to what he already knows. I'm certain the same is true for everyone here today. Nevertheless, I thought I'd begin my talk by saying a few words about our review and compilation of the related ideas we found in our survey.

'In Areho, and all the other countries of the continent we are part of, as far back as history is able to tell us, there has always been a small group of very powerful individuals able to preside over the rest of the population. Typically, members of the ruling minority were led by a king or emperor, and usually had badges of office, or titles, bestowed by him and related to the spheres of influence to which they were entrusted. In such ways, the ruling elite in each country was structured so that it could effectively manage and utilize the majority of the population. All other issues were subservient to this vital arrangement. Violence was used occasionally, but it was a very inefficient method of control, especially if the rulers depended heavily on the productive capabilities of the masses. It could also be very risky, especially at times when large numbers of ordinary people had access to weapons comparable to ones that could be used against them. Accordingly, violence was used only when necessary, as a last resort.

'A far more practicable and efficient method, developed and refined over very many centuries, involved directing, shaping and upholding the thoughts of the masses, especially if the ways of thinking thereby induced were able to engender widespread loyalty, commitment and devotion to the rulers. Very often the opinions and attitudes cultivated by the ruling elite harmonised with the beliefs and loyalties promoted by religious leaders, but not always. In several cases high ranking religious officials claimed comparable status to the secular rulers, and it was not unusual for friction between the two to occur as their respective leaders contended for supremacy. Each wanted to shape, consolidate and sustain how the masses perceived the world and its affairs. However, such disharmony was usually transient, and accord emerged when both sides realised they didn't need to compete. When it was seen that their respective realms of influence, the spiritual and the temporal, could coexist harmoniously, the discord evaporated, although usually with the religious authorities fulfilling supplementary roles and being deferential to the superior powers of the secular rulers.

'Although there have been slight variations from place to place and time to time, the general arrangement of a large majority, the masses, being conditioned by means of propaganda and indoctrination to serve the needs of a small minority, the elite, has seemed to be the way human beings naturally structured their societies. To thinkers who gave a lot of attention to the issue it seemed to be an intrinsic feature of human civilizations. It was thought that something built-in to human disposition, something that was given by nature, was the reason humans behaved in this way. It was considered to be one of a number of human characteristics attributable to nature. That there are such inherent aspects of being human, and they are universal, was an accepted certainty of expert scholars. However, following the discovery of a hitherto unknown continent on the far side of the Mighty Ocean, many have had to abandon the notion. In Yevad we find people who are not subservient to rulers. People in countries neighbouring Yevad, it seems, have similar arrangements. If the division of human populations into ruling elites and ruled masses is not an invariable and universal inherent feature of human beings, what, then, can be said of other human characteristics that have been thought of as having such qualities? Accordingly, the idea that human attributes are fixed and given by nature has been discarded by many thinkers. It's been succeeded by the notion that human characteristics are not invariable, but can be modified, to a variable degree, according to social circumstances. This may have profound implications for The Organisation. For example, if the idea that criminals are criminals because they are inherently evil is replaced by the idea that they are criminals because of their social backgrounds, too many questions might be asked about the localities from which law-breakers generally originate, and who is responsible for them being as they are. This is not an issue we would want to be looked into too deeply. You might want to discuss it later.

'Now, however, I want to say a few words about the particular narrative used to manage Areho's masses. When fractional reserve banking and related industrialisation emerged in a big way, it became necessary to bring The Organisation into existence. Supplementary beliefs were required so that bankers and business magnates could integrate with existing rulers. Financial and industrial moguls needed to be able to operate in conjunction with secular and religious leaders in fashioning the public's outlook. Luckily, establishing The Organisation was easily accomplished because one of the founders of the original banking business, Harold Indolder, was on very good terms with the easy-going King Walter II, and could easily direct his policies. As the centuries passed, largely by virtue of its command of the supply and allocation of money, The Organisation has been able to secretly infiltrate and influence all centres of power, both secular and spiritual. Now, operating as an invisible, persuasive force able to sway the thoughts and passions of the masses and their leaders, The Organisation is able to guide and harness political and religious sentiments, and overthrow and replace any dissenters that contravene its guidance.'

Harold's words were received by his audience with satisfaction. A mellow hum of approval circulated around the room. Harold waited until members were again quiet and attentive before continuing. When ready he went on to say, 'Except for a very few eccentrics who can easily be ignored, the masses have been profoundly influenced by the beliefs we've tailored for their edification. Well indoctrinated individuals automatically reject as being absurd any notions outside the boundaries of the convictions they've been guided to accept as true. They find comfort and reassurance within a collection of beliefs they regard as being beyond question. Just as a small child is distressed by any criticism of ideas he's been taught by his parents, adults find information that is incompatible with firm beliefs they've been led to accept as true to be disturbing and threatening. When confronted with ideas opposing those of its parents a child will become upset. It might cry. Similar feelings arise in adults if they encounter conflicting beliefs. They might become angry or even violent. They cannot consider information that conflicts with their deep-rooted, well-integrated complex of unquestionable beliefs, even if clearly seen supporting evidence is obvious. It would be too disturbing. It must be suppressed and rejected. Disruptive ideas are taboo, they cannot be allowed. They have to be denied. It's the way people respond when they encounter notions outside the boundaries of knowledge they've been conditioned to accept as true.

'I intend to tell you about an emerging trend The Institute regards as an issue we'll need to consider. It's known as experimental science. I'll tell you about it, and the concerns it gives rise to, in a while, but as we've been talking about deep-seated beliefs it seems an appropriate time to tell you about the findings of a few of its practitioners. They add corroboration to the things I've just been saying. After asking volunteers to discuss their deepest and most cherished beliefs, the researchers told them they were going to be told something that would threaten those beliefs. They were told it would not be something they'd need to worry about for it would be untrue. The experiment was to find out how the volunteers would respond even though they knew the disturbing information they were to be given was false. I'll not go into details – you can find them in literature you'll find in the lobby – but basically it was found that the heart rates of the volunteers, to a variable degree, and often significantly, increased after they'd been told things they knew were untrue but conflicted with their deeply held beliefs. Several teams of researchers conducted different versions of the experiment and all found similar results. These, and other comparable investigations, demonstrate what's long been known by The Organisation, and for which there are very few, if any, exceptions; once ideas and opinions have been firmly implanted into networks of deeply held beliefs in the minds of the masses they will stubbornly resist being unseated. Such networks of beliefs form the culture we've led people to regard as their heritage, the basis of their civilisation, the essence of their knowledge. I think it's worth saying a few more words about it.

'The beauty of the information from which the masses have constructed much of their knowledge is that none of it can be contradicted. By means of our clandestine control of schools, universities, institutions, churches, newspapers, books and magazines, we've been able to regulate the ideas, values and opinions by which they conduct their lives. We've had control of what goes into their heads, the material from which their beliefs have been formed, the substance from which they've gained their ideas of the world and its ways. Their beliefs consist of notions they've gained from artists, fiction writers, historians, theologians, playwrights, philosophers, poets, lawyers, romantics, travellers, musicians and many other creators of legend, including, of course, news purveyors. By means of our influence on the industries by which such stories and ideas are distributed, we've been able to shape the overall narrative within which the masses formulate their opinions and convictions. With our unseen influence in the background, they've constructed stuff they regard as sound, reliable knowledge. Profoundly influential parts of it are able to arouse very powerful feelings, yet our role in its making has been minimal. It's only been necessary to block material we didn't want included and have well regarded commentators enthusiastically praise any we did.

'Acting within the bounds afforded by these simple measures, creative sections of the masses have produced a vast quantity of cerebral material, some useful, some harmless. I'm going to call it artistic knowledge. I've called it that in order to distinguish it from scientific knowledge. Artistic knowledge cannot be contradicted, for it consists of the works of imaginative creators of myth, bias and fancy, and their critics. No one can claim that any part of it is false, only that some parts are better than others, and a person is regarded as a master of such knowledge if he, or she, is able to distinguish the good from the bad. Acclaimed aficionados are able to utilize inspirational prose with wide vocabularies to opine about works they admire or despise, and great significance is attributed to their assertions. In this way a corpus of wisdom from which the masses gain their understanding of good, evil, love, hate, beauty and disgust has been constructed. Included in this body of artistic knowledge is economics, a topic I think we should take a brief look at.

'Many years ago, new university departments covertly sponsored by The Organisation were given the task of studying the workings of the economic system with the aim of making it acceptable and understandable within the framework of existing wisdom. The legendary Baron Ranty coined the term economics for this new field of study, and now, although it has one or two critics, it is widely regarded as giving a credible and workable assessment of the economic system. Its advocates sometimes make public speeches, and compliant journalists listen to them when preparing stories for the popular media and pass on idiomatic versions of their ideas to their readers. The general public is influenced by such reporting. Many are inclined to believe everything they are told by such sources. They glean ideas and opinions from the popular media and, perhaps wanting to be seen as being well-informed, include them in their conversations. This, I believe, is the basic mechanism by which notions held within economics are transferred to the general public. They form the foundations of many popular ideas about national and foreign affairs.

'I know you are familiar with economic issues as understood within The Organisation, but I think it will be useful to take a quick look at what university economists have come up with. They have diligently fulfilled their given task of creating a branch of knowledge able to furnish the economic system with credible explanations of its functioning without delving too deeply into the role of banks. They have come to look upon the economic system as a collection of measurable variables which interact in ways comparable to the behaviour of parts of a machine. Principal variables, such as unemployment rates, price levels and income distributions, they say, find stable levels under the influence of forces arising from the competitive behaviour of participants in industrial and service provision activities. As required, they repeatedly describe such a system as the best of all possible economic systems. Dutifully, with the process of money creation heavily obscured, they briefly describe the role of banks as one of passively providing money when it is needed. With the same level of unwitting acquiescence to their unseen and unknown benefactors, they put forward the argument that the economic system will function most efficiently when interventions into its affairs by governments, bureaucrats or workers' representatives, are eliminated, or at least reduced to a minimum. They claim such a freely operating system provides the greatest possible benefits to society by virtue of its efficiency. They say that such a system is self-regulating since any fluctuations of important economic variables will be quickly brought back to their stable levels by virtue of competitive forces acting within the system. They see it as an ideal self-regulating machine. The economic system therefore, they claim, will automatically tend to a state in which the level of unemployment, under the influence of competitive forces, will find a stable level which will be minimal if the system is allowed to operate without interference.

'They casually account for the wide distribution of earnings, which progressively becomes scarcely populated as incomes increase, as the result of employers having to offer ever increasing salaries to attract employees with exceptional skills. They describe it as the operation of a market for human resources. Again, competitive mechanisms within the system are said to be responsible. To their way of thinking, inflation is the only variable requiring regulation, and it should be managed by a central bank able to operate without political bias. I'm going to call their teaching *popular economics,* to distinguish it from the clandestine thinking of the special economics units active within The Organisation's learned institutions.

'There's a lot more I could say about popular economics, but I think I've said enough for it to be clear that it doesn't exactly describe the system operating here in Areho, or in any of the countries of the CU. The reason is that many ideas within it are based on defective assumptions and flawed logic. The defective assumptions are primarily ones it makes about human behaviour. Irrespective of the huge efforts of advertisers aimed at cajoling buyers to spend, it considers the paramount, if not the sole, desire of humans to be insatiably consuming products and services. The existing low demand for such goods, it says, is due to the current lengthy, deep recession which, paradoxically, it argues is not possible because of the self-correcting features of the economic system. Soaring, unsustainable booms, and prolonged depressions, they say, cannot occur. Yet, in recent years, they clearly have. Areho is now in a long-lasting recession, which advocates of popular economics claim will automatically correct itself if the economy is left to its own self-correcting mechanisms without government interference. They are unable to see the evidence that this is not occurring. Ironically, their advice to the government has not been to allow the economy to correct itself, it has been to drastically cut its borrowing and spending. Unsurprisingly, this has had the effect of deepening and prolonging the recession. So, in addition to defective assumptions and flawed logic, we need to add inconsistency to the shortcomings of popular economics.

'In what I've just been saying we can see a clear example of evidence being stubbornly overlooked, ignored or denied because it conflicts with firmly held beliefs; beliefs, in this case, about popular economics. When their cherished beliefs are threatened, university economists are not different from the rest of the masses. They cannot countenance their complex of deeply entrenched ideas being unseated simply because they fail to give a satisfactory explanation of the behaviour of the economy. To them, their ideas are gratifying. They are at the heart of all they stand for. They are at the core of their professional identities. They cannot be contradicted. Evidence has to be overlooked. It is anomalous. It means nothing. Economics has not been blemished, they say. Nothing has changed.

'What, we might ask, is the cause of this situation? Apart from why do economists deny it, there is the question, why did they get it so wrong? I think there are two main reasons. The first is that the boom and following recession were unexpected. Their ideas could not predict the economy would behave as it did. They did not know, of course, that the events that had them confounded had been deliberately planned in great secrecy, engineered so that the old obstinate King would be ousted. It is not surprising, therefore, that their ideas could not account for them. The second reason is weightier, it goes to the heart of their central idea that the economic system behaves like a machine and will automatically return to a stable set of variables after being upset by unexpected events. The economy is clearly not returning to the way it used to be, and we all know why. Regarding the economic system as if it's a self-correcting machine is a mistaken way of thinking. It's a dynamic system in which the production and sale of goods and services must continuously increase roughly in step with the exponentially growing amount of borrowed money, or debt. To think of such a system in terms of stable variables is clearly paradoxical. Economic variables must continuously change as the debt grows. Other than for occasional brief interludes, they cannot be stable. This is why many ideas within popular economics are based on flawed logic.

'Why this is so is perhaps understandable. Economists were instructed by their paymasters to provide feasible explanations of the workings of the economic system without raising too many questions about the role of banks. While they stuck diligently to their given task their activities were adequately funded, but whenever their inquiries appeared to be wandering into areas The Organisation did not want examined, their supply of funds dwindled away. Consequently, the ideas they've come up with, while logically flawed, are nevertheless ideally suited to the needs of The Organisation. They meet the needs of Areho's democracy by providing the masses and their elected politicians with issues they can pointlessly argue about. Popular economics is, therefore, something we need to protect. We don't want it to be scrutinised too closely by methodical thinkers.'

Although his audience was clearly enjoying listening to stories it was familiar with - as devotees always do when listening to accounts of issues they enthuse about - Harold knew he had been talking for quite some time without a pause. He suggested the meeting should be briefly adjourned so that everyone could take a break. Several members took the opportunity to refresh their drinks, visit the toilets, or walk a while in the gardens.

Harold waited until everyone had returned to their seats before saying, 'Unlike popular economics, which, as I've been saying, was guided from its early beginnings by The Organisation, science in Areho has developed independently in a spontaneous and unfettered way. It has its origins in the activities of intelligent individuals endowed with high levels of curiosity. Perhaps inspired by common but inadequate explanations of observations seen in the skies at night, many developed new ideas about stars, planets, the Moon and the Sun. The world on which we live, they said, is a large sphere moving along a circular path around the Sun. It is one of several other spherical bodies, the planets, which also circulate around the Sun. While interesting, none of this was thought of as something The Organisation needed to be concerned about. The sky watchers claimed their ideas, unlike other explanations, accurately and logically accounted for the observable movements of the Moon, the stars and the planets. This claim, that their ideas were firmly anchored on observable facts, quickly became the prime feature of their methodology.

'That sound, reliable knowledge could only be gained by such an approach, by reliance on factual observations, became a widely accepted principle by many seekers of enlightenment. It soon became applied to questions other than ones found high up in the skies, to ones found closer to the ground, to ones of practical interest. By such methods, observable phenomena, such as the movements of small bodies on, or just above, the ground, gained credible explanations which previously had been absent or unsatisfactory. Scientists, as people involved in such inquiries became known, quickly found they could increase the number of observations they could make by purposefully arranging events they could observe. Such arranged observations, or experiments, greatly increased the range of their inquiries. They provided a firm foundation upon which a sizeable body of scientific knowledge has been built. Included are a number of applications, or related inventions, which we do need to be concerned about. I'll talk about these shortly, but first I want to say a few more words about science and scientists.

'Scientists, by means of observations and experiments, seek to gain an objective account of the natural world. Collectively, they form a fellowship united by a code of behaviour that requires them to follow strict rules of procedure. Three of the rules are particularly interesting. One is that clear and accurate accounts of their observations and experiments must be recorded and made accessible to other scientists so that, should they so wish, they will be able to reproduce their findings. Another is that any idea, or theory, suggested as an explanation for what is observed must be scrutinized by means of experiments designed to test its validity. To be valid, a theory must be able to predict what will happen in a related set of circumstances, and the scrutinizing experiments must be designed to test the prediction. If such experimentation is not able to show the predicted results then the theory must be revised or abandoned. A third rule is that theories, predictions, experiments and conclusions must be judged only on their objective merits, on their logicality and accuracy, not on the social status of the theorists or experimenters. We can now see certain clear distinctions between artistic knowledge and scientific knowledge.

A piece of artistic work is judged by human arbiters qualified by custom to give their opinions. This makes it very easy to manage the contents of artistic knowledge in our own interests. As I've just been saying, The Organisation is able to manipulate it with very little effort. It allows the masses to believe whatever they want to believe, provided it is not detrimental to our needs. By means of their own creative efforts, with very little guidance from us, the masses have constructed the values by which they live. They have created credible notions of justice, honour, righteousness, duty, patriotism and whatever else is appropriate for their contentment. We have allowed and encouraged such values to be fashioned because they satisfy our requirements. They make the masses manageable. Scientific knowledge is not so easy to control. As the three rules I've outlined show, scientists have refined their methods so that, as far as humanly possible, the natural world is the arbiter of their works. They ask nature to pass judgment on the quality of their work, not humans judged by other humans to be competent to give their opinions. This is contrary to the way we like things to be. Science might become very useful to us, but it might also become a threat. This presents The Organisation with a bit of a quandary. Science is something we need to keep a watchful eye on. Thankfully, scientific progress is now reaching a stage at which it becomes increasingly dependent on external funding, which, of course, we can control.

'We think science could become a threat because it promotes curiosity and investigation. Its existence creates a general awareness, without specific reference to science, that it is acceptable to ask sceptical questions. Because of its successes in providing convincing answers to many puzzling problems, science risks giving confidence to people who might query issues outside the fields in which its methods are appropriate, using ways of thinking that are not necessarily governed by its strict rules of procedure. Its explanation of the movements of stars and planets in particular has inspired faith in reason and a thirst for new knowledge. Consequently, it may well encourage astute individuals to question the values which keep the masses compliant. Many people regard such values as edicts that cannot be questioned. Some, if they think about them at all, consider them to be inborn principles given by nature. Most look upon them as essential constraints on behaviour, as vital regulators of good social conduct, and never think they can be questioned. This is how we like them to be regarded by the masses. They are convenient for our purposes, and it will not do for them to be scrutinised by self-styled truth-seekers inspired by developments in science.

'There are many ways such thinkers might approach their enquiries, but perhaps the most likely is that, without being aware of it, they will take from science's conventions the idea that people who guard and promote the rules of social behaviour should not necessarily be selected according to social status. This is very dangerous. If the values which regulate the masses can be questioned by anyone irrespective of age, sex, race, religion or social rank, and their ideas are to be considered only on their dispassionately judged logical merits, as in science, then it is likely that before long it will be asked, *who prospers from the way things are?* Exceptionally astute enquirers will then see that answers to the many questions their musings have awakened are to be found within popular economics. They will quickly see that economics is not scientific, as many of its advocates claim. It does propose theories, but if they are able to make predictions they do not do so with anything like the degree of accuracy demanded in the true sciences, and when it looks back to see how well its ideas account for events of the past it is found to be equally deficient. Diligent and intelligent thinkers, inspired by the general acceptance of sceptical thinking encouraged by the true sciences, will then look further into popular economics. Without too much effort, they will uncover many of its deficiencies. Amongst other issues, they will consider its claim that an individual's income is determined by his, or her, contribution to the economy. They will quickly see that such a claim is untenable. It is incompatible with the extremely wide divergence in the fortunes of the rich and the poor. They will see that it is not sensible to argue, as popular economics does, that the extremely wide distribution of incomes paid to employees mirrors the range of skills and abilities obtainable within the working population. It is simply not reasonable to maintain, by any rational measure of talent, that the worthiness for employment of one adult is very many hundreds times that of another. They will then undoubtedly ask how employees' talents are measured, particularly with regard to very highly paid executives, and will again be taken back to the question, *who prospers from the way things are?* We need to frustrate such thinking before it takes hold and gains momentum. It could easily steer shrewd thinkers towards a more credible explanation of the very wide gap between the wages of poorly-paid workers and the incomes of a relatively few extremely wealthy business executives.

'Although it may not be done exactly as I've suggested, we cannot risk heretical thinking, encouraged by the growing popularity of science, uncovering the illusions of reality we've let the masses believe. For the reasons I gave earlier, most will not believe *intrigue fantasists* who try to tell them the opinions they so firmly hold have been fashioned and fed to them by unseen influences. They will not allow their cherished illusions to be undermined. Even the few who are prepared to listen to the arguments will not accept them. Even if they are shown clear evidence, they will renounce it. However, with the growing popularity of logical thinking, encouraged by impressive achievements in science, we cannot rely on the number of people who will be influenced by such thinking being negligible. It is very unlikely their numbers will ever become large enough to seriously threaten our well-being, but if they become sufficient to spread serious doubts amongst a sizable portion of the population it may well give rise to bothersome civil disorder. Calling enthusiastic truth-seekers derogatory names has worked well in the past, but it might not be effective if their ideas gain too many followers. To forestall this possibility we need to effectively discourage logical thinking. We don't want people with enquiring minds awakening the masses. To put it succinctly, we need to counterbalance the undesirable influences of science. I'm going to suggest we inject into the public consciousness a stereotype of science and scientists designed to dampen the public's growing enthusiasm for their achievements and methods. But we'll need to do this without restricting science itself, for, as I'm now coming to, it is showing signs that it might become very useful.

'There are numerous scientific investigations currently in progress which may well lead to applications we'll find very useful, but I'm only going to talk about two of them as examples. One concerns efforts being made by engineers to construct machines that will use pressurised steam to produce motive power. They hope to eventually build steam powered engines able to drive industrial equipment or propel vehicles with considerable loads along suitable tracks. Trial steam engines, or locomotives, have been able to demonstrate the possibility of long convoys, or trains, of heavily laden wagons being pulled large distances on steel rails.

Trial steam engines were able to demonstrate the possibility of long convoys of heavily laden wagons being pulled large distances on steel rails.

'Although such engineering projects are not strictly scientific, they have aroused the attention of scientists interested in how such engines might be made more effective. They see steam engines as machines that convert energy stored in coal into mechanical energy, and want to know if there is a theoretical limit to the efficiency of the conversion, and how engines should be designed in order to achieve the greatest possible efficiency. We are confident that engineers and scientists working together will soon be able to construct steam powered vehicles able to quickly and efficiently transport very large loads of both people and goods over very large distances, and we've taken steps to ensure their efforts are adequately funded. The benefits of such railway transportation systems here in Areho and the rest of the CU are clear, but looking ahead we see them as being invaluable in our post-war development of Yevad and the other countries on the other side of the Mighty Ocean. I'll say more about this later, but first I want to say a few words about another scientific investigation currently attracting The Organisation's interest and funding. It involves experiments with magnets and metal wires.

It was thought that when wireless equipment had been fully developed it would be possible to transmit messages over very large distances.

'As most people know, certain solid materials are able to attract nearby small objects after being rubbed by dry cloth. The phenomenon of lightning, scientists have found, is closely related. They gave the name *electricity* to whatever is responsible and decided it was something they wanted to investigate. By conducting experiments using chemical solutions and metals able to produce electricity, they found it is something that is able to flow in metal wires and in doing so is able to produce some interesting effects. One property they were able to observe is the production of magnetic effects. This aroused considerable attention. Scientists wanted to know more. They set about finding all they could about electricity and magnetism and in doing so discovered several effects which promise to lead to very useful applications, including the production of light and motive power. Although they are extremely important, I'll not say anything more about them for I want to concentrate on an application of electricity and magnetism, if achievable, we think will have a great influence on The Organisation's security. It's in the field of communications. Scientists are already able to cause spoken messages to be transmitted back and forth between speakers and listeners along metal wires, but of even greater interest is the possibility of such messages being sent without the need for transmission wires. It is thought that, when the necessary equipment has been developed, messages will be able to travel through the air for very large distances, carried by electrical and magnetic ripples known as electromagnetic waves, at speeds so fast that they will be received at virtually the same time as they are transmitted.

'When this wireless equipment becomes operational, as I've been assured it will, I don't need to tell you how important it will be for The Organisation. Our armed forces will find the ability to instantly send and receive messages over very large distances invaluable, but of even greater benefit will be the advantage it will give to our ability to control the masses. Wireless apparatus will greatly enhance our ability to develop and secure popular beliefs at a time when, in all probability, they will be under threat. Scientists working on the project tell us that, when the system has been fully developed, they expect most households will be able to own inexpensive wireless receivers. They say listeners will not only be able to hear speech, they will also be able to enjoy listening to music. Wireless equipment, they tell us, will enable singing voices to be heard in homes throughout the kingdom. We'll need to be ready to take advantage of these amazing developments. They hold many promises. Intermingled with carefully crafted propaganda masquerading as news, home entertainments will reduce the risk of the masses being influenced by heretical thinkers. People will be distracted from the rambling arguments of *intrigue fantasists* by easily available amusements. Reporting progress of sporting events as they are happening by charismatic and enthusiastic commentators will, we think, be highly effective in distracting large sections of the masses away from unsettling questions about their living conditions.

'Clearly, we'll need to be fully in control of wireless provision from the moment of its inauguration. We have very good control of the print media, but it's likely we'll need to have even greater control of wireless for it will reach a very large proportion of the masses. Not all of them are able to read, and those that can do not always read what we want them to. They are the ones we think will be most susceptible to disruptive ideas promoted by heretical thinkers. Wireless will counter this. In addition to distracting entertainments, it will give them undemanding access to the information we will want them to hear, information with apparent official backing telling them what to believe, and warning them not to believe false stories of deception and conspiracy.

'There are problems that might arise from the introduction of wireless equipment, but they all seem to be manageable, with one possible exception: easily available transmitting apparatus.

If it becomes possible for messages to be broadcast far and wide, to be heard by any receptive listeners with inexpensive receivers, claims of government dishonesty will become very difficult to curb.

'If it ever becomes possible for almost anyone, including *intrigue fantasists*, to broadcast their heretical views, it might become difficult to uphold the official narratives we use to control the masses. It might undermine the comforting illusions we've promoted. However, scientists working on the wireless project tell us that the possibility of easily available, cheap transmitting equipment is a long way off. So we have plenty of time to think about how we might deal with the problem.

'Steam engines and wireless broadcasting are just two of the science and engineering projects we are currently encouraging. There are others, and they are all worthy of our funding. Yet, as I've tried to point out, the growing public appreciation of science brings unwanted consequences. It encourages widespread logical thinking and the associated danger of popular heresy. This risk could possibly get out of hand, and I'm going to suggest some ways by which it might be alleviated. One is to foster a widespread image of scientists as specialists who are very good at what they do, but are very bad at doing other things. In particular, we want the general public to see scientists as experts in narrow fields of study who, by virtue of their extreme specialisim, are rendered incompetent to make sound judgements outside the domains of science. Above all, we want scientists to be seen as naïve bumblers in matters of morals, politics and justice.

'In addition to our endeavours to propagate this stereotype, we'll need to focus our attention on schools and universities. Our aim here will be to create and spread an awareness of arts subjects as being superior to science. We'll promote prominent artistic achievements as high points of human culture and sophistication. We'll want pupils and students to see knowledge and appreciation of artistic creations as being significantly more worthy of admiration than familiarity with scientific issues. We'll know our efforts have been successful when supposedly well-educated individuals are able to flaunt their abilities to express esoteric literary quotations with pride, especially if their utterances are given in foreign languages, and yet feel no shame in their lack of knowledge of basic scientific ideas. Indeed, some might even use their scientific ignorance as badges of superiority. We can expect such individuals to see science students as being culturally deficient, boringly studious, socially inept and deserving of being referred to by derogatory names.

'Concurrently, we'll seek to create social conditions in which the public will clamour for schools to direct increased attention to educating pupils to have a better appreciation of their social responsibilities. With our guidance, educational authorities will respond by introducing subjects that will reduce the time pupils spend on mathematics and science. I'll have more to say about suitable subjects that might be added to the national curricula later. They will be intended to support our need for widespread ignorance and illogicality. We certainly don't want too many students who are able to think for themselves. There's no need to think such efforts will jeopardise our goal of benefiting from scientific developments by discouraging capable scholars from studying science. Evidence suggests that talented young people with an aptitude and interest in science and mathematics will choose to study them regardless of how they are regarded by other students. I'll come back to this in a short while.

'Now, I want to talk about a few issues James and I discussed at some length, issues James told me had been brought to his attention by Jeremy's probing questions. Fully appreciating how interest on bank loans necessitates exponential growth of the supply of money, Jeremy, well aware of the amazing consequences of exponential growth, repeatedly asked: *when will it end?* He realised that the economic system we all benefit from cannot keep on growing indefinitely. It might be thought that *'the end'* Jeremy asked about will happen at some time well into the future, as James reassured him it would, but it might occur sooner than we anticipate. The very nature of exponential growth means that, if things are left as they are, the amount of money in existence will reach astronomical levels in the not-too-distant future. It might well become a problem that will need to be addressed during our lifetimes; one that, if ignored, could easily lead to total economic collapse. It is clearly something we need to consider, and I'm going to suggest one or two ideas you might like to discuss. They depend largely on successful results in Yevad and the other countries across the Mighty Ocean.

'We've given a lot of thought towards governing Yevad after we've taken control there. It would be very foolish not to do so. Our aim, we think, should be to develop Yevad as an ideal society designed to impress its neighbours; a shining example of democracy, prosperity and freedom. We expect to be seen as saviours in Yevad, and we'll want people in nearby countries to see us in the same way.

'With Yevad demonstrating how beneficial our economic methods can be, we expect people in neighbouring countries will become interested. Acting as Yevad's governors, we'll invite them to visit as tourists, intending them to return home with very favourable views of their transformed neighbour. If this plan is successful, and I can see no reason why it might not be, we can expect the governments of Yevad's neighbouring countries to want to do business with us. It should then be very easy to persuade them to borrow in order to develop their lands. We intend railways to be one of the outstanding features of our plans for Yevad. We expect steam engines and associated equipment will become fully operational in Arcue soon after the hostilities in Yevad have ended. We'll then be able to export fully-developed railway equipment as we re-shape the war-torn country. Just as our canal and road building schemes brought business and huge profits as we expanded into the countries of the CU, likewise we expect railways will enable us to reap similar benefits as we bring Yevad into our economic orbit. Railways, paid for using money borrowed from us, will bring resources intended for export to us to Yevad's harbours, and take goods we'll want to sell deep into its interior. Railways, and all the other developments we'll be able to introduce, will transform Yevad into a model of economic success, a blazoned advertisement of our financial and industrial skills. Neighbouring countries will want what Yevad has. They will want railways and all the benefits of imports and exports they'll bring, and, in order to have them, they will need loans.

'Of course, we'll require them to absorb our ways before agreeing to let them borrow. We'll try to avoid infringing national customs and traditions as far as possible, but we will need them to incorporate laws, masquerading as international laws but effectively enforceable by us, regarding property, labour relations, debt obligations and all the other measures necessary for the well-being of business. Tough laws protecting intellectual assets will be particularly important, for it will not do for copies of our steam engines, or of any of our manufactured goods, being made by local businesses. Clearly, for these requirements to be effective, it will be essential that we have full operational control of their legislatures and judiciaries, and this, essentially, will require democracy and associated propaganda.

'It is, of course, possible that some countries, irrespective of Yevad's splendid example, will not want to take our offer of development loans. They might find our conditions too demanding, or they might have other reasons, possibly religious, for not wanting to borrow. It will then be necessary to exert a measure of persuasion. It's to be expected we'll easily gain sufficient influence in neighbouring countries to be able to apply trading restrictions on uncooperative governments, but if economic sanctions are ineffective then, regretfully, stubborn heads of state will have to happen upon unfortunate fatal accidents. Such accidents will need to be sufficiently theatrical to send appropriate messages to other non-compliant national leaders. The deranged lone gunman story is always popular, and the message it will send to dissident heads of state will be unmistakable. If, however, economic warfare and assassinations fail, as a last resort complete regime changes will be needed in uncooperative countries. It should not be necessary to use bandits from wild regions to initiate civil wars, as we planned for Yevad. We expect propaganda, playing on Yevad's ostentatious prosperity, will be able to generate sufficient national discontentment to provoke enough local hotheads - covertly supplied with suitable weaponry and other enticements - to create the required mayhem.

'However, just in case local would-be insurgents might need a little guidance and encouragement, we suggest sending suitable Esehems, acting as civilian refugees from Yevad, to settle with their families in the countries we plan to take over. Until their services are required they will live uneventful but well provided lives. They will be trained and equipped to assist local rebels, whenever the need arises, to do whatever is needed to replace uncooperative governments with compliant ones. In addition, ex-Esehem fighters, living in their wild regions, will be trained, equipped and kept prepared to be taken, perhaps by railways, to wherever their abilities might be needed to assist local rebels with problems in bringing their civil wars to successful conclusions. We don't think there'll be any difficulties in recruiting willing volunteers for this role, for the prospects of belonging to a band of cold-blooded mercenaries is usually appealing to adventure-starved feral young men, especially disaffected ones with recent experiences of civil warfare. Moreover, as our plans for the continent's interior are unfolding, we propose sending ships, based in Yevad, to explore its coastline. Their aim will be to determine the extent of the continent and to discover if any unknown lands exist beyond its far side. If any other countries or continents are found they will need to be incorporated into our overall scheme, for our plans necessarily need to embrace the whole world.

'As you will appreciate, the proposed sequence of events I've just described is highly speculative. We'll need to be adaptable in how we handle each successive situation, and, of course, if necessary, other means of persuasion will be available. However, no matter how we need to accommodate and adjust to circumstances as our plans unfold, our overall aim will remain unchanged. It will be to transform every country of the huge continent on the other side of the Mighty Ocean, and wherever else they might be found, into propaganda-controlled democracies, each wedded to popular economics and widespread consumerism. If we are successful, as I'm confident we will be, in the not-too-distant future every government and large business corporation outside The Organisation's direct control will be deeply in debt. When this has been achieved, we can take steps to ensure they become unable to service their loans. We'll need to be flexible according to circumstances in how we achieve this, but possibilities will be along such lines as engineering global shortages of vital resources, such as coal, water or corn, and using the resulting price increases as a pretence to raise interest rates. If this is done expediently, governments will become unable to repay their loans or to assist local companies facing insolvency. They will then have to negotiate new agreements. In all such circumstances, our ultimate aim will be to secure complete ownership rights to their natural resources according to laws introduced and administered by us. Bringing the scheme to fruition might take some time, and might have to be passed on to our successors, but by following such measures The Organisation can expect to eventually gain possession of the lands and resources of each and every country of the world. The planet will then be ours.

'The plan I've suggested is sketchy and provisional. I hope you'll discuss it and try to come up with suitable changes, but as you do so I ask you to keep in mind that the economic system The Organisation's founders gave birth to long ago cannot go on indefinitely. Eventually, its dependence on the exponential growth of fiat money will make its end inevitable. After lengthy discussions, James, myself and senior members of The Institute concluded that as the end approaches only two possibilities will be available to The Organisation: to go for world domination as I've suggested, or to abandon the economic system altogether. We could see no way in which members could retain their wealth and privileges if the second option is selected; accordingly the first option will be the only one The Organisation will be able to realistically choose. We'll be able to bring the economic system to a convenient end once we have total control of every country of the world. Remember, our forebears fashioned the system in order to gain wealth, privilege and power. When they found how easy it was to create money they probably regarded possession of money as a form of wealth, but they would have soon realised money was nothing more than a means by which they could attain their real ambitions. It was the key to their possession of privilege, power and tangible wealth. When The Organisation owns the whole world there will be nothing more to possess. There will no longer be any need for money as we now understand it.

'How The Organisation will govern the new world system will need to be discussed in detail as the final days of the fiat money system draws near. However, as the end approaches it's probable that we'll simply reduce, and then stop, lending. Civil disorder would then seem likely. As the economic system grinds to a halt, legal measures will be taken to persuade borrowers to pay-off their debts with the result that more and more money will go out of existence. This, of course, is simple speculation. It's impossible to say what will happen when money goes out of circulation; although we can be certain that the needs of our membership will be safeguarded. Nevertheless, once transition difficulties have been handled, we can expect that a few features of the new arrangement will be indispensable. One will be an unambiguous and wide distinction between The Organisation's membership and the masses. There will no longer be any need for individuals or families of intermediate rank. They are essential players in the illusions of democracy and economic righteousness, but as these pretences become unnecessary they will be phased out. All that will be needed will be a governing body able to manage the affairs of The Organisation, and a suitable one already exists. We are members of an elite inner circle of The Organisation, and have all been secretly selected by existing members because of our exceptional abilities and demonstrated loyalty to its values. Accordingly, we, or our successors, will govern The Organisation when it rules the planet; we will become an elite, exclusive section of the bureaucracy in control of the world and all it contains.

'As for the question of money, some form of it will be needed by members. Individual members and their families will own portions of the world in the form of estates, palaces and desirable artefacts, and an acceptable commodity of durable value to act as a means of exchange will be needed whenever possessions change hands. Although it's not possible to predict the future, it seems likely that gold will be the most convenient choice. A separate currency will be required for the masses, although it's to be expected that their needs will be rudimentary. Some will be needed as servants and labourers in mansions, estates and regions set aside for the enjoyments of Organisation members, and, of course, young desirable females and males for personal services will be required. As for the rest, they will be superfluous. They will have to be excluded from places reserved for members. We, or our successors, will have to determine what measures, if any, will be needed for their subsistence.'

Harold thought it wise to pause for a while, to allow his audience to grasp and exchange comments about the things he'd been saying. When he sensed that everyone was ready to listen he went on with his speech. 'I know it's enjoyable talking about how things will be when our ambitions have been realized, but we must now return to issues we'll need to face before they can be fulfilled. James told me about an interesting talk he'd had with Jeremy about the public narrative we'll need to sustain during the Yevad War. Jeremy thought we might have difficulties in maintaining its credibility if the War, as expected, proves to be prolonged. James reassured him they would not be ones we could not handle. I agree with James' assessment, but the concerns Jeremy expressed might not be so easily allayed when we are busy taking control of every country of the world. 'As we go about intervening in the internal affairs of country after country we must expect inconsistencies in the stories we tell the public to become increasingly difficult to avoid. Intrigue fantasists will notice them, and their cries of deception and foul play will gain added credence whenever our intrusions become chaotic and violent. Moreover, the emergence of railways will mean we'll not be able to depend on them being ignored or dismissed by the masses. The new transportation system will make it increasingly difficult to keep stories of deception and pretext from reaching the general public. When fully operational, railways will take perceptive individuals with alarming accounts of government iniquity from city to city and from town to town. It will no longer be possible to prevent such tales from spreading as we've always been able to. Also, when fully developed, long distance communications by means of fixed electrical wires will add to the difficulties. Trying to prevent the spread of alarmists' accounts of corruption by such means will, in all probability, increase the threat they pose.

'Furthermore, the inevitable development of low-cost wireless transmitters will greatly amplify the undesirable effects of the other innovations. When it's possible for messages to be broadcast far and wide, to be heard by any receptive listeners with inexpensive receivers, claims of government dishonesty will become very difficult to curb. Wireless communications will reach a sizeable audience, and attempts to block or outlaw them will be almost impossible without adding to the difficulties by clearly violating the promise of free speech given when democracy was introduced. Moreover, as stories of official deceitfulness gain credibility, as they surely will, astute thinkers will be able to realize that the government does not act alone. They will see that unseen actors must be influencing its decision making. Despite our efforts to keep our meetings secret, small but vigilant sections of the masses, without knowing our purpose, have long been aware that they occur. When they are able to perceive that the government acts outside their interests, at the behest of others who choose to remain concealed, they will easily deduce the involvement of our meetings. Our security and well-being will be endangered if we ignore this possibility. If intrigue fantasists attract too many supporters, as it seems they will do if we do nothing to counter their contentions, our overseas and domestic operations will be seriously jeopardised. Moreover, if they gain a sizable following, we must consider the possibility of exceptionally astute individuals amongst them being able to realize that the economic system must eventually come to an end. Once they are able to grasp that bank loans larger than ones taken out earlier must keep on being borrowed to enable ones taken out earlier to be repaid with interest, they will be able to work out that that the quantity of money thereby created must increase exponentially. Irrefutable logic will then enable them to conclude, as we do, that any economic system based on such a financial scheme must eventually come to an end. Since they will be fully aware that the government's concealed quest for world domination is being orchestrated by veiled influences, they will easily conclude that those behind the influences will be in control of the world when the economic system comes to an end, and will not be inclined to giving much consideration to the welfare of the masses. In view of these very real threatening possibilities, we need to ask, *what must be done?*

'I think we need to divide our approach to the problem into two parts: one directed at the masses and the other at intrigue fantasists. With regard to the masses, we've already talked about how we can seek to counter the growing popularity of logical thinking inspired by the remarkable achievements of science. But in view of the difficulties we are likely to encounter as amazing developments in mass communications coincide with our drive for world domination, we'll need to take far more effective measures to curtail the masses' enthusiasm for rational thinking. Widespread eagerness for common sense is the last thing we'll want. We'll need misleading distractions, ones that will divide the masses and simultaneously restrict the extent of their imaginations. We'll need to fill their heads with distracting thoughts. Large sections are very susceptible to emotive concerns that override their weak powers of logical thought. By looking out for opportunities, we'll be able to exploit this. Public issues able to arouse powerful emotional responses occur from time to time, and in some individuals they give rise to deep-seated passions. However, if no suitable concerns arise we'll get the media to invent one or two. With its help, we'll be able to stealthily inject a greatly exaggerated version of whatever the concerns are about into the public's consciousness, with a marked emphasis on the negative role of those who do not empathize with people who are passionately involved. With appropriate misinformation, we'll be able to generate an ongoing public debate with opposing sides.

'Acting on our directions, the media will promote advocates of one side of the dispute, giving them widespread sympathetic coverage, while suppressing and belittling their opponents. If the plan is successful, some well endorsed and ardently concerned individuals will become outraged by the views of their repressed rivals. They'll become so enraged by the thought of being opposed they'll organise public protests, or even engage in more dramatic communal remonstrations. Our furtive efforts will have caused a one-sided public controversy. Only a minority will be seriously involved, but very few will be unaware of what is happening and most will occasionally ask themselves if they should be concerned. Logical thinking, as inspired by science, will be of little relevance as they ask such questions. With well promoted publications, and occasional spectacular events, we should be able to ensure the dispute is prolonged for however long is required to divert the masses from being too concerned about wars on the other side of the Mighty Ocean. We will have successfully divided and distracted many individuals, and thereby limited the extent of their interests.

'If our plans succeed as intended we will have created a situation in which certain words, phrases or arguments will be regarded as being far too offensive to use. The assurance of free speech will then have to be modified or discarded, for we will have created a situation in which the right not to be offended will be considered to be more important. Voicing political views considered odious by sensitive individuals or groups will have to be suppressed, or even outlawed, and, paradoxically, anyone holding such views will be called demeaning and sneering names. Making jokes about politically sensitive issues will become repugnant, perhaps even prohibited by law. We will have created a state of political confusion and anger in which sensitivity to being offended will be central.

'Also, just as we did for the Yevad project, we'll make fear, linked in some way to the controversies, a vital element of our propaganda. We'll promote, without objective evidence, the idea that foreign terrorists, finding the new obsessions unacceptable, intend to attack targets within Areho. Introducing a measure of fear will be essential for nothing is more effective in disordering rational thought. To make the proposed threats seem real we'll probably need to stage occasional atrocities, and, as always in such operations, official statements will be needed to identify the purported culprits within a day or two of each event. Longer periods allow astute members of the public to come up with their own ideas of who, or what, might be responsible, and once such ideas have been formed they are not easily discarded. Early official announcements ward off such difficulties.

'Earlier, without specifying subjects that could be introduced, I mentioned the need for school curricula to be modified in order to reduce the time children spend studying maths and science. In the rousing atmosphere of strong and disagreeing views, with some opinions banned by law, we'll be able to consider new subjects for schools to teach. When, as intended, the raging public controversies have developed into a state in which fervent enthusiasts predominate, and their opponents are largely silenced, we'll be able to direct schools to teach related subjects with the aim of equipping pupils to appreciate popular disputes. If children and their teachers have their heads filled with such stuff they'll have little time for logical thinking. Outside classrooms the results of our efforts will spread to the general public, seriously curtailing the reasoning abilities of gullible individuals. It will blend in with all the other mind numbing stories we'll be able to use to shape the public's outlook.

'The measures I've suggested will easily distract politically minded sections of the masses away from matters we'll not want them to be concerned with, but dealing with intrigue fantasists will not be so straightforward. If their contentions seem to be attracting too many followers we'll need to befuddle and dishonour them, and the way to do this will be to give them misleading information. Searching for signs of government dishonesty is something they clearly find captivating, so the best way to discredit them will be to plant fake evidence. If the bait is seemingly concealed, as if it was never expected that it would be found, and it suggests there's an astounding conspiracy the government wants suppressed, they'll not be able to resist. I think we have something suitable.

'Soon after scientists enthralled the public with their explanations of observations seen in the skies at night, many storytellers started writing fantasy tales about strange creatures living on other planets. Such stories attracted many readers. The thought of intelligent beings living and conducting their affairs on other worlds seems to be fascinating to many people. This gives us a highly effective way of undermining the credibility of intrigue fantasists. By promoting countless fictional stories of human-like beings from distant planets, many involving interactions with people on Earth, we'll generate a widespread popular interest in visitors from other worlds. If we do this effectively, gullible individuals will start to wonder if it could really happen. Some will even want it to happen. They'll not believe it's just the basis of yet more fairy tales. If, in the throes of this contrived public fascination with visitors from outer space, with the media's compliance, we plant fake evidence showing they had already arrived, with a hint of concealed government involvement, intrigue fantasists will become fascinated. They'll not be able to ignore it. To many it will seem like the high point of all their efforts to uncover official corruption. But not all of them will be deceived. Despite our efforts to make it seem genuine, fantasists with sufficient intelligence will see that the planted evidence is flawed. However, for our purposes, enough will believe the evidence is authentic and make accounts of visitors from outer space, and the government's concealment of their arrival, part of the stories they try to persuade people to take seriously. Individuals whose intellectual faculties have been seriously impaired by our educational policies will believe tales of creatures from outer space acting in cahoots with the government. However, despite our efforts to seriously stunt the public's intellectual abilities, most will see such stories as evidence of the stupidity of intrigue fantasists. This will be the result we'll be wanting. It will discredit people who try to spread stories of conspiracies and high level deceitfulness. All the media's efforts to portray them as crazy fools with overactive imaginations will be justified.

'There's another way in which we'll be able to discredit intrigue fantasists, one we'll be able to blend in with the space visitor stories. A few dedicated intrigue fantasists seem to know when we plan to hold our meetings. They are informed by sympathetic locals who keep an eye on roads leading to the various venues we use for our conferences. Uncommon numbers of carriages travelling to one or other of our mansions reveals our intention of holding a meeting. We know this because we have been able to secretly infiltrate a few of the local groups of sympathisers. When informed that it seems we are planning to hold a conference, fantasists arrive, watch the roads carefully, and make notes of who arrives and leaves. We've tried to stop them from doing this, but abandoned the effort when we realised it was virtually impossible and that they could do no harm with the information they collect. However, from notes collected at various venues, they have been able to see the same individuals, often with their wives, attending many of our meetings. From this they have been able to discern that there is a distinct group of families

- our families - involved in whatever it is our meetings are for. This is not surprising, for, as you all know, from its early beginnings The Organisation has discouraged members from marrying outsiders. The Organisation is essentially an alliance of families banded together to further our mutual interests. We all know this, but to a few intrigue fantasists with overactive imaginations, and seemingly unquenchable thirsts for uncovering obscure conspiracies, the existence of a group of secretive families is vitally important. To them, it confirms that we must be plotting something very sinister, something profoundly evil, something they need to disclose. In the main they content themselves with trying to uncover the nature of this imagined wicked plot, but within their ranks there is a small section with very absurd beliefs.

'Since The Organisation's families have all been found to be linked together by marriage, this bizarre splinter group, for some totally unknown reason, has concluded that we must belong to a sub-species that exists apart from the rest of humanity. I know it sounds incredible, but it's what a small clique of intrigue fantasists firmly believe. Unbelievable as it may seem, we'll nevertheless be able to use it to our advantage. By exploiting the stupidity of this small group we'll be able to discredit intrigue fantasists in general. By being associated with a small clique of fantasists that are genuinely crazy, they will all be made to look ridiculous. Intelligent, methodical investigators who could seriously disturb our plans, people who know the government is being manipulated by secret influences and seek to find out how and why it is being done, will be thoroughly discredited by being grouped together with a coterie of misguided fools. All we'll need to do is to plant fake evidence that will apparently support the crazy clique's weird suppositions. When it's found, excited by the discovery, the clique will become determined to promote their bizarre theories, and in doing so they'll disrupt, discredit and confuse all conspiracy researchers.

'The sort of false evidence we'll need to plant is something we can be thinking about. Perhaps we'll be able to place an undercover intruder within the clique purporting to have irrefutable confirmation of their beliefs. But perhaps we'll be able to do even better than that. Gullible fantasists will be fascinated if archaeologists claim strange buried artefacts they've found show signs of having been produced long ago by visitors from another world. Fantasists attracted to the idea that we are not normal human beings will be delighted if the well-paid, dutiful archaeologists also claim the intriguing articles show clear indications of intimate interactions between their extraterrestrial owners and ancient humans. They'll readily come to the conclusion that our ancestors' fraternisation with prehistoric space visitors fully accounts for our supposed biological divergence from the rest of humanity.

'To make the deception seem credible we'll need to ensure that little, if any, of the story is told to the public. With our unseen support and encouragement, the archaeologists entrusted to make the claims will publish a book about their incredible discoveries. This will be essential to inform intrigue fantasists of their assertions and to make them believable, for it would be very suspicious if no such publication was made after such an astonishing find. Intrigue fantasists would sense that something was amiss. Newspapers reports, with our guidance, will cover the story with a generous helping of scepticism. They will claim the archaeologists' interpretations of the signs on the artefacts could be wrong, for there could be other, equally possible, but far less incredible, explanations. As for the government, in response to questions, it will announce that its policy is not to comment on unconfirmed speculations. Other than these sceptical and dismissive announcements, very little more will be said publically about the unusual articles found deep in the ground. Allegedly to prevent unwanted speculation, the artefacts will be withheld from unrestricted viewing and locked away in some undisclosed location. The general public will quickly lose interest, for they will be used to archaeologists digging up relics of ancient times. But to intrigue fantasists, the government's and media's scant and indifferent treatment of such an amazing occurrence will suggest that information is being withheld. To many of them it will reinforce their beliefs about secret government dishonesty. It will confirm that something truly incredible has been uncovered, something they will have to reveal to the public. They will not know, and will deny it if it is suggested, that the whole story of visitors from space, and their involvement with the biological and political development of humans here on Earth, had been fabricated by us to undermine the efforts of intelligent researchers who could seriously disrupt our activities.

'By making intrigue fantasists in general seem ridiculous, we will have effectively stymied their efforts to convince the general public that there are things it should know. Any members of the public who become sufficiently interested in what intrigue fantasists have to say will want to learn more about them, but when they find they include people who believe beings from outer space have been interfering in the affairs of humans here on Earth they will conclude the news media is correct in what it says about them, that they are seriously deluded idiots with overactive imaginations. Determined, intelligent researchers will not then be taken seriously. They'll be unable to disrupt the affairs of The Organisation. They'll not become nuisances we'll need to be concerned about.

'Gentlemen, I've talked for longer than I intended so I'll finish now by simply reminding you that we cannot be certain of how the future will unfold. We can only consider the problems we might encounter as we move closer to our final goal. I've tried to suggest a few ideas we can be thinking about as we look beyond our conquest of Yevad. As we move inevitably closer to world domination, keeping the masses distracted and intrigue fantasists discredited will become increasingly difficult. Expected developments in wireless transmission equipment will make it easy for fantasists to exchange information, and controlling this without blatantly tearing away the remnants of the free speech illusion will not be easy. We're still a long way from having to deal with such problems, but it's not too early to start thinking about them. Perhaps as we consider the difficulties ahead, new ways of keeping the masses uptight about overblown issues, and intrigue fantasists discredited so their assertions will be ignored, will become apparent. These are questions we can all be thinking about. That's about all I have to say right now. I understand James' staff have prepared a magnificent spread for you in the main dinning hall. So I thank you for your attention, knowing you'll mull over and discuss the issues I've put before you as you continue enjoying James' legendary hospitality.'

Chapter Fifteen

Newspaper sales soared when one of the ships returned with news of civil war in Yevad. As intended, they provided readers with believable accounts of atrocities committed by wicked rebels previously reported as the work of Yevadians. They made it abundantly clear that all the terrorist outrages, including the assassination of King Thomas IV, had been committed by an insurgent band known as Esehems who were opposed to the legitimate, peace-loving, Yevadian government. Tensions had been building up as a result of Esehem terrorism and finally the country had been plunged into civil war. No explanation was given for why King Thomas had been assassinated. The question was overlooked. The Prime Minister, on behalf of the government, expressed his dismay, offered his support for the people of Yevad and condemned the rebels. King James declared his deep shock on hearing the news and added his sincere wishes that the difficulties would soon be resolved peacefully. No military action was proposed, but in view of the supposed continuing threat of Esehem atrocities in Areho, the armed forces were called to a heightened state of alert.

Fighting started in Yevad when four Yevadian soldiers were ambushed and killed by a squad of Esehem fighters hiding in thick undergrowth.

The returning ship's captain, reporting directly to the inner circle of The Organisation, described the war as proceeding exactly as planned. Action started when four Yevadian soldiers, on patrol in peace-time recreational uniforms, were ambushed and killed by a squad of Esehem fighters hiding in thick undergrowth. Thereafter, sustained by weapons covertly supplied in carefully considered measures to the Esehems, the war proceeded at a steady pace with neither side gaining advantages. As intended, the killing and destruction was relentless but indecisive. Having delivered his message, the captain returned to his ship. It was being prepared for a return voyage to the war-zone with fresh supplies of guns and ammunition.

Using the new field guns, the Esehem rebels attacked Yevadian border fortifications.

The war was unremitting. Supplies of weapons, provisions and ammunition to the Esehems were increased if they showed signs of being war-weary, and decreased if the Yevadians seemed to be suffering from the same difficulty. In this way Areho's Special Forces, without being directly involved in the fighting, furnished the war with the means and inducements it needed for its continuation. Slowly, bit-by-bit, Yevad's civilisation was dismantled and destroyed. A steady succession of fast ships sailing back and forth across the Mighty Ocean took news of the conflict to Areho and the requirements of warfare to Yevad. Eventually, after more than three years of brutal fighting, news reports indicated that the war was waning. Both sides were noticeably weakening, and no changes in the supply of weaponry were able to influence it. In Areho, without publicity, troops started to assemble in Arcue's naval dockyards. When given orders, unseen by onlookers, they started to go aboard awaiting ships.

Unseen by onlookers, troops started to go aboard awaiting ships.

The same day, when it was nearly dusk, explosions occurred in Arcue Cathedral's towers. Far from the building two men dressed in garments characteristic of the Esehems were found running away. They were arrested. Soon furious flames could be seen coming out of the towers' windows. People gathered around to gaze at the spectacle. After a while the flames subsided and thick black smoke could be seen issuing in their place. At first it seemed the fires were burning themselves out, but after a while it became clear they were spreading from the towers to all parts of the building. Suddenly a huge explosion, far more powerful than the earlier detonations, occurred from deep inside the Cathedral. Subsequent smaller explosions caused the two weakened towers to collapse, and a short while later the building was destroyed totally when the rest of its structure crumpled. When smoke and flames had cleared all that could be seen was a smouldering pile of rubble surrounded by the bodies of onlookers who had been killed or injured by flying pieces of masonry. People nearby, lucky enough to have survived the almighty blast, screamed in shock and horror as dreadfully maimed casualties around them cried out in pain. Their anguish became amplified as they looked upon the debris that had once been their cherished Cathedral, the sacred focus of their hallowed spirituality.

Two men dressed in garments characteristic of the Esehems were
found running away from the burning Cathedral.

The following morning the front pages of all leading newspapers showed dramatic pictures of the Cathedral, before and after its final moments, topped by headlines that ranged from *Terrorists Dead* to *Bombers Resisted Arrest*. Columns below reported that the two men who had been arrested soon after the first explosions had attempted to escape from custody and had been shot when they'd refused to stop. Lengthy accounts of the supposed exploits of the two men were supplemented by emotional accounts of the old King's assassination and reviews of previous articles about shocking atrocities attributed to the terrorists. Only one journalist questioned, in a half-hearted manner, why it had been necessary to use seventeen bullets, all fired within the confined interior of the police station, to halt the would-be fugitives. None reported that both men had strenuously denied having anything to do with explosions and each had stated that they had been paid to pose beside the Cathedral wearing fancy costumes so that pictures of them could be used in advertisements.

As intended, the public was enraged. People were left in no doubt that the Cathedral, a revered symbol of their sacred traditions, had been wilfully destroyed by evil Esehems. Newspapers stressed that the destruction of the Cathedral, along with other recent terrorist incidents, including the old King's assassination, was clear evidence that the Esehems intended to bring their campaign of evil to Areho. No reasons were given as to why they wanted to do this, but people believed it. Many voices cried out for war. The Prime Minister and the King both gave their support for a military expedition to Yevad to provide humanitarian aid to the terrorized people of Yevad. The following day, amidst a blaze of publicity, ceremony and waving crowds, a fleet of ships filled to capacity with weapons and heavily armed troops headed out to the Mighty Ocean.

Thick black smoke could be seen issuing from the Cathedral's towers.

Huge crowds gathered in the following days to gaze at the wreckage of the Cathedral. Cordons had been erected to keep them from getting too close. Soon after daybreak they started to assemble, many with flowers to toss to the still smoking remains of the once-revered building. Feelings of deep sorrow mingled with intense anger. It was in such a crowd that a small boy stood with his father.

'Why did it blow-up?' the boy asked.

'Because of the fire,' his father replied.

But the boy was not at ease with his father's answer. He had heard nothing about the two men supposedly from the distant lands and only considered what his eyes could see. He looked at his father and said, 'But there were only wooden pews inside. They couldn't have caused the whole Cathedral to explode. Why didn't they just burn out?'

Suddenly a huge explosion, far more powerful than the earlier detonations, occurred from deep inside the building.

People around overheard. Several whispered the boy's questions to others who had not been able to hear. The crowd became hushed, listening for the father's answer. Feeling uncomfortable, aware of the attention his son had attracted, the father turned to the boy and firmly said, 'Don't ask silly questions!'

Knowing that uncomfortable feelings had caused him to react so sternly, and that his son would resume wanting answers when he'd recovered from the unexpected and unpleasant surprise of being told his questions were silly, the father took the child's hand and walked him away from the watchful eyes and ears of the people around. The eavesdroppers were left whispering. Many, their minds filled with rage and sorrow, were unable to consider the boy's questions rationally. Had he not been so young they would have reacted loudly and angrily, not in whispers. A few onlookers, however, knew the boy had not been silly. But they could not admit it. They grasped the logic of his questions but knew they needed to keep quiet about it. Doubting any part of the official account of the Cathedral's destruction – that it had collapsed because of fires caused by evil Esehems – would not only be unpatriotic, it would be sacrilegious. Not just any building had been attacked; it was the hallowed Cathedral, the sanctified symbol of the people's sacred faith. Rational considerations of its fate could not be tolerated. However, memories of the boy's questions were soon forgotten, even by the few who knew they were based on sensible reasoning.

People were outraged, they cried out for war.

In Yevad, the required regime-change occurred exactly as planned. Any surviving Esehem fighters were ushered back to the wild regions by their Special Forces advisers, to be retained, supported and trained for future campaigns, perhaps operating under a new name. They would be needed for actions in countries still outside The Organisation's control.

When all traces of hostilities had sufficiently faded away, a suitable governor was appointed and shipped over to Yevad to supervise its introduction to democracy, propaganda, debt and interest. He took with him a sizable staff of bureaucrats, all carefully selected by The Organisation.

They were fully familiar with the difficulties they were likely to encounter in their task of governing the new Yevad. Along with them were a number of experienced journalists, sent over to establish news media able to provide the misinformation requirements of democracy.

'Why did the Cathedral blow-up?' the boy asked. 'Why didn't it just burn out?'

As intended, Yevad was soon exporting fine textiles, delicate pottery, unusual foods and spices and basic raw materials to Areho and the wealthier countries of the CU. This enabled it to re-pay, with interest, its post-war debts to Areho's banking corporations. The provisional government, with its cabinet of unelected bureaucrats, ensured sufficient export income was retained for buying needed goods and services from Areho. As anticipated, the people regarded the foreigners in their lands as benevolent liberators. Not only had they saved them from certain defeat by barbaric Esehems, they were helping them to recover from the devastation of war. In Areho, the intervention in Yevad was seen by the public as a great humanitarian achievement. The Prime Minister and his government were praised by the news media for the magnificent achievement of the armed forces. *"Well done, lads"* proclaimed the headlines of one newspaper. Others expressed similar praises for the country's soldiers and sailors.

So history books recorded the story of the dreadful day when terrorists attacked and destroyed Arcue's Cathedral, and how brave Arehoian forces liberated Yevad from brutal tyrants so people there could enjoy democracy and trade freely with the rest of the civilized world. As The Organisation intended, people in Yevad were soon deeply in debt. The bankers were very pleased. They had created the money owed to them out of nothing more than the gullibility, unawareness and conformity of people, both in Yevad and Areho.

In Yevad, as planned, Esehem leaders were instructed to withdraw their fighters and return to the wild regions.

There were still, however, unconquered countries of the distant lands that were not in debt and The Organisation was not going to rest until they were. Its debt-based economic system could not continue to function for very long if it ever stopped growing and it was thought it could keep on growing as long as more and more lands could be conquered. In Fairy Tale World this could happen. In the real world things are not so simple. But that's another story.